SEA DRAGON

DEPTHS OF MAGIC
BOOK THREE

EMMA SHELFORD

SEA DRAGON

Kinglet Books
Victoria BC, Canada

ISBN: 978-1989677650

www.emmashelford.com

First edition: January 2023

CHAPTER 1

A suction cup tickled my shoulder through my dyed-blond hair. I swatted it away, laughing.

I know you're there, I said to Squirter, my octopus friend. *Want me to chase you?*

Chase, he replied. His graceful body floated midwater in front of me. Lean muscles slid under a layer of textured skin colored red, cream, and orange. Squirter gazed at me with his greenish-yellow eyes for a moment. When I grinned and reached out for him, he gathered himself and jetted away.

My eyebrows rose at the little octopus's speed. Was he faster than usual? He was only a baby, after all. I supposed it was natural that he would gain strength and size at some point.

I'd never catch him if I didn't try. I pushed my body forward through the water with powerful undulations of my legs. Even though I'd lived on land for over a year, the ocean was still my element.

Squirter disappeared into the murky green water of the upper water column, but I didn't need to see him. Faint currents caressed my pale skin and painted a far more vibrant picture than the one my eyes gave me.

A school of perch flitted to my left, and an outcropping of rock jutted up from the seafloor, covered in anemones and giant barnacles. In the waves above, driftwood rolled and plunged. Squirter was ahead, and I pushed harder to catch up.

Grace, the substance that pale folk like me ate to

maintain their underwater abilities, flowed through my veins. I could feel its power driving my limbs. My mind drifted to the rogue faction from the underwater city I'd called home for twenty-four years. Were they still vent-bent on stopping all Grace from leaving the Seamount? I'd heard no news since we'd rescued the kidnapped half-sirens and demolished the army of mer folk holding them hostage.

I shuddered at the memory of stabbing the seal shifter Selo last month, then I put it from my mind. Rehashing that act of brutality and the shark feast that had followed wouldn't help, and I had a wayward octopus to catch.

Squirter paused to look for me, and I caught up and squeezed the tip of one arm. He crawled over me in his delight, and I tickled his mantle between the eyes.

A large body emerged at the edge of my skin sense. Had my thought of sharks conjured one out of the depths? It was large, a blue shark at least three times as long as me, and it moved slowly but purposefully in my direction. I frowned and scratched Squirter's mantle again. I wasn't nervous—my ability to compel and control other creatures was strong enough that I didn't have to worry about the intentions of the shark—but it always paid to be wary of large predators.

Squirter finally noticed the shark's approach, and he stilled. I gave him a swift hug.

It's fine, I said. *You're with me.*

He curled the tip of an arm around my ear, but his eyes continued to face the threat. I swam downward with the nervous octopus gripped onto my shoulder and trailing his unattached arms behind me like loose seaweed.

The shark changed direction to follow us. My heart rate quickened. What did the predator want? I glanced at Squirter tucked close to my body and decided to compel the shark.

I hummed deep in my chest, a soft sirening of disinterest and redirection. It would turn the shark away from its path without disturbing the creature much. I'd overdone sirening before, and now I aimed for minimal interference.

The shark twitched but kept coming. A flicker of alarm jolted my stomach, and I increased my sound from gentle to strident. The shark slowed slightly but continued to swim directly toward us.

My sirening wasn't working. I could figure out why later. For now, I needed to get us away from the approaching menace with teeth like bone knives and a single-minded intent. I turned and undulated to my right, where a kelp forest loomed in my skin sense. If sirening wasn't working, maybe old-fashioned hiding would.

I didn't give up my song, though. Instead of misdirection, I belted out a call to stop and turn around. Subtle wasn't what I strived for anymore. I wanted our pursuer gone.

My skin sense told me what my forward-facing eyes couldn't see: the shark growing ever closer. I desperately undulated my body. The forest was too far away for comfort. Squirter pressed himself against my back to make himself streamlined.

The shark darted forward, and it was only my heightened skin sense that alerted me to the movement. I jerked my leg out of the path of the shark's mouth and dived in a zigzag pattern to disorient the animal. My body flushed with the heat of exertion and fear.

The weight of Squirter on my shoulder disappeared, and my heart nearly leaped out of my chest. I spun around to both see and feel the scene behind me.

Squirter was grasping the shark's head with his suction cups. By the way the shark twitched, I guessed that Squirter's sharp beak was biting the giant fish with all its might.

My jaw dropped at Squirter's aggressiveness. He was so small that he usually relied on me to protect him. What had prompted this display of bravery?

One of his arms dangled, forgotten, in front of the shark's mouth. The animal snapped at it and almost made contact. Squirter slithered the arm out of reach. The close call jerked me out of my shock. My friend needed help.

I screamed a blasting call of disorientation. Squirter drifted off the shark, momentarily stunned. The shark paused. Then it faced me—reminded of its larger target—and lunged.

Whoops. I backpedaled toward the kelp forest, but I was nowhere near fast enough to escape the shark. Zigzagging movements wouldn't work for long. Could I make it to the forest?

A cloud of ink, larger than any I'd ever seen Squirter make, ballooned over the shark's eyes. My skin sensed the animal pause in confusion, and a small creature jetting toward me. I turned in relief and darted into the wavy fronds of the kelp forest, Squirter close behind.

I kept my skin sense on high alert, although it was hampered by the kelp stipes brushing against my arms. We were lucky that this patch of bull kelp was still here since winter storms hadn't yet arrived to tear their holdfasts away from the rocks.

I glanced back through the murk, but nothing followed us. The shark must have finally decided that we weren't worth the hassle of chasing.

That brought my thoughts around to why the shark hadn't responded to my sirening, at least not until my powerful blast at the end. It could have been an animal resistant to compulsion—although resistance was rare, it could happen naturally—but my mind drifted to another threat that had been lurking ever since the battle for the kidnapped half-sirens.

Marina Highcave, daughter of the siren Seamount Protector, pledged lover of the man I'd killed, and avowed bringer of Seamount justice, had seen me. I'd faked my death last year, and she'd bought the story until she'd seen my face a few weeks ago. It was only a matter of time before she avenged her loss. If a strong siren had already compelled the shark, that would explain my inability to stop the animal.

Maybe I was being paranoid. Why wouldn't she come herself to end me? She was powerful, after all.

Because the upper echelons don't like getting their hands dirty, a little voice whispered to me.

Squirter touched my arm, and I came back to the present moment.

Big ink, I said to him. *Good job.*

Squirter's skin flushed a bruised purple with pride.

But too dangerous, I added, in case he was getting ideas of grandeur. He was too little to know when to back away from a fight. He needed my firm hand to guide him. *We need to stick together next time.*

Squirter changed color again, but this time with the paleness of anger.

I frowned. My words were reasonable, weren't they? I only wished I could be close enough to everybody I cared about to protect them the way I could Squirter. My mind drifted to my friend Levi Storm. He didn't even live in the city, and I hardly saw him, let alone knew when he needed help. It was frustrating.

You'll be big one day, I told Squirter. *But until then, let me help you.*

I was cautious leaving the kelp forest, but only lingcod and pile perch greeted my expectant skin sense. Still, we didn't linger in the open. I headed straight for the shore with Squirter close behind me, his eyes peering backward every few seconds.

Come with you, he said in the language of hums, clicks, and gestures that we shared. *Shark.*

Yes, I said, eager to remove Squirter from whatever the shark had wanted with us. The shark wouldn't likely bother with the little octopus, but I didn't want to take that chance.

Squirter waited in the heaving shallows while I crawled above the crashing waves and coughed water from my lungs. When my hacking ceased, I dripped over to my backpack and extracted Squirter's container from its pouch. I splashed back into the surf swamping the jagged rocks, wincing as sharp stones dug into my feet. With a dip of the container, I scooped Squirter into the opening.

He slithered inside. Was it my imagination, or was it a tighter fit than usual? With no bones, even big octopuses could squeeze into the tightest of spaces, but I was sure he was larger. For how much longer could I take him home and play with him in my tub?

In an ideal world, I'd own a seaside house like the Lodge's dockside rooms. But that was an unlikely dream, given the way my debt loomed over me. Besides, dry folk valued oceanside properties, and I could never afford one on my salary, even with my creditor Branc Driftwood out of the picture.

I heaved Squirter's container to my pile of clothes and quickly dressed. I'd have to find a solution another day. Squirter still fit in my backpack today, and that would suffice.

The clouds opened on my way to the bus, and I spent the ride soaked. The cold and wet didn't bother me, but I received plenty of concerned glances from motherly types. I merely hugged Squirter's backpack closer and tried to revel in the lingering Grace-high still flowing through my veins. It was difficult when adrenaline from the shark attack kept hitting me with aftershocks, leaving me alternatively wired and drained.

What if the attack hadn't been a fluke? Was I in danger entering the sea?

My racking coughs interrupted the fruitless pondering. When I emerged from the bout, the latest concerned citizen leaned toward me.

"Are you all right, dear?" she said, her glasses winking in the gloomy light streaming from the window. Her brow creased, and the earrings pulling her earlobes downward swung heavily with the relentless pull of gravity. "Do you have a place to get dry?"

"I'm almost home." I wrestled out a smile for the woman. "I got caught in the rain, that's all."

The woman sat back, mollified, and I pressed the button for my stop. The cold weather and my wetness had nothing to do with my cough. It had cropped up last week and hadn't stopped since. Coughing was a new, unwelcome feature of life on land, and I didn't know how to fix it. Hopefully my body would take care of the infection by itself soon enough.

I heaved Squirter's backpack to my apartment building with grungy carpeting and stained walls and jiggled the key in the door until it let me in. The mess that greeted my eyes wasn't a surprise, but it grated on my nerves. My friend Cetus had been staying with me ever since he'd arrived from the Seamount a few weeks ago, and signs of his habitation were all too present. Blankets draped over the couch, dirty clothes gathered in a pile on the floor, and dishes from his breakfast lingered on the counter.

I sighed and shut the door behind me. Although I was happy to help Cetus get on his feet, putting up with his mess without the aid of our mutual friend Pelagia to nag him into submission was wearing on me. He had a job now—my friend Byssa Sweetcurrent had helped him get a dishwasher position at the Crispy Prawn, the Japanese restaurant where she worked as a line cook—and although it didn't pay well, it was enough to find a basement suite somewhere with a roommate. Not me, though. He'd been making friends under the wing of Byssa's brother Hades, and he was resourceful enough to find a new roommate.

But that was tomorrow's problem. Cetus was out, and I took a deep breath to revel in the quiet. That set off another coughing fit, which took a minute to subside.

I stumbled to the bathroom and poured Squirter into the bathtub. Byssa had hauled in a fresh container of seawater for Squirter yesterday, and the little octopus stretched his arms luxuriantly across the tub.

I tossed in a few toys for him to play with, then changed my wet clothes and picked up my keys again. The shark's attack had distracted me, but I tried to push it from my mind. I had other concerns vying for my attention today.

I'd asked everyone I knew about the Seamount story singer Hades had told me lived on this coast, but I'd come up blank. Story singers were the historians of our people and held an exalted place in Seamount society. I hated to approach Branc, but he was the person most likely to have an answer to my question.

And I wasn't willing to let it slide. I wanted to know more about the sea dragon that had saved me from the

serpentine ligan a few weeks ago. The story singer was
my best chance, but to find her, I needed Branc.

CHAPTER 2

Branc's club Abyss was closed mid-afternoon, but the bouncer Reef opened the back door when I knocked. He was always there, and not for the first time, I wondered whether his debt was so large that he'd be working it off forever, or whether he liked his job. The pearl stud in his ear gleamed when his bald head nodded at me.

"Hi, Lune. Branc's at the bar with someone, but he'll be done soon."

"Thanks, Reef."

I loitered in the hall after Reef disappeared into a back room. When I grew tired of waiting, I ventured into the main room of Abyss. Brighter lights glowed than were usually on during opening hours, and they made the usually elite and swanky club look garish and tacky.

A murmur of male voices floated toward me from the bar. Branc wouldn't take kindly to eavesdropping, so I sat at a far table and tapped my fingers with impatience.

The man Branc was talking to was thick-necked and oily-looking. If he had any pale folk blood in him, it was buried deep. Likely, he was a dry folk contact. Branc had his fingers in a lot of anemones.

Branc's eyes landed on me, and I gave him a little wave with my fingers. He spoke for a minute more, his eyes flickering to my corner occasionally, then he put his hand on the other man's shoulder and steered him to the exit. Branc strode over to me after the man left.

"What do you want, Lune?" he asked abruptly. "I'll call if I have a job for you, you know that."

"I know, I'm not here for a job." I waved at the now-empty doorway. "Who was that?"

"It's just business. None of your concern."

"Is the rogue faction still trying to stop Grace distribution from the Seamount to shore?" Just because Branc didn't offer any information didn't mean I couldn't pry.

Branc tightened his lips. "It's been quiet lately," he admitted. "Nothing since the thwarted kidnapping. I don't trust the silence, though. The faction is only regrouping, I'm sure of it. I'm taking actions against their return."

"Like what?"

Branc's eyes flashed. "Just because we worked together at the battle doesn't mean we're partners, or that I'm obliged to tell you the minutiae of my business dealings."

I raised my hands in surrender. "Fine, fine. A girl can only ask."

"About that battle." Branc stared at me with an intense gaze. "Has Marina Highcave approached you?"

I stared at Branc, my mind whirling. What did he know about my connection to Marina Highcave? I'd never told him the reason I'd left the Seamount, but Branc always knew everything. He could have found out if he'd wanted to.

"Why would she?" At Branc's raised eyebrow, I shifted my eyes to the bar to avoid his gaze. "No, she hasn't."

It was true. As far I as knew, the shark was an unrelated incident, an anomaly among sea creatures. I couldn't assume that it was being controlled by Marina.

"Marina Highcave is stubborn and won't let go of something once she's put her mind to it." Branc rubbed his forehead in an unconscious gesture that drew my eyes back to his face, fascinated by his uncharacteristic show of distress. Again, I wondered how he knew Marina. "She can get deep in your head if you let her. She's dangerous. If I were you, I'd take a break from swimming for a while. She isn't comfortable on land, but if she hasn't returned to the Seamount, she might be waiting in the waves."

"Well, that's not an option," I said with an incredulous shake of my head. "I'm not about to stop swimming. Might as well stop breathing while I'm at it."

A spasm crossed Branc's face.

"But I can be more careful," I allowed, curious about what had triggered Branc. "Go to unexpected locations, swim with others. That's good sense."

"I see you know Levi Storm," Branc said, picking invisible lint off his sleeve while he changed the topic. "Has he had any disturbances in his Grace shipments in the past few weeks?"

I crossed my arms. "Really? You expect me to act as an informant for you? Let's get this straight right now: asking me anything about Levi is off limits. Got it?"

Branc gave a dismissive wave, as if the subject meant nothing to him. "Fine. But us shore-dwellers are in this together. You may take issue with my methods, but I'm fighting for the same thing you are: the chance to live on land with the Grace we need to survive."

"Noted." I sighed to release the tension caused by Branc's inquiry. In a way, he was right—we did have the same goal, even if our methods often differed drastically—but that didn't change my stance about Levi, the manager of the vacation destination for sirens called the Lodge. And my friend. Hopefully more than a friend, one day.

The Branc situation was already fraught, and my relationship with Levi unclear. I had no desire to work behind Levi's back, no matter how much it might pay off my debt.

"If you're not here for a job," Branc said, "and you're not here about Marina or Levi Storm, what do you want? I have things to do."

"I'm looking for a story singer, and rumor has it there's one on the Sunshine Coast. No one knows exactly where, though. Do you?"

Branc narrowed his eyes at me. "Why do you want a story singer?"

"I have questions," I said vaguely. "Things I want to know, things I never learned since I grew up in the ghetto and didn't get a fancy education like the upper echelons got. I figured it's time to even the playing field now that I can."

"You'll be disappointed." Branc sniffed. "What they learn isn't that interesting." Before I could ask him how he knew, he continued, "Yes, I know where the story singer is. I can tell you, for a price."

I pursed my lips. Branc's stance wasn't unexpected.

"What do you want?"

"A small job," he said. "Compel some information out of a contact. I'll call when I'm ready for you."

I breathed a sigh of relief at the request. It was nothing I hadn't done before, and Branc could have asked for whatever he wanted. "It's a deal."

"Good." Branc walked to the bar and reached under the counter to pull out some paper and a pencil. He scribbled directions and handed the paper over to me. "Few people know where the story singer lives because she likes her privacy and lives as a hermit. Don't make this information common knowledge, for her sake."

"Noted." I tucked the paper in the pocket of my jean skirt and nodded my goodbye, pleased to receive the story singer's address. "See you later."

It was almost time for my dinner date with my friends Byssa and Hades, so I turned my steps toward The Crispy Prawn. My thoughts drifted to Levi after Branc's reminder. What was he doing now? Was he having dinner in the staff dining room at the Lodge? What was he wearing? Was he thinking of me?

I shook my head to rid it of wistful thoughts. We'd parted amicably after the battle to free the captives, but I'd destroyed his trust in me when I'd tried to siren him in the summer. I'd wanted him to tell me why he'd been avoiding me, but compulsion hadn't been the way to go about it.

I didn't know if I could repair that hurt, and it was awkward to try long-distance. I'd done my best to keep up a back-and-forth of texting, sticking to light, inconsequential topics. Levi had responded well, but it was hard to judge from words on a screen.

I missed hearing his voice. On a whim, I pulled my phone out of my pocket and dialed his number before I could wimp out. I suppressed my cough while I waited for him to pick up.

"Lune." The gladness in Levi's voice squeezed my throat until it was hard to speak.

"Hi, Levi." I released the breath I hadn't realized I'd been holding. "What are you doing?"

"Right now? Shoveling mashed potatoes into my mouth in the dining hall. I have a pile of paperwork that needs to happen tonight."

Distant words drifted past Levi's in a voice I recognized as Sandy's, the middle-aged receptionist at the Lodge. "Your papers can wait, Levi."

I grinned. "You have your orders."

"I thought I was the boss around here," Levi said with a smile in his words. "But Sandy's known me since before I could talk, so she runs loose with the hierarchy."

"Sounds like she speaks sense." I sidestepped a dawdling child and his mother on the sidewalk. "Papers will always be there, but I'm a special occasion."

"That's true," he said quietly.

I'd meant the comment as a flippant observation, but Levi imbued his words with more depth than I'd expected. It was encouraging, but also left me not knowing where we floated. I floundered for something to change the topic.

"What's happening at the Lodge?"

"A couple of new employees, but that's about it. Pulling the smaller boats ashore for the winter. How about you?"

"I have a week of holidays coming up, actually." My fingers fidgeted with my belt loop. "I'll be heading in your direction. There's a story singer somewhere north of the Lodge whom I want to see. Her location is top-secret, but I managed to wrangle the address out of someone. I have a few questions for her. I hope the bus makes it up there, otherwise I'll have to swim, and I don't know if I have enough holidays for that."

"Why don't you stay at the Lodge for a few nights?" Levi suggested. "I can drive you to this story singer, if she's not too far away." He released air through his teeth. "If I can move around my duties here, of course."

"The Lodge will be fine without you for a day," Sandy's voice called out from the background. I bit my lip to avoid chuckling aloud as she continued speaking. "Honestly, Levi, you're too young to be so tied up in work here. Enjoy yourself."

"I guess I should have gone outside for a private conversation," Levi muttered. "Anyway, the offer's open."

My stomach jolted at Levi's invitation to stay at the Lodge. It was the place where I'd rediscovered the joys of being pale folk, where I'd made friends and a community of sorts, where I had a touchpoint of comfort. A warm glow ignited at the thought of returning.

If the comfort of the Lodge warmed me, Levi's presence there turned my stomach into a writhing nest of eels, in a good way. And that he had invited me—did that mean he forgave me?

"That sounds great," I said with far more outward composure than I felt inside. "I'd like that. If Sandy says it's okay, of course."

Levi huffed, as I'd hoped he would at my cheeky comment.

"I'm the boss here," he said.

"You keep telling yourself that."

After promising to keep him updated on when I would arrive, we hung up and I slipped my phone back in my pocket. My feet were light, like floating in water. This was a chance to see Levi, to revel in his presence once more. It was a chance to prove myself trustworthy again in his eyes.

I didn't know what would happen at the Lodge during my visit, but I was yearning to find out.

CHAPTER 3

Hades was in our usual booth at the restaurant, tucked in the corner away from other patrons. Dim light from a hanging lamp above the table illuminated his pale face. I slipped in across from him then did a double take at his expression.

"I don't think I've ever seen you look so down," I said. "What happened? Did the shops run out of your favorite hair gel?"

"Ha, ha," Hades said. He leaned back and crossed his arms. "No."

"Then what?" I stared at my friend. The hair gel comment had been a good guess. His usually immaculate hair—today long and black on top with buzzed orange sides—was limp and unstyled, and his already pale complexion was wan.

"It's nothing."

I kicked him gently under the table, and he winced with a glare at me.

"It's not nothing," I said. "Spill. You expect me to tell you everything these days. You might as well return the favor."

Hades released a long-suffering sigh, then he dropped his head on to one hand and leaned his elbow on the table.

"It's Rachel," he said quietly.

"Uh oh, trouble in paradise. What's going on with you and the perky aquarist you've been dating?"

"She found out about me." Hades waved his arm

vaguely. "You know, what we are. In part, anyway. She caught me swimming, and I guess she pieced the rest together from clues."

My stomach dropped for Hades's sake. "I take it the talk didn't go well."

"She freaked out," Hades whispered. "Couldn't handle the fact that there's a hidden world she knew nothing about, that science knows nothing about. Accused me of lying to her—although I don't know when I was supposed to tell her," he said with spirit, lifting his head from his hand. "'Hey, Rachel, want to go out with me? By the way, I'm part pale folk. You don't know what that means, but let me tell you all about it.' Great topic for a first date. I would have told her eventually, but not right away."

"Apparently, that was the right call." My forehead creased at Hades's distress. "She clearly needed more time than this. I'm sorry. Why don't you siren her, confuse her about what she saw? She won't forget, but with enough suggestion, she can mistrust her own memories. You don't have much sirening juice, but you have enough for this. You know what, let me do it. My abilities are stronger and probably more precise."

"Thanks, but no." Hades clasped his hands and looked down at them. "I do want her to know. I wish I could have controlled the timing, but now the secret's out, I don't want to take it back." He looked up at me, and the longing in his brown eyes was clear. "I really like her. I think we might have a future. At least, I owe it to myself and to her to find out. This is a test of our relationship—a big test—and if we pass, we'll be stronger for it. I'll know we were meant to be."

"But why don't you compel her now, then you can reveal what really happened at a time of your choosing? Seriously, I don't mind compelling her. I can find a quiet place at work. It's no problem."

I didn't understand Hades's motivation. Sirening was the ultimate undo button. Granted, I'd learned the hard way that I should only use it under the direst of circumstances, but wasn't Rachel's freakout dire enough? Surely, sirening her would calm her down and benefit her.

"But then I'd have to tell her later that I'd compelled her," Hades said. "I never want to lie to her, and then she'd always wonder if I would do it again. No, I'll give her space to process this revelation, and if she comes back, we can go from there."

I leaned back against the bench, pondering Hades's words. He was deliberately letting Rachel choose him, secrets and all, and allowing the currents to sweep him where they would. I didn't like the thought of relinquishing control to fate. Did Hades really feel it was a worthwhile gamble?

Before the silence could grow too deep, Byssa approached the table. Her straight black bangs shifted above the petite features of her smiling face, and she carefully balanced a platter of sushi in her hands. The lanky young man with shaggy brown hair who followed her highlighted her diminutive height.

"You remember Jules?" she asked me, jerking her head toward the man, whose expression looked as grim as Hades's.

"Of course." I scooted closer to the wall so he could sit down. "Works in the kitchen here. Friends with that sick half-siren, Zeb. I remember."

"Zeb's a quarter, I think." Jules shrugged. "But yeah, that's me."

"How is your friend doing, anyway?" Hades asked. "Now that he has some Grace in his system?"

"Miles better," Jules said with a fervent glance at Byssa, who ducked her head at the attention. "He would have died without Byssa's help."

"I'm so glad we caught the problem in time." Byssa snapped open her chopsticks and waved at the platter. "Eat up, everyone. Our break only lasts fifteen minutes."

We dutifully loaded our plates with sushi, sashimi, and nigiri that Byssa had prepared for us. It was only after the soy sauce had been passed around that Hades cleared his throat.

"Jules, you found out about Zeb at some point, right? How long have you known he was different?"

Jules shrugged and swallowed his mouthful. "It was obvious once we'd spend most of the summer at the beach as kids. I wrangled the truth out of him, eventually."

"You were pretty young, then." Hades looked crestfallen, and Byssa squeezed his forearm. "Kids and teens are probably far more accepting of weird stuff."

"Yeah, maybe." Jules dipped his roll in soy sauce. "Personality, too. I don't think I would be too bothered if I found out now, you know? But everyone's different."

"My girlfriend found out," Hades said. I frowned at him. It had taken me a fair bit of prodding to get that information out of him, and here he was volunteering it to the whole table. "She didn't take it well."

"That sucks, man," Jules said. "Hopefully she comes around. I feel you. My girlfriend and I just broke up, too."

"I'm sorry to hear that," I said, although I wasn't, not really. From Byssa's studious attention to her sushi, neither was she. "Break-ups are tough."

"Yeah, it was time," he said. "The long-distance thing was hard on her."

I read that as she had broken up with Jules, but I didn't mention it out loud.

"I thought he might like company tonight, which is why I invited him to our dinner," Byssa piped up.

"That was a good idea," I said. Byssa glared at me, knowing what I was getting at, but the others were oblivious.

"It totally was." Jules smiled at Byssa. "And look at that. I feel better already."

Byssa's cheeks flushed with a faint rose, and I hid my smile with another bite of food.

We spoke of light topics until the end of the meal when a mention of the battle a few weeks ago brought Marina to my mind. Since the others didn't want me to hide things, I might as well bare all.

"A shark attacked me this morning," I said.

Byssa gasped, and the other two stared at me.

"I got away, and it was fine," I quickly added. "No harm done. I just don't understand why it didn't respond to my compulsion. It could have been one of those rare immune fish—they do exist—but I'm worried a stronger siren sent it to target me."

"Who wants to target you?" Hades said. "You think it was someone from the rogue faction? But why only you? I haven't heard of other attacks lately."

I worried my lower lip. I'd never told them about my history with Marina, indeed had never mentioned the reason I'd left the Seamount. Now was as good a time as any.

"Marina Highcave saw me at the battle a few weeks ago," I said. "She's the siren Protector's daughter. More importantly, she chased me out of the Seamount last year after I killed her man, Shoal Highcave. It was self-defense, but still."

If Byssa's eyes could have grown any wider, they would have filled her face. Jules grew pale, and Hades blinked a few times.

"So that's why you left," Byssa breathed. Her eyes filled with tears. "Have you been hiding that terrible secret all this time? What a burden. You silly blowfish, you could have told me before."

My heart warmed at Byssa's reaction. I couldn't have asked for better friends. When I told them I was a murderer—albeit one who'd acted in self-defense— Byssa worried more about my own state of mind.

"I know that now," I said with a smile at my friend.

"Why hasn't Marina come after you before?" Hades asked. "She's had a year, after all."

"I pretended I died during the chase to shore." At Hades's incredulous look, I shrugged. "A last-ditch effort. It worked, though. Put her off the scent until she caught sight of me underwater. Now? I don't know what she'll do. Revenge has crossed her mind, I don't doubt."

"How do we keep you safe from her?" Byssa fidgeted with her chopsticks, her sushi forgotten. "Maybe you should swim down at White Rock for now, instead of your usual spot."

"It's too far away, and I don't have a car." I waved away Byssa's worried look, although I didn't feel nearly as sanguine as I pretended. "I'll be careful, that's all. And I won't go back to where the shark found me. Besides, I'm on holiday next week, and I'm heading to the Sunshine Coast."

As expected, Byssa perked up at this news.

"To the Lodge?" She gave me a knowing glance. "To visit Levi?"

"Among other things," I said vaguely, but it was hard not to smile at Byssa's satisfied expression.

I took a breath to say more, but a fit of coughing overtook me. When it finally eased, I put my hand on the table to steady myself.

"That sounds pretty bad," Jules commented beside me. "Might want to see someone about it."

"Jules is right." Byssa frowned at me. "That's been lingering for a week. Go see Dr. Mazzaella before you leave, okay? I want a report afterward, otherwise I won't believe you went."

"Okay, okay." I leaned back against the bench, tired from the effort of coughing. Maybe Byssa had a point. "I'll go see the doctor."

I called Dr. Mazzaella that evening using the number Byssa had pushed on me before she'd returned to the kitchen. The doctor told me to stop by before work, so the next morning, I presented myself at the basement door of the doctor's residential house after passing through a wooden arch with the nautilus shell carved into it.

"Come in, come in." Dr. Mazzaella ushered me across the threshold when she opened the door. The familiar office with brightly colored cushions and posters of sea life on the walls relaxed me. "I don't have long before my hospital shift, but I can take a quick look at you."

The doctor listened to my breathing with a strange metal and plastic instrument, then she placed her hands on my upper chest and back and hummed gently. I closed my eyes as the sensation washed through me. She then performed a few other tests, but her expression showed no confusion.

"Just a touch of dust-lung," Dr. Mazzaella announced. "It's an irritation of the lungs from too much dryness. You'll find it comes and goes with the seasons." She rummaged in a cupboard and drew out an inhaler. "Puff on this twice a day for the next week—it's only saltwater vapor—and it should ease your lungs enough for them to heal on their own."

"What if I breathe underwater?" I asked.

"Even better. Do both, and you'll be fine within days."

I thanked the doctor, tucked the inhaler in my pocket, and exited the basement clinic. A woman stood at the gate, gazing at the nautilus sign. Did Dr. Mazzaella have another client? I looked at the newcomer's face, then my heart stuttered. Even with her white hair dry in loose waves around her face, so different from how it looked underwater, I instantly recognized her.

Marina Highcave glanced at me, and her eyes widened.

CHAPTER 4

Before I could react, Marina slammed into me and pushed me against the wall of the house. Wooden boards dug into my back and hips.

"You," Marina hissed in a hoarse voice unused to speaking on dry land. She accompanied her single word with clicks and hand gestures in Seamount lingo. She heaved for breath. "You're the cause of Shoal's suffering. I will end you, but not before I erase you in Ramu's eyes."

My blood grew icy in my veins. Death was one thing—and something I certainly had no desire for—but to be excommunicated, not allowed to join our goddess Ramu's endless sea after death? That was a fate I couldn't endure.

"It was an accident," I whispered, too frightened to speak louder. "I didn't mean to hurt him."

"But it still happened," she hissed then released a racking cough. "And you need to face Seamount justice. We're going to do the erasure ceremony as soon as I get you underwater."

I released a hum of compulsion, but it was as futile as it was involuntary. Marina laughed with disbelief despite her labored breathing.

"You think you can best me with compulsion?" She shook her head. "Oh, my poor little half-human. You're out of your depth."

Marina hummed, and the power in her vibrations took my breath away. They traveled through her restraining arms and into my body, thrumming in my very core until every part of me shook with her will.

She was powerful, as powerful as any female siren I'd ever encountered. The upper echelons valued compulsion abilities, and centuries of breeding between the strongest pale folk had resulted in people like Marina. As well, children of the upper echelons trained for years to perfect and optimize their innate abilities to increase their strength and the longevity of their effects.

Marina had all the advantages, and she wasn't shy about using them to achieve her ends. I floated under her spell, uninterested in breaking free, drifting at ease in the wash of her song. I would follow her anywhere, contentedly and at peace with my actions. If she wanted me to offer myself as shark bait, I would do so with a smile and a whisper of gratitude.

Marina's cough interrupted her hum. Her face reddened with the attack, and my mind snapped into clarity. But before I could wrestle free of her hold, she resumed her hum. I fell into the spell of her command.

Marina's eyes bored into mine, cruel in their satisfaction. My cheeks rose in a beatific smile in return.

"Stop!"

A harsh voice disturbed the pleasant, numb fog I floated in. Marina's hum stopped, and it was as if I'd been slapped into awareness. Oxygen flowed into my chest like the shocking first breath of an infant, and I gasped.

Marina twisted her head toward the voice, and my gaze followed. Dr. Mazzaella stalked toward us along the path that ran between her house and the fence, her eyes flashing and her brow thunderous.

"What do you think you're doing?" she spat out. She accompanied her words with jerky gestures to get her point across. "Release Lune at once. You are at my place of healing. I'll remind you to respect that, even if we're on land."

Marina took a step back, her face twitching with the first indecision I'd seen on her. She heaved for breath again, and I wondered at her struggle for air. I edged closer to Dr. Mazzaella, terrified that Marina would ignore the doctor and turn on me again.

I shouldn't have worried. Marina, for all her faults, was Seamount nobility through and through. The hierarchy was all-important and absolute to them, and they exalted healers above all others. I could count on Marina to respect an important position.

"Apologies, healer," Marina said in Seamount lingo. "Lune and I have unfinished business. I shouldn't have tried to complete it on your threshold. I am here for your healer expertise."

Dr. Mazzaella pointed down the path behind her. "Wait for me inside the door," she said in clipped tones. "I will attend to you shortly."

Marina walked past us. She shot me one last, venomous glance, her breath stuttering, then disappeared into the clinic. The doctor sighed once she'd left.

"Are you all right?" she asked me. "Did she leave a compulsion on you?"

"She was going to take me somewhere," I said in a small voice. "But she didn't finish, so there's nothing pulling me, no."

"Good." She rubbed her forehead. "Thank Ramu that healers are respected."

"Why did you leave, if life was so great at the Seamount?" I asked with curiosity. Now that Marina's looming presence was gone, I had the mental space to ponder things other than my death.

"I wanted to know more. The Nautilus Academy for healers isn't interested in change and learning, and I'd heard fascinating reports of dry folk medicine. I couldn't contain my curiosity." Dr. Mazzaella chuckled. "My colleagues thought I was crazy—I got quite the reputation from my decision—but isn't the pursuit of knowledge worth a little craziness? Marina Highcave must have heard of me and sought me out."

"Maybe. Thanks for intervening." I rubbed my arms. "It's been a while since such a powerful siren compelled me. I can't say I've missed it."

"Are you going to be all right?" Dr. Mazzaella tilted her head in concern. "She doesn't look like she'll easily quit her vendetta against you, whatever it is. Although I'd wager that she won't come back on land anytime soon. She has the worst case of dust-lung I've ever seen. Way worse than yours. When it's that bad, no amount of inhalers will cure it. Dry air must be torturous to her."

"I'm leaving town shortly," I reassured her. "Just for a few days, but hopefully it will put her off the scent and give her time to cool down. I presume she'll be heading back to the Seamount soon. She has no desire to live on land, and apparently her body agrees."

"Stay vigilant," Dr. Mazzaella warned.

I said my goodbyes to the doctor and hurried toward the bus stop, unwilling to meet Marina on the street again. At our next encounter, I wouldn't be nearly as lucky. I had to avoid her at all costs.

It wasn't until I walked into the Vancouver Aquarium to prepare for my work shift that I thought to wonder what Marina was doing here visiting Dr. Mazzaella. What could have convinced her to visit a traitorous healer on land, the antithesis of everything the rogue faction stood for? Was something wrong with her, something that Seamount healers couldn't fix?

My mind wandered to the creature I'd encountered last month. The long, dragon-like animal had licked my wound and miraculously healed it. What else could it heal?

Not that I cared about Marina and her dust-lung. I didn't owe that wretched siren anything, certainly not information about a strange creature that I'd seen once and never again. Marina could go back to the Seamount where she belonged, and good riddance.

Two days later, I entered Branc's club Abyss again. Branc had already given me all the information I needed for my assignment. After changing in his empty office, I headed straight for the bar with quick steps. A man with a thatch of light-brown hair wearing a loud shirt with pineapples on it sat drinking alone.

I adjusted my top—a sparkly number that my human friend Mireille had insisted I buy last month for a concert—and slid onto the bar stool next to the man. He was older than he looked from the back, and his eyes crinkled at the corners when he smiled at me.

"Hello, lovely," he said. "What are you drinking tonight?"

I laid my hand on his arm. No point in prolonging this encounter. I wanted the job done so I could get out of this club with its pounding music and flashing lights. It might have been an enjoyable place if I hadn't associated it with my debts. As it stood, I wanted to leave as soon as possible.

"Hello." I hummed a vibrating song of compliance so that it shook the man's arm. "Tell me what you know about Moray. Where was he last week?"

"Moray told me to keep it a secret," the man said with a glazed look. "But he met with a delegation on Tuesday. I don't know who. They were strange. Didn't talk to anyone. Moray hustled them into a back room quick enough. I only pour the drinks, I don't know anything else. Moray ordered extra salt on their margarita rims, though. Oh." The man held up a finger. "Moray got me and the other bartender to carry a stinking, wet sack to his boat. Dirty job. I found this on the dock after we loaded."

He passed me a small, white disk, polished smooth, with the familiar curl of a nautilus shell on it. It was the insignia of the Seamount Protectorate, but I didn't know what the disk meant. Branc probably would, though.

That was enough. I'd done what Branc wanted. Feeling a little dirty from the job, but happy to be finished my sirening, I sauntered across the main club area and skirted gyrating couples and laughing patrons until the staff-only hallway appeared. The door to Branc's office beckoned, and I gratefully pushed my way in.

Branc must have been watching for me, because he followed me inside a moment later.

"Did you get it?" he asked.

"Moray got a package from some Seamount folk. 'Stinking and wet', our friend said. Tuesday last week. That's all he knows. Oh, and he found this on the dock after loading the package."

Branc tucked the polished bone disk I handed to him in his desk drawer, looking especially smug. I slipped off my slinky shirt and replaced it with a tee shirt from my backpack that I'd left in his office. It was inscribed with the words "I love it when you talk nautical to me". I hoped Branc wouldn't mistake the words as being aimed at him.

The memory of the man's slack-jawed expression hit me like I'd been walloped in the stomach. That had been me yesterday, when Marina had cornered me. She was still out there, searching for me. Vancouver was a big place, and I was leaving tomorrow, but what if she met someone who knew me? It would be a simple matter for her to compel information out of them.

I turned to Branc once my shirt was on. He watched me with narrowed eyes, as if he could sense my upcoming question.

"Branc, how do you avoid being compelled?"

"I'm allowed my secrets," he said in his gravelly voice. "It's on a need-to-know basis, and, well…"

"I don't need to know," I finished for him. "Yeah, I get it. Tight-lipped as always. It's just that Marina Highcave cornered me yesterday, and her sirening is so strong. There's no way I would ever be able to resist it, and she wants me dead. Excommunicated and then dead, specifically. The next time we meet, it'll happen." I swallowed, and my hands grew clammy. At least I was leaving tomorrow, but what if she was still in town when I returned?

Branc tapped his fingers on his pant leg, clearly thinking.

"I'm just saying," I said in the hopes of getting him to tell me his secret, "I might not be around for much longer to siren people for you unless I figure out how to protect myself against Marina."

Branc stared at me, his black eyes unfathomable. Then he sighed, and my stomach unclenched.

"There's a substance prepared from seagrass roots at the Seamount, by a complicated and secret method. It gives protection from compulsion. It's mainly used by high-ranking males, as they're the only ones who can afford it."

I wondered again what Branc's story was that he knew of this substance. He was half-human like me, so how was he so well-informed of the upper echelons?

"Where can I get some of this stuff?" I asked. However Branc knew about it, the substance would certainly solve my problems.

Branc's lips tightened. I sighed in exasperation.

"This is my life we're talking about. I don't want to die, and you don't want me to die so you can keep using my skills. Giving me some of this substance is a win-win situation."

"It's too expensive to give it away," Branc retorted. He drummed his fingers on his pant leg again. "But you're right, I don't want to lose a powerful asset. I'll add it to your debt, and you can work it off."

My heart sank. "How much will you charge for it?"

"It's practically priceless. So, you can owe me for a future job, details of my choosing. No negotiations when I require your skills, nothing except compliance."

"You want me to promise to do something for you, but I don't know what it will be?" I pursed my lips, frightened of the ramifications, but not seeing another way out. "I agree, but with a few conditions. I will do your future job, as long as I'm not pimped out, or forced to cause death or physical harm to anyone. Oh, and it can't involve anyone I care about. And it needs to be within the next few months. I don't want this hanging over me forever."

And I especially didn't want my debt prolonged just because of this stupid agreement. A bundle of cash waited under my bed for the day when I could hand over the entire sum, hopefully soon. I didn't trust that Branc wouldn't find some way to artificially inflate my debt if I paid it off bit by bit.

Branc studied me for a moment. "Deal," he said at last. He pulled an envelope out of his jacket pocket. It looked like the waxed paper of a Grace envelope, but the markings on it were unfamiliar.

Carefully, he shook out five shapeless slivers onto his gleaming wood desktop. He quickly tucked the envelope into his pocket again then rummaged in his desk drawer for another, unmarked envelope. He swept the slivers into it and passed it to me.

"Chew and swallow half a piece every two days," Branc instructed. "That dose will prevent you from being compelled, as long as the siren isn't touching you."

"Thanks," I said, still nervous about what I'd promised but not seeing any other options. "I'll try my best to stay alive so I can do my payback job."

"See that you do."

CHAPTER 5

I went to work the next day, but this time I packed overnight clothes to prepare for my trip to the northeast. I took Squirter to the aquarium and let him play in a crab tank while I scrubbed. At the end of the day, I squeezed him into his backpack and hoisted it on my back. He'd insisted on coming with me this way, and I didn't have the heart to deny him. I would open his lid from time to time and give the water a stir to introduce oxygen. Maybe I could refresh his water at the ferry terminal.

On the way out of the staff doors, I spotted Rachel, Hades's former girlfriend and the cause of his current woes. It would be so easy to erase the source of those feelings. Hades would thank me later.

I strode in her direction, but a hand clamped on my forearm.

"What do you think you're doing?" Hades hissed. His usually bright, mischievous eyes narrowed with suspicion.

"Just thought I'd say hello to Rachel."

"You were going to siren her for me, weren't you?" When I didn't deny Hades's accusation, his breath exploded from his mouth in a forceful exhalation. "For the last time, don't. If I wanted to confuse her into mistrusting her memories, I have enough siren juice to do it myself. Letting her come to grips with this on her own is my choice. Don't take that away from me."

"Fine, fine." I raised my hands in surrender. "I

promise I won't compel Rachel. Satisfied?"

Hades dropped my arm and nodded. Then he spun around on one heel and stomped back into the building.

I released my own breath in a sigh and shook my head as I walked to the bus stop. I still didn't understand the big deal, but now I'd promised. I only hoped Rachel would come around soon. I wasn't as optimistic as Hades.

The bus ride through West Vancouver was uneventful, and I caught the last ferry to the Sunshine Coast. Although that stretch of shoreline was part of the mainland, too many mountains made a road impossible, and so the ferry continued to run.

I stood outside the whole time, enjoying the wind on my face and smelling the salty tang of ocean. I was mostly alone since the cold autumn winds had driven everyone else inside.

A crackling noise preceded an announcement over the loudspeakers.

"Attention all passengers. Due to mechanical failure, the bus from the terminal to Sechelt will not be running tonight. Please find alternate transportation."

I pursed my lips. That was how I'd planned to travel to the Lodge. Now what would I do? I could call Levi, but it was a long drive to the ferry.

Heaving waves far below my feet caught my eye. What if I spent the night underwater and swam to the Lodge? I was stocked up on Grace, I had a drybag for my clothes, and Squirter was with me. It would also do wonders for my cough. A heady delight stole through me. It had been ages since the cool embrace of water had surrounded me during slumber. Maybe this was my chance.

At the ferry terminal, I walked past a group of irate passengers arguing next to a lone taxi and headed for the nearby beach. Daylight was only a faint hint on the western horizon, and no one else stood on the wave-tossed stones. No one ever visited this beach, it looked like. It was too close to the noisy ferry terminal for casual beachcombing.

I found a pile of driftwood above the hightide line and shifted it around until I exposed a small patch of sand. I dug a hole deep enough to store my backpack. My shirt and skirt came off, then my boots, until I stood in my undergarments in the dark, windy evening.

My feet curled over stones as I picked my way to the water's edge with Squirter's container. Once he'd slithered out to wait for me in the shallows, I traipsed back to the driftwood pile and put clothes, shoes, toiletries, and my inhaler into the yellow drybag that I always kept at the bottom of my backpack, ever since Hades had told me his story of swimming too far in a storm and needing to bus home in his undergarments.

I chewed a piece of Grace and rolled with the overwhelming sensations that flowed through my body as the substance took hold. A quick text to Levi told him I would arrive at the Lodge tomorrow morning. I tucked the eelgrass substance in my drybag without ingesting any, since I was leaving Marina behind in city waters. Then I squeezed air out of the drybag and tied it around my waist. I covered my backpack with sand and logs until it was out of sight, then I splashed into the waves.

Squirter was waiting for me, and his arms wriggled with happiness. After I coughed out air from my lungs and filled them with cool water, he pointed toward the deeps. I was happy to oblige.

Darkness robbed my eyes of their vision, but I didn't need to see. My skin sense painted a picture in my mind, as clear as in daylight, and I followed my eight-armed friend through the blackness. My drybag bobbed behind me, slowing me down slightly, but having dry boots when I emerged at the Lodge would be worth the inconvenience.

We swam through the blackness for a leisurely hour. Squirter eventually started to flag, and he crawled onto my shoulders for a ride.

Time to sleep? I asked him, and he made a gesture of agreement. I looked for a good place to curl up for the night.

Since we were in water, a bed wasn't the necessity that it was on land. But to avoid floating away in my sleep, I needed to tuck myself into the right sort of cavity in the rock. That, and I didn't want a rude awakening by something looking for a snack. I could compel most things—aside from that one shark—but I needed to be awake for it.

Squirter's suckers gripped my bare shoulders tightly, and he pressed against my body to streamline our silhouette. One arm snaked out and grabbed my floating drybag to stop its incessant bobbing behind me. I grinned and dived closer to the rocky slope.

Anemones waved and squat lobsters clacked their claws upward as they sensed our passage. A deep crack in the rock caught my attention, and I undulated closer. With a shrug of my shoulders, I dislodged Squirter, and he wandered toward the hole to scout it out.

He returned swiftly and settled onto my shoulders again. *Small,* he said sadly. *You are big.*

I pressed on and was rewarded a few minutes later by an even larger hole. No currents escaped from its opening, and I felt confident that nothing lurked inside that would endanger my friend. After a minute of exploration, Squirter returned and touched my arm.

Inside, he commanded.

The hole wasn't large, and rocks pressed inward with jagged protrusions, but it was big enough to curl up inside without danger of floating away. I found a good position then relaxed. Squirter crawled around the rocks for a while, exploring, until his tiredness made him creep onto my stomach and attach himself there. Two arms held onto the stone wall to anchor us for the night.

The water was soothing on my beleaguered lungs, and Squirter pressed against my stomach was comforting. I fell asleep almost instantly as gentle motion from the ever-moving water lulled me into slumber.

A faint glow from the cave mouth was the only sign

that dawn had broken. That, and porpoises frolicking in the water outside.

Squirter wasn't on my stomach anymore, but he crawled through the opening shortly after I awoke. One of his arms carried a wriggling sea urchin.

Food, he said, and held it out to me.

I took it with a gesture of gratitude and cracked the sea creature open. Its white flesh was sweet and tender on my tongue, and I ate it quickly, hungrier than I'd expected to be.

Go? Squirter asked.

Yes, let's go. The sooner I arrived at the Lodge, the sooner I could see Levi's handsome face, immerse myself in his scent, and fantasize about touching his hair. My brain squashed thoughts of more, but hope was a persistent animal.

Squirter led the way, energized by sleep and breakfast. We were in familiar waters after an hour, and the taste of the Lodge area grew stronger. At the southernmost beach of the Lodge, Squirter paused.

Visit soon? he said to me.

I tickled his mantle. Now that we were away from Vancouver and Marina's threatening presence, I felt comfortable leaving him alone. *Of course. Be safe. Have fun.*

He jetted off and soon disappeared from my skin sense. I turned my body toward shore. Moments later, I emerged at the Lodge's southern beach which was covered with slimy rocks encrusted with barnacles. I pulled on my tee shirt and skirt, shoved my feet into socks and boots, and shook out my hair. Too bad I couldn't dry it, but this was me. He would have to learn to like it if he wanted to get to know me better. Presumably he was used to the drowned-rat look growing up around sirens, even though he was dry folk himself. One coughing fit later, and I was ready to walk on land.

Rays of sun lanced across the sky and hit trees on islands in the strait. The Lodge at the top of the mildly sloped lawn was quiet and still in the dawn light, its wooden siding dark in the shade. The windows of the upper restaurant were black holes facing the water. I stopped and pondered. Where would I find Levi? Should I wait in the Lodge's lobby until he turned up for work? Should I see if the staff dining hall was open yet?

No. I knew where Levi's apartment was. He was expecting me today. Not this early, of course, but still. I could knock on his door and say hello. Maybe I could catch him in his sleepwear, whatever that might be.

I sternly told my inner self to stop giggling and strode toward the main Lodge building, shaking my hair out as I walked. The door to the long-term employee apartments was unlocked, and I slipped inside and stepped quietly along the deserted hall. When I reached Levi's door, I paused. What if he had moved into the larger suite once his parents had vacated? Would I be disturbing someone else's early morning?

I hesitated, my fist hovering at the door, then I gritted my teeth and knocked decisively. I would have to take a gamble and apologize if Levi didn't answer my knock.

Silence greeted my summons. I knocked again, hoping that Levi could hear me from his bedroom. My imagination pictured him sprawled on sheets, his limbs long and muscled, his hair tousled from sleep...

A lock clicked, and my body tensed. A disheveled Levi blinked at me from the open doorway, and my abdomen cramped with pleasure at the sight of him in the flesh at last. And there was plenty of it on display, since he wore only navy-blue pajama pants. My gaze crept over his muscled chest, and I had to clench my fists to stop myself from reaching out to touch him.

My eyes met his, and my shoulders tensed for a different reason. Gone were the flat blue contacts. For the first time, I saw what color Levi's eyes truly were.

Blues, greens, and silvers swirled in mesmerizing whorls and stripes throughout his irises in a dazzling array that I'd never seen on any dry or pale folk. They mesmerized me with their beauty, and I could hardly look away. Recognition flashed through me.

They matched the sea dragon's eyes perfectly.

CHAPTER 6

"Lune?" Levi said in a sleepy, surprised voice. A smile slowly grew on his face, and he opened his suite's door wider. "You're here. Early."

I blinked to break the frozen spell his eyes had foisted on me and pretended that I hadn't noticed anything strange. Was Levi the sea dragon? Could he shift into another form? I supposed it was possible. Seal shifters changed their shape, after all. My mind whirled in the background while I tried to act normally.

"The bus wasn't running yesterday when the ferry docked, so I spent the night underwater." I shifted my drybag on my shoulder. "Hope you don't mind me being so early."

Levi stepped aside and waved me in. "Of course not. You know, you could have called. I would have picked you up."

"It was nice to spend the night underwater. It's been a while. And Squirter was with me."

I wandered into his suite. Levi dashed ahead of me and shuffled a laptop and a few dirty dishes off the couch. I hid my smile.

"Just—hang out here for a minute," he said with a hint of frazzle. "Let me get dressed."

I wanted to say I didn't mind him as he was, but we weren't there yet, so I let him be. When he ensconced himself in the bathroom, I sat on the couch with a sigh and pulled out my phone.

Got to the Lodge safely, I texted Byssa.

A few seconds later, she replied. *Good. Enjoy your time with Levi. ;)*

I grinned then shoved my phone in my pocket. A few minutes later, Levi emerged from his bedroom, unfortunately fully dressed. My eyes glanced involuntarily at his eyes, but his usual blue contacts covered the mesmerizing swirls of blue and green. I wondered if he'd noticed my noticing. He'd been very sleepy, so possibly not.

I wanted to confront him. Was he the sea dragon? Why would he keep it a secret?

He must have had a good reason, but I hoped I could gain his trust enough for him to tell me himself. I sat up straight, determined to mend what had broken between us so he could trust me.

Levi grinned shyly at me, and I patted the couch. "Come keep me company. I've only spoken to an octopus for the past day."

"Are you hungry?" Levi nodded toward the dining hall. "We could grab some breakfast."

My stomach rumbled at the mention of food. "Yes. My early-morning urchin wore off ages ago. Lead the way."

A few staff members were already in the dining hall, and sounds of clanging and singing filtered from the kitchen's open doorway. Sandy looked up from her newspaper when we entered and waved at us. Levi wandered over to her and I followed.

"Good morning," she said in a cheery voice. Her short white hair bobbed above her tanned, smiling face. "Lovely to see you, Lune. I hope you're going to take

Levi somewhere fun today." She gave Levi a stern look. "He works too hard."

"Well," he said with a guilty glance around. "Probably not the whole day."

"Of course, the whole day." Sandy shook her head and pointed at me. "You make sure he doesn't come back until dinnertime."

I grinned at the twinkle in her eye. "I'll do my best."

"You're sure you can handle everything on your own?" Levi said.

Sandy waved him away. "I've been running the front desk for over a decade. I think I can handle a few wayward guests. Go!"

"You heard the lady." I dragged an unresisting Levi away while Sandy winked at me. "Let's grab some food and get out of here."

"Where are we going, anyway?" Levi changed our direction to pull me toward the kitchen. "Something about a story singer?"

"Shhh," I said, not wanting others to hear. "I'll tell you outside."

Levi nodded and poked his head into the kitchen. "Martin, could you pass me a paper bag? And is there any sandwich bread we could steal?"

"You need lunch?" Martin glanced at me. His hair was still in the same green spikes from the summer, although it had grown longer since I'd seen him last. "Lunch for two, got it. Give me a minute."

"It's good being the boss," I teased Levi when we were at the buffet table filling our paper bag with muffins and fruit. "Lunch, sir? Yes, right away, sir."

Levi nudged me with his elbow, and I closed my eyes at the comfortable contact. I wanted more of that warmth.

"Martin's a good guy," he said. "But I feel like Sandy pre-warned him. Is everyone conspiring to make me take a day off?"

"Maybe you should take a hint." I broke off a piece of muffin and popped it in my mouth. "The Lodge is running great. Sandy can handle anything."

"I guess." Levi grinned at me. "So, what are you planning for our day away from the Lodge?"

I glanced around, but no one was nearby. Still, I drew him to an empty corner away from the buffet table.

"The story singer," I whispered. Levi ducked his head closer, and I breathed in his salty warmth. "I want to find out what she knows about that sea dragon I saw."

Levi's entire body stiffened, and he didn't meet my gaze.

"Ah," he said with nonchalance that didn't mask his repressed interest. "Okay. You have the directions?"

My shoulders slumped in disappointment. I had hoped Levi would have told me then and there, but I supposed sharing secrets in a public dining hall wasn't wise. He didn't know how I would react. Besides, I hadn't earned back his trust yet.

"Here's your lunch," Martin called out from the kitchen door. Levi straightened and moved to grab the paper bags the cook held out for him, and I mastered my face to remove any traces of regret.

I followed Levi out of the dining hall. Outside the door on the wet lawn, a familiar pale figure with short, dark hair walked toward us.

"Morning," Levi said to his younger brother Austin.

"Hi, Lune," he said. "Nice to see you again."

I blinked. The last time I'd seen Austin, he'd captured Byssa and then ran off after Levi had fallen in the water. Granted, he'd been under compulsion for his role with Byssa, but the fact that he hadn't helped his brother hadn't endeared me toward the younger man.

"Yeah," I said lamely. "Sorry, got to go."

I pulled Levi's arm up the grassy slope toward the parking lot. When we were out of earshot, I hissed, "What is he doing here?"

"I guess I didn't tell you." Levi rubbed the back of his neck. "He came back a week ago. Finally felt safe, that the sirens who'd compelled him weren't chasing him anymore. He apologized, wanted to make up for his mistakes."

"And you let him stay at the Lodge again?"

"He's my brother." Levi twisted his mouth. "I have to give him a chance. He made a stupid mistake, then the pale folk wouldn't let him leave."

"He tried to burn down the Lodge." I shook my head. "That was with his own free will. How can you trust him again?"

"It's a work in progress," he admitted. "He's very repentant and is trying to work hard. Which, let me tell you, is entirely against his nature. And don't get me wrong, I'm not totally blinded by our relationship. I have all the staff keeping an eye on him. Think of it as a sort of probation period." Levi nodded toward a truck with the Lodge logo on it. "I want him back, so I'm willing to give him a second chance."

"I hope it works out for you," I said. Levi wouldn't have appreciated what I really wanted to say, so I kept my words minimal. I swung into the passenger's seat and buckled my seatbelt, and Levi did the same on the driver's side. "Now, head north."

"Yes, ma'am."

Levi turned the truck on and backed out of the stall. Once on the highway, and after a brief negotiation with me over the radio station, Levi spoke.

"This story singer," he said. "What's her background? Why do you think she would know anything about the creature you saw?"

"Do you know what a story singer is?"

"Vaguely," he replied. "Oral historians at the Seamount, right?"

"Exactly. Paper isn't exactly a hot commodity underwater, so our history is recorded through story singers. They're highly respected, and all the upper echelon children learn from them." I drummed my fingers on the truck armrest. "If anyone has heard of a sea dragon before, it will be a story singer."

"Okay." Levi changed gears and roared up a hill. "Then let's talk to this story singer and get some information."

I gazed at Levi's profile as he drove. His voice had been eager as if he wanted information about sea dragons as much as I did. But why, if he was one himself?

For that matter, where were his biological parents? His adoptive mother Seafoam was pure pale folk, and his adoptive father Kane was human. Levi said he'd come to the Lodge as a toddler. Did he not remember his biological parents? My heart squeezed for how lost he must feel, being the only sea dragon among people who didn't even know he existed. No wonder he hid his true self.

Levi glanced at me, and his eyes crinkled with a smile.

"Like what you see?" he teased.

My traitorous cheeks warmed, and I crossed my arms. "You forgot to comb your hair," I lied. When Levi raised his hand to pat down his head, I chuckled. "That will teach you for being vain."

We settled into comfortable chatter while we munched our muffins and fruit. He asked about my swim from the ferry, and I asked about people I knew from the Lodge. Our talk drifted into more personal topics—my favorite food, Levi's hopes for the future— and I relaxed into my seat with every passing kilometer. A warm glow of happiness lodged itself in my stomach and flickered brighter with every chuckle, every passionate word from Levi's mouth, every gesture of his hands as he spoke. I wished I could have stayed in this truck, forever driving with Levi, no one but us and nothing we needed to do.

But all good things must come to an end, a phrase that Byssa sometimes quoted from her human aunt. Before long, I directed Levi off the highway and onto a dirt track that plunged into the woods. The track grew narrower and more overgrown until branches screeched their needles across our windows. Levi slowed to a crawl to avoid bottoming out in the muddy potholes. Rain drizzled through the foliage, and the window wipers added their own rhythmic thumping to the branch symphony.

"I guess we keep going," I said.

"Nowhere to turn around." Levi's jaw was tight, and he peered ahead intently. "This old truck has seen worse roads."

"Really?"

"Not really. But it's tough."

The road—maybe too generous a term—ended at a small clearing barely large enough to turn the truck around. Beyond, an overgrown path wound through thick bushes that dripped with rain.

"Now, we walk," I said with a confidence I didn't feel. "The story singer's place can't be far, surely."

"I can hear the ocean." Levi pointed westward. "That's where she'll live, I presume. Being pale folk and all."

"Good point." I pulled on my raincoat and stepped out of the truck, squinting at a patch of sky peeking through the tree branches. "Come on. Let's hope she's at home after all this."

Levi slammed his door shut and led the way down the narrow track. Despite my best efforts—I didn't have many clothes to spare on this trip—my skirt grew soaked within a minute of pushing through wet leaves, and water dribbled down my bare calves and into my sturdy boots. Levi's sodden jeans clung to his legs, although I didn't mind seeing his muscles move beneath the fabric. I would have worried for his warmth, but that was before I'd guessed he was the sea dragon. If he could swim in local waters without getting cold, a bit of rain would barely register.

Not even birds sang in this wet. For fifteen minutes, we trudged through forest undergrowth thick with the scent of damp soil. I had two coughing fits during our walk. Levi glanced at me with worry in his eyes, so I waved my inhaler at him.

"Dust-lung," I said weakly after I'd recovered. "The doctor said it will go away soon if I use this."

He waited until I puffed on my inhaler twice.

"Happy?" I said.

He snorted and continued down the path.

The ocean's quiet roar separated into distinct waves when the trees finally opened and the trail spat us onto a rocky beach. We balanced on driftwood piled thickly at the hightide mark and glanced up and down the beach.

"North, I think." I looked at the instructions Branc had written down for me. "Yeah, keep walking north. We should see it soon."

"Is that it?" Levi pointed up the beach. I peered in the direction of his finger.

What I'd thought was a huge pile of driftwood taller than Levi was upon closer inspection a house of sorts. It looked like it was about to collapse in the stiff wind blowing rain in our faces, but at the same time, like it had been there forever. Now that I was looking, crab traps and hung fishing lines were obvious.

"I can't imagine who else would be living out here." I carefully walked along the driftwood log I was on and jumped to the next. "Let's see if she's at home."

More details emerged the closer we drew to the strange dwelling. Some pieces of driftwood that looked like random protrusions from the house resolved into statues of ravens, eagles, and fish. A windchime made of shells clattered mournfully in the breeze. Trees encroached on the beach from a steep cliff behind and loomed over the house-like pile of driftwood as if daring it to come nearer.

"Hello?" I called out when I couldn't take the suspense anymore. "Anyone home?"

I glanced at Levi, who gave me an expectant look. Then his gaze shifted past me.

CHAPTER 7

An old woman clambered toward us, her wrinkled face contorted with fury. Her ragged dress flapped in the breeze, and she shook her fist at us.

"Get away from here," she shouted in a voice hoarse with age and disuse. "Begone with you!"

"Wait!" I held up my hand to stop her. "Please, we mean you no harm. I'm looking for Marea the story singer."

"How did you find me?" The woman's scowl only deepened at my words. Long, scraggly white hair tossed in the wind. "Leave now, never speak of this place again."

"Branc Driftwood gave me directions," I blurted. How could I calm the old woman down so she would tell stories instead of raging at us? "Please, I only want to ask you a question about history."

Marea stopped, her chest heaving with exertion. She stared at me.

"Branc Driftwood sent you, did he?" Her voice, now that she wasn't shouting, was calm and measured, although still hoarse. She shook her head slowly. "Foolish boy. Well, come along, then. If Branc sent you, you must be all right."

I blinked at the old woman, who turned and hobbled back to her hut.

"Are we talking about the same Branc Driftwood?" I whispered to Levi.

He shrugged, his expression as confused as mine.

56

"It's not exactly a common name."

"Hurry up," Marea called back to us. "The tea is ready."

I didn't want to waste a minute of the mercurial woman's goodwill, so I leaped from log to log until I reached the hut. Levi followed close behind, and we approached the dark entrance to the dwelling.

Marea shuffled out with three mugs of hot liquid.

"Sit, sit," she chided us. "Find a log. I don't stand on ceremony, not out here." She pushed a mug at my chest. "Here. Made from fresh seawater and boiled with things I found in the forest. What won't kill you will make you stronger, as the humans love to say."

She cackled and settled on a tree stump perched against the wall of her house. I gripped my mug and sat gingerly on a log opposite her, and Levi sat next to me with his own drink. He sipped it before I could remind him that Marea had brewed it from seawater—a liquid far too salty for dry folk to drink—then I bit my tongue. Levi drank it without wincing, and I remembered his alter ego. Of course, he would be fine with the salt levels, if he could live in the ocean.

A faint hum startled me from my preoccupation with Levi. It emanated from Marea, and I recognized the faint vibrations as a song of thanks. The familiar tune brought a lump to my throat. We had sung the same notes before every morning meal to show our gratitude for the food. It had had extra meaning to us since I hadn't always been able to provide food for every meal.

The song was a little taste of home and a reminder

of the friends I'd left behind. What else would Marea be able to tell us?

"Why did Branc send you here?" the story singer said after a gulp of her salty tea. "What is it you wish to ask me? I'm a crazy hermit, after all. I left the Seamount ages ago, after spending too long teaching the upper echelons' offspring their histories."

"Why did you leave?" I asked with curiosity. Bitterness swept through me at the mention of her teaching duties. I'd never received an education like that. The ghetto was a far less privileged place.

"Bored," the old woman said with a shrug. "I wanted to experience some of that world I'd only learned about through stories. Teaching sassy children grew tiresome. But you didn't come all this way to ask about my past. Tell me, what do you wish to learn?"

"I saw a creature in the water last month." It was uncomfortable talking about this with Levi beside me. I was certain that he was the sea dragon, but doubt would remain until I saw conclusive proof or he told me otherwise. "It looked like a dragon that swam underwater. I've never seen anything like it before, nor heard of anything. Do you know what it was?"

Levi was tense next to me, and he leaned forward to hear the story singer's words better.

"Oh, yes." Marea took a deep breath and released it. "I'm sure I have something. Give me a moment to access it."

She closed her eyes and fell still. A minute later, Levi nudged me.

"She's finding the stories in her memory," I

whispered in his ear. The warmth of his body touched my cheek when I leaned close. "She has a lot memorized, but it can take a while to find the right one."

Levi nodded, his eyes trained on the motionless story singer. Another minute passed, then Marea took a deep, shaking breath.

"Hundreds of sunsweeps ago," she said in a measured, lilting voice, "A strange creature swam to the Seamount. The barrier was not as tightly controlled then, and the mer folk patrolling allowed him to pass. He appeared harmless, and they had never seen anything like him. When he spoke in an ancient dialect that only the story singers understood well, and when he shifted to a legged form like a seal shifter, the mer folk knew to bring him to the Protectorate.

"Many came to see the strange creature. He became known as a sea dragon, from myths the pale folk had heard from dry folk they'd visited. The sea dragon spoke of a land of fire and ice. As a gesture of goodwill, he offered to heal the Shifter Protector's young son from a wasting illness of which none could cure him. Something in the sea dragon's saliva healed that little boy, for he swam with his old vigor within moments of treatment.

"The Protectorate then knew they had an immense power in their hands. They treated the sea dragon with the utmost respect by giving him caves in the highest reaches of the Seamount, offering him the choicest foods, and speaking to him at length of his history and his people. Those stories have been lost to time. The sea dragon returned their favor by healing those who were in need.

"But the power to heal came with a cost. The sea dragon grew weak with every healing and needed time to recover. When he started healing those he found in the lower reaches of the Seamount, thereby neglecting the needs of the upper echelons, the Protectorate was pressured into capturing him. Once he was restrained, they forced him to heal only those presented to him.

"At first he refused, crying out in his haunting, mournful calls unlike those of any other creature. But as he grew weaker, he became easier to bend to their will. Eventually, the cost of healing became too great, and he died after a healing. No one has seen or heard of a sea dragon since."

I was barely breathing by the time Marea finished her tale. Levi's face was as rapt as my own, and grief for the long-dead sea dragon creased his forehead.

I wasn't immune to the sadness, but how much more must Levi feel? Now I understood why he hadn't told me his secret, why he had blown up at me when I'd attempted to siren him. How much of this history had he known or guessed?

The silence billowed after Marea's tale while we digested her words. A fascination coursed through me. What other races populated the oceans? I'd never left the Seamount until last year, and I'd been woefully ignorant until then. Ghetto children learned how to survive, nothing else. In this land of fire and ice, were there others besides sea dragons, just as three human-like races inhabited the Seamount? I knew so little, and it both frustrated and excited me.

"Where is the land of ice and fire?" Levi said into the silence of crashing waves. "Where the sea dragon came from?"

"If we once knew, that knowledge was lost," the story singer said quietly, her now-open eyes gazing out to sea with a faraway look.

"And you have no more stories of them since then," he pressed, his gaze on Marea intent. "Nothing at all."

"You have the extent of my tales on the subject," she said calmly. "Unless a sea dragon has visited the Seamount since I left, that is everything pale folk know of the matter."

Marea had no more to say about sea dragons. Although I would have liked to stay and learn more about my people's history, I didn't want to push Levi's patience. His gaze had turned inward, and he was quiet during our trek back to the truck. It wasn't until we pulled onto the highway, the truck dirty and scratched but in one piece, that he shook himself out of his thoughtful state.

"It's still early," he said, "and Sandy will have my hide if we get back this soon. Want to take our picnic to the beach?"

"I'll never say no to an ocean visit."

The beach Levi picked was in a park, so it was devoid of houses. At this time of year, with rain threatening and a cold wind blowing off the water, it was also empty of park visitors. He led me down a disused path until a beach spread before us, this one sandy and shallow. Small waves lapped against the shore, and I sighed happily.

"Not bad," I said. "It will do for lunch."

Levi spread out a large towel that he'd grabbed from his truck—I now had a sneaking suspicion I knew what he used it for—and we sat close together, facing the water. Levi pulled out the paper bag from the kitchen, and we peered into it.

"Salmon sandwiches," he said at last, pulling one out and handing it to me. "Apples, and cookies. It's not fancy, but it will fill us up."

I wriggled closer to Levi while he was preoccupied unwrapping the waxed paper from his sandwich. I didn't get close enough to touch, but the heat from his body radiated toward mine. With food in my stomach, Levi's warmth next to me, and the lapping of waves on the shore, a mindless, blissful happiness stole over me. It was such a foreign feeling that I almost jerked myself out of it, but the moment soothed me.

I wished I could see Levi's eyes again. Desire to gaze into those swirling depths consumed me until I clenched my hand on the towel. He would show me when he was ready, and I was willing to wait. Keeping a secret like this—about something wonderful instead of terrible—was a pleasant change.

Remembering the secrets I'd kept in the past, including the man I'd killed, sobered me quickly. Marina and her threats rose to the forefront of my mind, and I shivered. I was suddenly, fiercely glad that Levi had kept his secret so closely. I didn't want anyone like Marina Highcave finding out about him. She would never learn about Levi from me, that was certain.

"Are you cold?" Levi frowned. "Never mind, you don't get cold."

"No, I'm not cold. Just thinking about Marina Highcave." I twisted my fingers around the edge of the towel. "Remember, she was the one whose man I killed, and she saw me a few weeks ago. She cornered me at the doctor's office the other day. She would have dragged me off to the ocean to excommunicate and kill me if Dr. Mazzaella hadn't stepped in."

Levi stared at me, his jaw tight and his eyes hard. "She did what?" he spat out. "I thought you said it happened in self-defense. She has no right to carry out vigilante justice like that. Where is she now?"

A warm glow filled my chest at Levi's eagerness to jump to my defense, but I placed a hand on his tense shoulder.

"She's back in Vancouver waters," I said soothingly. I was nervous about returning to the city, but Levi didn't need to know that. "Far away from here. I'll deal with the situation once I'm home. For now, let's not let her ruin our beach visit."

To distract him, I ran my fingers down his arm. My eyes didn't leave his face to judge how he took my advances. I wanted nothing more than to fling myself on him and press my body hard against his, but I still wasn't certain about his stance concerning me. Was he interested? Did he trust me enough yet?

He shivered, and his eyes half-lidded at my touch. Emboldened, I traced his arm along the edge of his shirtsleeve, ending on the tender inside skin. A sigh escaped Levi, and he wet his lips. His eyes rose to gaze at my mouth.

That was all the invitation I needed. I leaned forward and pressed my lips against his. He responded instantly, his eager mouth soft yet firm against mine, the barest hint of stubble grazing my skin. His fingers cupped the back of my head, drawing me closer to him. He tasted of salt and sweetness, and the combination squeezed my insides with intense pleasure. I'd known that kissing Levi would be worthwhile, but I hadn't expected the fireworks in my stomach.

I laid my hand on his chest, reveling in the warmth and hard muscle under my fingers. A far-off corner of my mind rejoiced in my ability to last for ages without breathing. I didn't plan to come up for air anytime soon.

Levi showed no signs of wanting to pause, either. His warm hand traveled over my thigh and pulled my leg over his. I slid into his lap and pushed his chest down until he lay on the blanket with me straddling his hips.

He groaned under my mouth. I caught myself inadvertently humming a siren song of pleasure, and I suppressed it quickly before Levi noticed. It had slipped out without thought. I didn't want to spoil the moment with the reminder of my previous transgressions.

Levi's hands ran up my thighs, squeezing them and traveling high under my skirt. I writhed against him, wanting more, wanting to be closer to him than this. My own hands ran over his chest, the muscles of his upper arms, and the gorgeously soft hair on his head. I clenched the locks in my fists when his fingers grew closer, closer…

Shifting rocks and the bark of a dog froze Levi's motions. Regretfully, we parted lips.

A man was walking toward us along the beach, throwing a stick into the water for his dog to fetch. I didn't know if he'd seen us, but it wouldn't be long before he did.

Levi sighed with a groan of frustration and pushed himself to a seated position. I wiggled off him, but my lips formed a pout of their own volition.

"Do you care if someone's watching?" I asked.

Levi closed his eyes briefly, then he gave a strained chuckle. "I forgot, you grew up at the Seamount. Privacy isn't such a big deal there, is it?" At the shake of my head, Levi said, "Having an audience is kind of a mood killer for me. Sorry."

I traced my finger around the shell of his ear, and he shivered.

"That's okay," I whispered. "Anticipation is its own special pleasure."

Levi made a strangled noise and jumped up. "Come on, let's get back to the Lodge. I should relieve Sandy." His glance at me was heavy-lidded and intense. "But I'd like to continue this 'conversation' later, if you do."

I stood—slowly and leisurely while Levi watched my movements—and faced him.

"I'll be waiting."

CHAPTER 8

We were quiet on the drive home. I didn't know what Levi was thinking about, but my mind wandered in delicious places, helped by my hand roaming his shoulder, his neck, his supremely touchable hair. From time to time, his heavy gaze landed on me with a smile of promise.

It was mid-afternoon when we pulled onto the long driveway of the Lodge. A dark-haired young woman was trimming a hedge beside the parking lot, and Levi jerked his chin in her direction.

"A new employee. Come meet her, she's fitting in well here."

I followed Levi out of the truck, curious why he was introducing me to his new employee. He did treat the Lodge people as family, so maybe that was why.

The woman straightened as we approached. Her dark hair reached midway down her back in soft waves, and pieces of it framed her oval face. Her large, almond-shaped eyes lighted on Levi with a happiness that put me on guard. She was too pretty to show that kind of interest in Levi. Granted, Levi was a catch, but he was my catch.

"Hi Pipa," Levi said when we drew near. "How's the trimming going?"

"You tell me," she said in a melodic voice. She waved at the hedge behind her.

Levi grinned. "Looks great. Hey, I wanted to introduce you to Lune, she's staying here for a few days."

Levi didn't address me as anything—not friend, girlfriend, anything—and it rankled. Not that I knew what I'd say to introduce him, but still.

"Nice to meet you, Lune." Pipa held out her hand. "I'm Pipaluk, but everyone calls me Pipa."

I grasped her hand and tried to shake it, although I'd never figured out the rhythm properly. To my surprise, Pipa's shake was as mediocre as my own, and we let go quickly.

"Hi, Pipa." I wracked my brain for something to say. "You work here now? I assume you're part pale folk, then."

"I don't look it, do I?" Pipa gave a tinkling laugh that sounded as sweet as bells but grated on my nerves like a screeching dolphin. "I got most of my traits from my human mother. I can't even swim, really. A poor excuse for a siren, but we can't choose our heritage."

"We don't have any requirements for our employees," Levi assured her. "Just that they know about the hidden undersea world. I mean, no one's booted me out yet."

Pipa gave her laugh again and smiled at Levi. I gritted my teeth. I'd had enough of chatting with perfect Pipa. Time to move on.

"It was lovely meeting you," I said sweetly. I slipped my hand into the crook of Levi's arm and was gratified when Pipa glanced at it. "But Levi wanted to check in with Sandy as soon as we got back."

Levi said goodbye and followed me willingly enough. I steered him to the front entrance, eager to put distance between us and the too-friendly Pipa. I didn't like how chummy Levi was with her, and how Pipa reciprocated. A little distance wouldn't be a bad thing.

"Oh good, you're here," Sandy said to Levi as soon as we entered the lobby.

I deliberately turned my back to the gas fireplace, which was burning hideously on this cool October day. Maybe if I ignored it, I could forget about its terrible presence. Why would anyone want a fire in their wooden building? Dry folk were so strange.

Sandy continued, "Can I have a hand for a minute if you're back? I have a line-up of phone reservations, and customers in the restaurant need reassurances about allergens."

Levi was instantly alert. "I'm on it," he said. Turning to me, he squeezed my hand with an apologetic look. "I'm sorry. Will you be okay on your own for a bit?"

"I'll be fine." I waved him off. "I'll go for a swim, but I'll be back for dinner. See you then?"

"Absolutely." He dazzled me with a heartfelt smile before he whisked away to the restaurant, smoothing his windswept hair as he went.

A pang of regret lanced through my body, but I sighed it away. Having Levi all to myself on our trip to Marea's had been blissful, but that wasn't how life worked. He would always have the tidal pull of other influences, as would I. That didn't mean I liked it, but it did mean I had to accept it.

Although, I could do without the influence of Pipa.

My bag was still in Levi's suite, so I wandered downstairs and let myself into his unlocked room. A brief rummage in my drybag produced a package of Grace, and I bit off a tiny piece and chewed. I didn't need much today, since I'd eaten some last night before sleeping underwater, but a little top-up wouldn't reduce my meager stores too much.

After the initial effects of the Grace lessened and I could stand upright again, I wandered outside. A chill wind tousled my hair and dampened it with droplets of rain, and autumn waves hit the beach with resounding crashes. I enjoyed the wildness of stormy weather—it was so different from the calm placidness below the waves—but I looked forward to the muted timbre of sound that being underwater would bring.

Pipa emerged from a storage building to my left and strode with sure steps toward the southern path. It led to a small beach away from the prying eyes of human guests.

She'd said she could hardly swim. What was she doing down that path? My curiosity about the new woman, with her silky hair and tinkling laugh, reared its head. I was heading in that direction anyway. I might as well find out what she was doing. She was a little too friendly toward Levi for my liking, and it couldn't hurt to learn more about her.

But by the time I entered the wooded path, Pipa was out of sight. I hurried to the tiny beach, but no clothes were piled on the logs, and no splash showed that I'd missed her entry. Defeated, I set aside my tracking for now. I had a swim to take.

I stripped off my outer clothes and boots and tucked them in the shelter of a driftwood log. Then I splashed through the shallows and past the breaking surf.

Underwater, I released my air and sucked back clear, cool water. After the hacking transition, I dived deeper to escape the relentless tug and pull of wave action. Below, all was still, and I breathed a deep sigh of relief. A lingcod eyed me with sleepy wariness from below, and a crab scuttled past to hide under a rock.

Was Squirter around? I hummed loudly with the special call I reserved for him. Although I repeated my call many more times, no familiar blob jetted toward me, arms streaming behind him.

Eventually, I gave up and focused on enjoying my swim. Squirter was probably off hunting for food. With the amount he'd grown lately, I didn't doubt his hunger. I wondered if he was growing more adventurous and striking out into deeper waters. I bit my lip, then shook my head. He was a very capable little octopus. I couldn't fret about him.

Still, I missed his company. I hoped he was having a good time. My little friend had been trying to catch a perch for months, now. He would lie on the seafloor, camouflaged, and wait until one of the schooling fish swam directly overhead before pouncing upward in a flurry of arms. He hadn't caught one yet, but maybe today was the day.

Lost in reminiscences of Squirter, a dreamy unconcern stole over me. It was pleasant drifting in the water, feeling tiny currents tickling my skin sense, noticing the three seal shifters approaching me in human form. Two were males and one female, and all three were naked, as was common among Seamount shifters. One of the males had scars across his chest and side like some huge beast had dragged its raking claws across him. The female was very young, maybe sixteen sunsweeps old, dark-haired and brown-skinned with speckles across her body. The other male had patches of pale skin among his speckled coloration.

A hum I hadn't realized I was hearing grew louder, enveloping me in a warm cocoon of comfort. When the seal shifters took my wrists and tied them together with kelp ropes, along with my ankles, I smiled dreamily at them. Who were they? It didn't matter.

The shifters transformed into seals then tugged me gently to the north, and I floated behind them without resisting. Why would I resist? Everything was as it should be. My eyes fixated on tiny ctenophores drifting in the water, their grape-shaped bodies glimmering with rainbow stripes. I smiled and gently prodded one of their tentacles with my nose as I floated by.

We didn't swim for long. The shifters deposited me close to an old anchor half buried in silt and covered with giant barnacles. A tiny grunt sculpin fish peeked out from an empty barnacle, and I cooed at it. The two male seals flicked their tails to swim away, and the female shifted into human form and fastened my bonds to the anchor. I moved my ankles closer to the metal to oblige her.

Once they'd tied me up, the gentle humming that thrummed through my body abruptly stopped. Awareness flooded my system. My head jerked up. A burst of rage and fear filled my chest, and panic licked at the edges. I was trapped through the skills of a master siren. There was only one person who wanted to capture me.

Marina was here.

CHAPTER 9

I fought to free myself of my bonds, but the knots were firm in the kelp ropes surrounding my limbs. I bared my teeth at the shifter beside me in her human form.

Get me out of here, I hissed. When she looked away with a grimace, I shouted louder. *Marina! I know you're here. Face me.*

Leisurely, a figure emerged from the dimness. I felt her before my eyes saw her, and my hands trembled with fury and fear.

She emerged from the murk. Her pale hair and face blended perfectly with the expensive white seaweed dress that floated around her thighs in a graceful swirl.

Be still, she said, her face set with determination and a quiet satisfaction. *We'll come for you soon enough.*

What are you doing? I shouted after her. She ignored me and floated to join the two seal shifters. They weaved their bodies in a circular pattern, dropping pieces of shell and stone at intervals on the sandy floor.

I frowned, then my eyes widened. They were preparing a sacred space. Seamount folk created these temporary spaces with reverence to honor the event taking place within. Births took place in a sacred space, as did two people pledging to each other. But there were other, more terrible practices that used a sacred space.

The erasure of a person in Ramu's eyes happened within a prepared circle. Removal from the path that pale folk swam from life to death was final. Severing that connection between a person and her goddess was the ultimate punishment. No one truly knew what happened after death, but I didn't want to risk not swimming in the peace of Ramu's endless sea when I died.

But that was the fate Marina now prepared for me. And after this excommunication, death would swiftly follow. There was no greater punishment I could imagine.

You can't do this, I shouted. *This is insane.*

Marina ignored me, as I'd known she would. I glanced at my guard, who stared at the preparations with a twist of her mouth in an expression of distaste. While she was distracted, I sent out a low hum of compulsion. I needed her under my spell so she could untie my ropes.

She continued to stare at the others with a frown. Why hadn't my sirening worked? I hummed louder. With a start, the shifter looked at me.

That won't work, she said with sympathy threaded through her words. *You can't compel me. Marina got there first.*

She was immune to my abilities? I bit my lip hard, thinking frantically for another solution.

Please don't let me die, I said to her. *Please. You know this is wrong. What I did was an accident. I don't deserve to be erased and killed for it.*

The shifter glanced at me with indecision in her eyes. I held her gaze, internally pleading with all my strength that she would waver in her convictions. I didn't know why she was here, but I had no other options.

I can't, she said with a defeated gesture. She glanced at Marina, and the hate and fear that crossed her face told me plenty. Marina had something on the shifter, otherwise she would have already freed me.

Stumped, I watched Marina and the other two shifters in their seal forms complete their preparations for the erasure ceremony. My fists clenched.

Please, I said to the shifter again. *Please. Don't let this happen. Don't let Marina's quest for vengeance end me.*

The shifter's lip quivered, and she threw an agonized glance my way before gazing at the others once more. My shoulders slumped and my eyes grew warm with tears that mingled seamlessly with the sea.

Marina swam over to me, her expression hard and satisfied. My legs kicked frantically. I strained against the ropes that bound me. If this was it, I wanted to die trying to escape. My warm eyes prickled, and I let out a sob.

Please, I forced out. *Don't do this. I didn't mean to kill Shoal. It was an accident, I swear. I'm so sorry it happened. He was threatening me, and things got out of hand. Please don't end me.*

Marina stared at me with her head tilted. *He's not dead,* she said at last. *But he might as well be. I've kept him hidden for the past year—you know our ways, he would have been sent to the abyss with the injuries he had, and I couldn't bear to give up on him—but he was so badly wounded. He's been weak and unable to speak or care for himself since then, and the healer on land says he won't ever recover.*

I stared in disbelief at Marina, trying to process what

she was telling me. I hadn't killed Shoal? My heart lightened a fraction. Not that his current state sounded much better, but when there was life, a sliver of hope remained. I wasn't a murderer after all.

I need a miracle to cure him, Marina continued. *But they are hard to come by. I'll settle for justice instead.* She gestured to the shifters. *Bring her.*

I struggled wildly when the seals approached me. Their jaws closed gently but firmly around my upper arms to tow me along, and I shrank from the press of their sharp teeth. I tried to kick at the scarred one, but he was too deft and strong. The patchy male tightened his bite on my arm.

I screamed a siren song of defiance and chaos. The seals didn't blink an eye. What was with these shifters? Had Marina already compelled them so my song wouldn't work on them?

Stay still, Marina commanded with a hum of persuasion that she maintained while swimming around the circle. I glared at her, but my limbs stopped moving at her command, no matter how hard I tried to force them into motion. The seals swam out of the circle of shells and stones and drifted out of the way. The shifter who had guarded me kept her human visage. Her expression twisted with indecision.

Marina didn't notice. Her eyes fixed on me.

Finally, she whispered. *You will pay for what you did to Shoal. It's not enough—nothing will ever be enough to atone— but at least it's something. Ramu!* She shouted into the water in an invocation that made my skin crawl. *Cast aside your daughter. She is not worthy!*

I recognized the beginning of the erasure ceremony. The two male seal shifters weaved around the edge of the circle with a hypnotic, ritualistic rhythm while Marina chanted. Her calls, clicks, and vibrations grew louder and more insistent the further into the ceremony she went.

The seals changed their movements and now glided gracefully over the circle in a dome shape, preparing the space for my presence. Soon, they would place me in the center, where Marina would chant the final words to sunder me from Ramu.

I thought frantically, but no plan sprang to life. I was trapped, by rope and by my own mind that wouldn't obey me anymore. No one knew where I was. The seal shifter hadn't released me.

I was stuck.

I released a long wail of desperate calling. Could I entice another creature here to at least disrupt the ceremony now underway? My feeble song was all I had. I opened my mouth and let it pour out.

Be quiet, Marina snapped during her litany. The order came with an increase in her humming compulsion. My mouth sealed shut without my consent. My eyes grew hot again as I resigned myself to my fate. Dead, and forever sundered from my goddess. A dark, dry void of nothingness yawned at my life's end, which was approaching too rapidly. I closed my eyes to block out the hateful sight of my enemy.

A disturbance hit my skin sense like a jet. My eyes flew open. The movement was too fast to distinguish, but a large body darted toward Marina with the speed of a swordfish. My eyes caught the flash of silvery-blue scales before Marina screamed and black blood poured out in a cloud from the arm she now cradled. The long, sinuous body of the sea dragon that had attacked her shot into the dimness beyond.

Levi.

With Marina's hum disrupted, I could speak and move again, but I was still tied with ropes. I struggled futilely. Gentle hands touched my wrists.

Stay still, the female seal shifter whispered to me. *I can untie you now.*

I held still while her deft fingers released my bonds. The sea dragon soared in for another attack on Marina, whose jaw dropped at the sight. Recognition flared in her eyes, along with a heart-stopping look of triumph and greed.

Marina knew what the sea dragon was. As an upper echelon child, she'd been educated by story singers. She knew that sea dragons could heal, and she had Shoal hidden away in a coma.

But the sea dragon story ended with capture and death at the hands of sirens. I bit my tongue hard enough to bleed when Marina screamed a song of rage and control.

It didn't faze the dragon, who circled her then opened his mouth. With a mighty roar, massive clouds of billowing blackness shot from his throat like midnight fire. Water surrounding the deep shadows shimmered with heat. The cloud enveloped Marina, and she screamed in pain. Flecks of sparkling light flickered dizzyingly in the darkness like stars on a cloudless night.

The blackness spread to engulf the sea dragon, Marina, and the two seal shifters who had dived to help the siren. The shifter with me released the last bonds around my ankles and tugged me away.

Hurry, she said. *Before Marina notices.*

The shifter transformed into a seal and swam between my arms. I held onto her sleek body gratefully. Although I swam quickly, we would be three times faster if she took over our forward motion. I could do nothing to help the sea dragon. Hopefully, he would use the inky blackness as a distraction while he escaped. Surely, he could only repel Marina's song for so long.

I clung to the shifter, but my skin sense checked behind me for any hint of the sea dragon. Finally, a long figure darted away from the billowing cloud of darkness and disappeared from my sensing. I dropped my head in relief, then directed the seal toward the beach where I'd left my clothes. We needed to leave the water before Marina found us again. At least on land, Marina would be out of her element. I was used to air, but she could hardly breathe. I needed all the advantage I could get.

The ground grew shallower, and the broken mirror of the water's surface appeared above us. I let go of the seal and kicked to shore.

Come with me, I invited her. *Hide from Marina on land.*

The seal transformed into a girl once more, but frowns wreathed her face. *Are you sure?*

Of course, I said with assurance. *I live there. I don't know what you've heard, but it's not that bad, I promise.*

She glanced at me with mistrust but kicked toward

the surface after me despite her misgivings. Whatever Marina had done to her, she didn't want to encounter it again.

My head burst above the surface, and I coughed out water until air flowed into my lungs. After watching my antics, the shifter did the same. She spluttered and dipped under the water again, so I dived and held up her legs while she expelled the contents of her lungs. When she stopped convulsing, I let go and we swam the last few strokes to the rolling surf.

The shifter rose on unsteady legs, not helped by the waves pushing against us with every step. I grabbed her arm and drew her toward the driftwood log that hid my clothes. Since she was completely naked, I helped her into my shirt and skirt. I would have to make do with my towel and undergarments. Hopefully, no human guests saw me and wondered about my stormy October swimming habits.

I put my shoulder under the shifter's arm and helped her up the path that led to the Lodge. She concentrated on putting one foot in front of the other, so my mind was left to wander.

My gut squirmed in terror for Levi. Marina had seen him as a sea dragon, and she clearly knew what that meant. If Marina got her hands on the sea dragon she'd seen, Shoal could be healed.

Part of me thought that Levi should just offer to heal him so that Marina would leave us alone, but I knew that it wouldn't end there. If history was to be believed, my people wouldn't hesitate to entrap a sea dragon and force one to use its healing powers at their leisure. I didn't trust Marina as far as I could push her.

But now Marina would be after him. I shuddered. She might not know that Levi was the sea dragon, but she would be watching for him. Greed had been stamped on her face.

I was the reason Levi was in danger now. I had to protect him from my past mistakes and the enemies I couldn't shake.

CHAPTER 10

I managed to sneak the seal shifter into the employees' supply room without anyone catching sight of us. The stormy weather helped since no dry folk braved the cold weather. I handed her a skirt and blouse with the Lodge logo on it, and she passed over my damp clothes.

"Why did you help me?" I asked in English as well as in our common language of clicks and gestures. I'd learned with Cetus to include English in every sentence so a newcomer could learn more quickly. Seal shifters didn't have the pale folk ability to pick up languages quickly, but she would eventually learn.

She responded in her own fashion, her gestures clumsy and jerky out of water. "You were going to die. I'd had enough of Marina and her orders." She flapped the blouse in front of her until I took pity and fastened her buttons. "She came to my colony last week and took three of us away from our harvesting duties. Told us that she had a special job and that she would reward us. The other two puffed up with importance that the Siren Protector's daughter chose us." Her mouth pursed. "I didn't want to leave, so I refused. Well, that wasn't an option. Marina said that she needed three, so she put a siren song on me that made me follow her orders until we captured you and started the erasure ceremony."

"You couldn't help me until then." I shuddered at the long-lasting and far-reaching power that Marina could wield. "Will she come after you now?"

"I hope not. Hopefully, she thinks you dragged me along as a hostage." The shifter adjusted her shirt with a grimace of discomfort. "Is this really what dry folk wear?"

"Better get used to it," I said with a grin. "Modesty is a big thing up here. What's your name, by the way?"

"Echo," she said in our language.

I twisted my mouth in thought, then translated the word into English and said it aloud. "Echo. That works."

"Echo," she repeated in English with a doubtful expression.

Now that Echo was dressed and we were out of danger, I had the leisure to think of Levi. The last I'd seen of the sea dragon, he'd been zipping away from the black cloud engulfing Marina and her cronies, but I didn't want to trust that Levi was safe. Should I dive under to search for him? What if Marina was lying in wait for me? I couldn't count on Levi rescuing me a second time. But what if he was in trouble?

I wrung my hands as we exited the storeroom. To my intense relief, a familiar figure traipsed across the lawn toward us, clothes dry but hair dripping. Levi's eyes brightened when he saw me, and he broke into a jog.

"I've been looking for you," Levi said when he skidded to a stop in front of me. "It's past dinner, and I was getting worried. Where were you?"

I blinked at him. Was he still hiding his true nature? I suppressed a sigh—I had promised myself that I would let him tell me his secret when he was ready—and answered. "Swimming. Then Marina captured and tried to kill me. The sea dragon distracted her, and Echo and I escaped." I jerked my thumb at my companion, who ducked her head at Levi in the shy way many shifters—and teenagers—had. "Marina threatened her and forced her to follow. When the compulsion ended, she fled."

Levi stared at Echo, who shuffled her feet at his scrutiny. He wasn't buying her story, and I didn't blame him. It would be easy for Marina to plant someone to follow me.

But he hadn't seen what had happened between us underwater, and Marina had had no time alone with Echo before we'd escaped. I was certain that Echo was being honest.

But precautions weren't a bad idea, and I didn't argue when Levi came up with a plan to have her watched.

"Good to meet you, Echo," Levi said carefully with English and gestures. "Let's find you some dinner, and I'll get my brother to keep you company. I need to speak to Lune."

Echo nodded again, and Levi led the way to the staff dining hall. Austin was still there, chatting with an employee I recognized as Henry, but he immediately stood when Levi waved him over.

"Austin, this is Echo," he said. "She's new on land and doesn't speak English yet. Could you get her some food and keep her company while I talk to Lune? Set her up in the bunkhouse if we're not back soon."

Levi gave his brother a significant look, and Austin

nodded.

"Hi, Echo," he said in the mix of English and Seamount language I'd been employing. "It's your lucky night. The kitchen made sushi."

Austin led Echo away after she glanced at me for reassurance. I nodded and watched them walk toward the buffet table. Levi tugged my elbow.

"Can we talk outside?" he said quietly.

At my nod, he drew me forward and into the darkening night. Stormy winds whipped my shirt's hem and whistled through the creaking trees overhead. Levi's hand ran down my arm and slid into my own hand, and I clutched its large warmth in my fingers. Memories of our beachside intimacy rushed through my body. I ached to hold him closer than this. What would those hands feel like running over my back, up my thighs again, squeezing me…

A splash of reality brought my thoughts back to the current moment. Marina had almost killed me. But how had she traveled from Vancouver so quickly? For that matter, how had she known I was at the Lodge? The ocean was a big place, and to pinpoint my location so exactly spoke of insider knowledge. But only Byssa, Hades, and Levi had known about my vacation destination.

Wait, Branc had also known. But what would he gain from telling Marina where I was going? Because he would gain something, that was for sure. Branc never did anything without it benefiting himself.

Levi spun me around to sit when we reached the relative shelter of a bench within an arched trellis. In the summer sun, this must have been a tranquil, picturesque spot to enjoy a view of the glittering bay. Now, it was surrounded by whispering trees and dimly lit by porch lights from the nearby dockside rooms. Shadows flickered over Levi's face as branches bobbed in the wind between him and the light.

"Do you want to hear more about what happened under there?" I asked, not sure why he had pulled me away from the dining hall. "Or talk about Echo?"

"No, I…" Levi ran a hand through his damp hair, making it stand in tousled spikes. I sat on my hands to prevent them from reaching out to touch him. While I would rather do other things than talk, he clearly had something to spit out. I didn't want to distract him.

"What is it?"

"I have something to tell you," he said in a rush. "But I need you to promise me that you won't tell anyone else. Ever. It's really important."

My stomach clenched. Was this the moment? Had Levi decided that I was worthy of trust, of his most vital secret?

"I promise."

"I'm not human," he breathed. "And I'm not a siren, nor a seal shifter. I'm something different. You know the creature that helped you with the ligan last month, and the one that distracted Marina today?" He took a deep, shuddering breath and stared into my eyes. "That was me."

I stared back, wondering what to say. I wanted to throw my arms around his neck at my joy that he'd trusted me with his secret. I didn't know how I'd proved deserving, but I was going to revel in it, regardless.

But he didn't need to know that. I leaned back on my hands and tilted my head at him, feigning nonchalance.

"I figured," I said casually.

Levi recoiled with mouth agape. He clearly hadn't considered my reaction possible.

"You knew?" he whispered. His head shook as if to clear it. "How? And if you know, does everyone? It's not safe, you heard the story singer Marea. No one can know. I'll have to leave if anyone else finds out."

"No, no." I grabbed his hand and squeezed it between both of my own. I had to calm the wild terror that flowed off Levi in waves of distress so strong I could almost feel them vibrating through my body. "You're so careful. There's no way anyone else knows. I only started putting the pieces together after you saved me from the ligan. I had suspicions, especially since your hair was sometimes wet with seawater but you said you didn't swim, but it wasn't until I saw your eyes without contacts this morning that I was sure. They're so—"

"Freaky," Levi muttered, although his hand didn't leave mine.

"Mesmerizing," I finished with a finger squeeze.

"Why didn't you say something?" he demanded. "We were alone all day."

"I wanted you to tell me yourself," I said quietly. I didn't explicitly mention my hope that he would find me trustworthy. Levi must have read the subtext, because he gripped my hands tighter.

We sat in silence for a minute, both lost in our own thoughts. I stared into the darkness, wind whipping the sea into frothy peaks that glinted in the black of night. I had too much to say and no idea where to start. What did he know? Where were his birth parents? Did his adoptive parents know everything? What was the black fire he'd distracted Marina with? What happened when he shifted?

"I really want to swim with you," I blurted out.

Levi caught my gaze with his. His eyebrows rose.

"That's what you want?" he said in surprise. "That's all you have to say?"

"I have a thousand questions," I admitted. "But yes, I really want to swim with you. It's where I feel at home, and not sharing that…"

"It was a barrier, I get it." Levi sighed and slipped out of my grasp to run his hands through his hair again. Then a wide smile slowly developed on his face. "Yeah, let's swim. I've never swum with anyone except my parents and Austin."

"They know?"

"Hard to keep that a secret from family. Although I didn't start shifting until I was twelve. That's when the eyes turned, too." He waved at his face with a dismissive motion that hurt my heart to see. "Before then, I looked like a typical human kid. After that, anytime I get in the ocean, I can't stop the change."

"Why would you want to?" I whispered. His sea dragon form was so fantastic.

"It's hard to keep a secret in a place full of sirens

when you can't swim in front of them." Levi huffed a mirthless laugh. "I've had my fair share of teasing, let me tell you."

"I can imagine that." I drummed my fingers on my thighs. "We can't swim here, though. Marina saw you." I gulped as the full import of my words sunk in. After the madness below, dealing with Echo, and Levi's revelations, I'd forgotten about the incident. "She *saw* you. And she was raised on story singer tales. She knows exactly what you are. Oh, by the way, the man I thought I'd killed? Not dead. Shoal is Marina's pledged lover, and he's in a sorry state that the doctor thinks he won't recover from. And now that she knows you exist, nothing will stop her from hunting you down to heal him."

"I've never tried anything much more than a cut," Levi said. "But maybe I should heal him and move on. Will she forgive and forget her vengeance against you, do you think?"

"No way. I don't want her anywhere near you. It might start with her man, but you heard the story singer. Marina would absolutely drag you back to the Seamount. You didn't see her face when she realized what you were. And her compulsion ability is so strong, you wouldn't stand a chance."

"Sirening doesn't affect me," Levi said with a grin. "Not since I started shifting. Well, it can if I'm not paying attention, but I can protect myself against it. I'm not worried about that."

My jaw dropped. "Not at all? And you let me wallow in my guilt for weeks?"

"Rightfully so." He quirked an eyebrow at me. "You tried to control me. Just because it wouldn't have worked doesn't mean it was okay to do."

I sank against the back of the bench, defeated by his logic. Guilt threatened to wash over me again, but I pushed it down firmly. I'd floated in that current before, and Levi had forgiven me. No point in opening old wounds.

"But still." I straightened, back on my original point. "She'll be after you. And she knows the sea dragon is likely to be someone close to me, since you saved me. It won't be long before she figures it out. We can't let that happen, not on my watch."

"So, no swimming here." Levi's shoulders slumped. My stomach squirmed with pleasure that he wanted it as much as I did.

"What if you come to Vancouver for a bit? Throw Marina off the scent?"

"She followed you here. What's stopping her from following you back?"

I drummed my fingers again. The wind howled above us. "I still don't know how she traveled here so quickly, and how she knew where to come. I can't imagine her taking the ferry, but it's a few days' swim up here."

Levi shook his head, as perplexed as I was.

"But still," I continued, "it will keep her guessing."

"I don't know," he said. "I don't think the Lodge—"

"Sandy is immensely capable," I said firmly. "And we can leave in a few days, it doesn't have to be tonight. Marina will have to figure out a plan, and you can use that time to make sure everything is ready for leaving.”

“Austin could use some more responsibility,” Levi mused aloud. “Properly supervised, of course.”

“There you go,” I said, eager to push the visit. “It would be good for him. Show him that you trust him. A little.”

I wanted Levi safely away from Marina, but him visiting Vancouver would also give us more time together. Even more after his revelation, I wanted to explore us. Explore him. I wrenched my thoughts away from that topic when my cheeks warmed.

Levi tensed at shouting from the Lodge. I turned my head to see what was wrong.

CHAPTER II

A branch from the wildly swaying trees overhead had fallen, and its weight had crashed into an outbuilding near the Lodge. Now, three figures stood around the oversized branch and the hole in the outbuilding's roof.

Levi growled in frustration. "I need to deal with this."

"Do you want help?"

"No." He leaned forward and kissed me firmly on the lips. "This is your vacation. I'll rustle up some staff. I don't know how long I'll be, though."

"Do what you need to do," I said with an inward sigh. It looked like my plans of exploration would have to wait. "I should make sure Echo is okay, anyway. See you in the morning?"

Levi growled again, and the sound cramped the muscles in my torso with a pleasurable ache. He slid a hand around my hip and kissed me again, pressing hard against me as if he could release some of our tension that way. I wriggled closer, opening myself to him.

Another shout froze his movements, then he tore away from me with an exasperated release of air.

"Go." I pushed him away to stop his teasing. I'd have to go for a swim at this rate just to cool down. "Go fix the Lodge."

His smoldering eyes were eloquent, but he strode into the night without another word. I heaved a tremendous sigh and gave myself a moment to unwind from Levi's presence.

Once my heart stopped racing—although nothing would halt my mind from following interesting paths—I walked to the staff suites' entrance. Levi had left the door to his suite unlocked for me, and I entered and grabbed my drybag. I tried not to look at his bed as I left. The cozy blue duvet was so inviting, but tonight hadn't gone as planned, and I wanted to do things right. The bunkhouse would do for now, but tomorrow?

I grinned. Levi had better watch out. Just because I couldn't siren him didn't mean I wouldn't lure him in by other means. From his glance at me as he'd left, he was already ensnared and liked it.

The door closed behind me with a sad click, and I stumped off to the dormitory after grabbing a plate of sushi from the dining room. It was only now that my early morning and kidnapping by Marina were catching up with me. My eyelids drooped, and my mouth opened in a jaw-cracking yawn. The dorm beds sounded inviting with every passing minute.

The low building that housed seasonal workers was tucked into the trees on the south end. I'd stayed here in the summer with Byssa and Hades, and the handle opened with familiar ease under my fingers. Inside, the hallway was dimly lit by a lamp that remained on all night.

A door at the end of the hall opened, and Pipa stepped out with only a towel wrapped around her torso and her hair wet. Skin on her neck glistened with dampness from her shower. She blinked at me in surprise, then a knowing look stole over her features.

"Hi. It's Lune, right?" She smiled. "Have a good day?"

"The best," I said, hating the way she looked at me. Her thoughts were as clear as tropical water. Why was I here and not with Levi? Were we not that close? Did Pipa have a chance?

I wanted to say she absolutely didn't—and Levi's actions today agreed with me—but a niggling doubt wormed to the forefront of my mind. He'd been very friendly with Pipa, almost a little too interested in her, and she certainly wasn't turning him away.

I gave her a big, fake smile. "So great. Don't let me keep you. A friend of mine just arrived and I want to make sure she's settling in okay." I laughed lightly. "Levi will just have to wait. Do you know which room she's in?"

"That one." Pipa pointed at the closest door. "There's hardly anyone here this time of year, so she took her own room."

"Okay, thanks, good night!" I waved at her and knocked at Echo's door, eager to escape Pipa's smirking face. I didn't know if she'd bought my story, but her expression told me she hadn't. My jaw clenched, and I pushed into the room to leave the dark-haired woman and her annoying, smug, too-pretty face behind.

"Lune!" Echo sat up in her bunk from where she'd been lying, staring at the top bunk above her. Her eyes were moist, but she sniffed and gave me a watery smile. "I didn't know you would be here."

"Sorry for leaving you alone like that." I sat on the

bunk opposite her and dropped my drybag on the ground. My feet kicked my boots off with relief, and I wiggled my toes. "I had to talk to my friend Levi about something. He's the manager of the Lodge, which is where we're staying."

Echo gave me a blank look. "Lodge?" she repeated in English.

"It's a place where people stay when they visit other places," I explained. To someone from the Seamount, the notion of traveling was a confusing one. I knew from experience. "Dry folk stay here for fun, and so do upper echelon pale folk sometimes. Levi isn't pale folk, but he knows about us and helps keep our secrets from other dry folk."

"Is he dry folk?" Echo asked.

"There are lots of half-humans here," I said vaguely without directly answering her question. After becoming the recipient of Levi's trust, I would protect it as hard as I could.

"Yes, like Austin." Echo nodded, a pleased smile on her face. Every few words, she attempted a word in English to accompany her gestures, and Austin's name was one of them. "He is Levi's brother? He kept me company at dinner." She made a face. "Very strange food here. Odd textures."

I laughed. "That's the cooking. I eat a lot of sushi for that reason. Are you okay, though? You looked sad when I came in."

Echo shrugged. "It's been a long day. A long week, actually. And I miss home. My family must be so worried about me. And I can't let them know I'm all right because I can't return to the Seamount, not with Marina patrolling these waters. She won't let me go that easily."

"What did she have on you?" I asked.

"She threatened to compel me further, said she'd make me hurt my own family if I didn't obey her. She could do it, too. Her compulsion is so powerful." Echo glowered. "No offense, but sirening sucks for the rest of us."

"Yeah, I get that." I took off my socks and laid down on the bunk, still facing Echo. "I used to live in the pale folk ghetto and had my fair share of oppression. So, Marina forced you along to do what?"

"Take care of Shoal, mostly. We had to drag him with us across the ocean. It's not like Marina was going to do it herself. And he needs feeding softened food every few hours. Apparently, Marina had someone caring for him at the Seamount, but they grew ill themselves and had to quit. That's what prompted her to leave and try finding a cure outside the Seamount. She'd heard rumors of a healer who'd left years ago to study dry folk medicine."

"Dr. Mazzaella." I nodded. "Yes, I know her. I saw Marina visiting her. Turns out there's nothing she can do for Shoal."

"Ugh." Echo flopped back onto her bed. "I was hoping she could fix Shoal, and we could all go back to the Seamount together. He doesn't even want to be here, I can tell. He doesn't hum or click, but he makes feeble gestures that almost look like words. I'm pretty sure he wanted to be sent to the abyss like he should have been, but Marina wouldn't hear of it. She's keeping him alive against his will." Echo sighed. "I don't know whether to appreciate or be disgusted by her actions. Now I have to escape somehow, and then avoid bumping into Marina for the rest of my life in case she wants to retaliate."

All this talk of Marina reminded me that she was still out there and angrier than ever. I leaped up and locked the door. Marina might have powers of persuasion, but her abilities didn't extend to mechanical things. A lock should keep her out while we slept, in case she felt the urge to prowl around without thinking up a proper plan like I expected her to. And who knew what she might send her seal shifters to do?

To be on the safe side, I dug out Branc's eelgrass concoction from my drybag and nibbled a dose. It was sweet with a hint of bitterness, but I would have eaten anything to protect myself from Marina's compulsion.

I texted Levi to remind him to lock his own door. When he didn't reply immediately, I sighed and shoved the phone back in my pocket. He was probably still dealing with the broken roof. Hopefully, Pipa was keeping to her room this evening.

"I'm heading back to Vancouver in a few days," I said to Echo to distract myself from sour thoughts of Pipa. "It's a dry folk city to the southeast. You could come with me, over land, and swim back to the Seamount from there. You'd avoid Marina that way."

Echo's eyes brightened. "You think that would work?"

"I don't see why not. Then you could see a bit of

land before you go. It's worth checking out, especially if you're going to spend the rest of your life cooped up at the Seamount."

Echo nodded, her gaze reflective. I shuffled to the bathroom and got ready for bed. When I slipped between the sheets, my body ached for the warmth of someone else, a particular someone.

Despite my tiredness, sleep was a long time coming.

In the morning, I accompanied Echo to the staff dining hall and helped her find food that she could stomach. Although my eyes scanned the room every minute, Levi didn't show up. I tried not to be too disappointed—even as my gut clenched every time someone new entered the room—and I vowed to search for him after breakfast.

"What should I do?" Echo asked me once we'd finished eating and I stood from my bench seat. It must have been clear that I wanted to get away.

"Wander," I said. "Explore. Get steady on your feet. Just don't get lost, and keep your eyes open for Marina and the other shifters. I might leave for a bit, but I'll be back by dinner. Come here when you're hungry, especially when the sun is halfway across the sky." I peered out the window at the steely gray clouds overhead. "Scratch that. Come here when you're hungry, and someone in the kitchen will help you out. Okay?"

Echo nodded and glanced out the window with interest. Now that she wasn't weepy and frightened, her curiosity about the world she'd unexpectedly found herself in was showing. That would serve her well.

I waved goodbye and trotted to the front desk through the interior of the main Lodge building. Echo's boredom wasn't my responsibility. I'd set her up with food and shelter, and the rest was up to her.

My stomach flopped when I caught sight of the back of Levi's head bent over papers on the front counter in the bright lobby. I gave the hated fireplace a loathing glare—it was lit, and flames were flickering with evil delight—then I turned my attention to Levi, who was pointing at numbers on the paper. Sandy stood next to him, nodding at whatever Levi was saying. When she saw me, she grinned and put her hand over the paper.

"I understand," Sandy said with tolerant patience to Levi. "And I'll take care of it right away. But, for now, it's time for you to leave."

Levi stared at her in bewilderment. When I cleared my throat, he spun around, and his face broke open in a wide smile that felt like a warm current on my face.

"Lune, you're here." He turned back to Sandy with a frown. "But what about—"

"I've got it." She made a shooing motion with her hands then handed him a paper bag. Had she packed us lunch? "Honestly, Levi, it's shoulder season. It's quiet here. If you don't take a little time off now, you never will."

Levi hesitated for a moment, then he grabbed the lunch and a set of keys from a rack on the wall and took my hand. I adored how easily our hands slid together, and how casually he made the connection happen. He tugged me outside and toward the Lodge truck he usually drove. I didn't know where we were going, but I didn't care, as long as we went together.

"Good morning," a silky voice said from our left. Pipa stood with garden shears next to a scraggly bush along the driveway. She glanced at each of our faces and then our linked hands. Her smile grew more forced.

"Hi, Pipa," Levi said. "We're off for a while, but I'll be back later."

"Have fun." Her glance flicked to me again, and her mouth tightened.

Levi pulled me to the truck, and I allowed myself to be propelled forward. Once we were seated and Levi had backed out of his parking spot, I tried to put Pipa from my mind. She was far too interested in Levi for my comfort. The other woman had designs, and I promised myself to keep an eye on her. She wanted something from Levi, and it was my job to make sure she didn't collect. Protecting Levi from Marina's greedy hands was paramount, but keeping him safe from Pipa's clutches might prove the more difficult task.

"Pipa is around a lot," I said with as much delicacy as I could muster.

Levi glanced at me. "Yes, because she works at the Lodge. Why, what are you thinking?"

"Nothing, nothing." I drummed my fingers on my knee. "She just acted strangely toward me last night."

"I think you're feeling paranoid after Marina's

attack," he said firmly. "Don't worry about Pipa. I'm sure she's fine. It's natural to feel on edge after what you've been through. Focus on our upcoming swim. I hope you're still game."

I didn't like Levi's blasé assurances but resolved to put my dilemmas aside. We were driving away from Pipa's schemes, Marina's searching, and the Lodge's ever-present pull on Levi's attention. He and I were going for our first swim together, and that was worthy of being in the moment for.

"Of course I'm still game. Where are we swimming?" I asked, turning on the radio. "Somewhere far from the Lodge, I hope."

"We'll go to Skookumchuck Narrows." At my raised eyebrow, Levi chuckled. "They're rapids at the entrance to Sechelt Inlet, north of here, so it's a long swim from the Lodge. There won't be as much sea life to check out, but it should be safe from Marina."

"Then it sounds perfect." I leaned back and tried to whistle along to the song on the radio. It came out as breathy as always.

"Don't laugh." I swatted Levi's arm when he chuckled under his breath. "Whistling is hard. I need to practice."

"Tighten your lips more," he instructed. I tried and blew harder, but the sound was still breathy. He reached over with only a quick glance away from the road to make sure his hand was over my mouth, then he wrapped his fingertips around my pursed lips. "Tighter, Bah, I don't know how to teach whistling."

I was less interested in whistling than in Levi's hands

on my mouth. I relaxed my lips and reached my tongue out to lick the side of his finger.

He froze, then the wet fingertip ran along my bottom lip. He inched it into my mouth, and I let him explore my tongue.

The truck swerved. Levi snatched his hand back to grip the wheel when a car honked at us.

"Distracted driving," he said hoarsely with a grin at me. "I'm putting that one on you."

"I can handle it." I crossed my legs and resumed my whistling practice, missing Levi's touch on my lips.

CHAPTER 12

We drove for almost an hour, and I was ready for a stretch by the time Levi pulled into a nearly empty parking lot past the Skookumchuck Narrows sign. He grabbed two towels from behind my seat then hopped out of the truck.

"This way." He pointed at a narrow path that led east. "The water's not far, and there's a private beach we can swim from. I come here when I want to jump in the water, because no pale folk bother to swim over here."

My heart squeezed for Levi. How many years of lonely swims had he endured, never able to tell anyone about himself? I slammed the truck door and followed him with eager footsteps.

The path wandered under towering conifers until water glinted between trunks beside the path. Levi turned down a track that was hardly wide enough for deer to pass along. It meandered away from the main trail to the water's edge. I looked behind us, but no one was watching our progress through the light rain. Humans weren't very fond of getting wet, so we had the park almost to ourselves.

We emerged in a stony cove barely long enough for three people to lie end-to-end on. Steep, rocky banks dripping with ferns and brilliant green moss surrounded the cove, which provided a sense of shelter and privacy. Toward the water was open, but across the way were thick stands of conifers that melted into green hills behind. Little wavelets lapped at the sand, untouched by wind and storms at sea. To our left, standing waves and swirling whirlpools spread across the narrows.

"It's perfect," I breathed. "No one will ever see us here, and pale folk won't dare to cross the rapids. So, how does this work? How do you change?"

"It happens in the water." Levi pulled off his shirt, and I stopped to watch the show. When he caught me ogling him, his cheeks grew faintly pink. "Shifting isn't something I can control. When I'm immersed, I change. When I come ashore, I turn back into this."

"Can you shower?" I imagined Levi curled up in his sea dragon form in a tub.

"Yes, it has to be salt water. I can swim in a lake, and that doesn't trigger it."

Levi paused his undressing, so I stripped off my own clothes and tucked them under the cliff's edge since the show was on hiatus. When I turned around, Levi still had his jeans on, although he tucked a contact lens case in his towel.

"I'll meet you in there?" he said.

"You're feeling modest, are you?" I stepped forward and rubbed his cheek. His mesmerizing eyes gazed at me with uncertainty dancing in their depths. I swallowed then smiled to push away the squirming sensation in my gut. "Clearly, you've been raised among humans. Fine, I'll see you in the water."

I had every intention of seeing Levi as the gods had made him, but if he wanted to delay, then I would savor every moment of anticipation. I splashed into the water and dived under the mild waves, resisting the urge to turn around and watch him get in, but I couldn't turn off my skin sense. Although my transition to breathing water was distracting, I caught a general sense of Levi's transformation as a twitching, twisting flurry of limbs until a sinuous sea dragon writhed behind me. One day, I promised myself, I would watch his change with my own eyes.

Levi swam around me in a circle, one blue, green, and silver eye on me all the time. I reached out with a tentative hand to brush his skin. When my fingers made contact, his silvery-blue scales shivered under my touch. The scales shimmered in the dim light, and I marveled at their opalescent beauty.

Levi's tail whisked past me, then his head was back. I breathed in the scent of him, a rich taste hinting of hazelnuts. I ran my hand along one frond-like appendage that emerged from behind his eye. It must have been sensitive, because he shook his head to dislodge my hand.

Too much. Clicking startled me. I peered at Levi.

Can you talk under here?

A little. He positioned his body so his head was level with mine. Now that his face was visible, with its craggy brows and gleaming scales, his eyebrows and mouth expressed more emotion. A choked sort of humming emerged from his throat. The meaning came out garbled, and I strained to understand. *It's hard.*

You can understand me, because you grew up with Austin and your parents, I guessed so he wouldn't have to explain. *But your body isn't made for communicating like we do.*

Levi nodded. I touched his nose, and he reared back in surprise. A laugh escaped me.

He growled and twisted away. I turned to see what he was up to, but my skin sense only felt a rush of water before his body appeared between my arms. Reflexively, I squeezed.

We shot through the inlet at dizzying speed. Water rushed past my skin sense, too chaotic to feel anything of our surroundings. I didn't care. Riding on Levi's back was thrilling. I tucked my legs around his form and pressed against his back to streamline our passage. My hair fluttered behind us, and his fronds occasionally tapped me on the head. I laughed aloud for the sheer joy of it.

Levi dived through waters that grew clearer the deeper we swam. He hadn't been lying when he'd said that not much lived in the inlet, and we passed plenty of silty seafloor with only the occasional sea pen waving or sea cucumber nuzzling the mud.

But I wasn't here for the scenery. Levi's back was warm against my stomach, and his body twisted from side to side in a gentle undulation that shifted me back and forth with the motion. I closed my eyes, relishing the sensation of his slippery scales against the tender skin of my inner legs.

Aside from his adoptive parents and brother, I was the only one who had ever seen him like this. The thought made me squeeze him tighter and press my cheek against his scales. His trust in me was overwhelming, and I hoped I would live up to it. I promised myself that I would never reveal this to anyone, ever.

Pipa would want to see this, I had no doubt. Her smug face popped into my head. I scowled then pushed her malevolent presence out of my mind. Pipa wasn't going to spoil this moment, not even in my thoughts.

Levi slowed, then he gently shook his body where I clutched him. I let go and swam to the front of his head.

Watch, he said. I knew his mind was as sharp as my own, so it was strange to hear him speak with no more clarity than Squirter. Still, I had plenty of practice understanding my little octopus friend, and I nodded.

Levi turned his head to the side, opened his mouth, and exhaled sharply. I stared in surprise.

Inky blackness billowed from his mouth in dark clouds of black fire. The water shimmered, distorted by heat. Within the clouds, tiny flickers of light sparkled and twinkled like stars in the sky.

Is that bioluminescence? I asked incredulously. When Levi nodded, I shook my head in amazement. *But why?*

Makes it hard to see, he replied. He twisted his head in a figure eight, the expression in his eyes frustrated. *Makes it confusing.*

So, if you blast someone with your breath, they'll see a hot, black night full of distracting stars?

Levi nodded vigorously. I reached out with tentative fingers to touch the cloud. The water was warm, but no hotter than dry folk might run a bath.

Not hot, Levi said. *Gets hotter.*

I turned and gazed into one of his beautiful eyes, and my finger traced the hardened scales of his brow. He held still, eyeing me.

Thank you for showing me this, I said softly. *And trusting me. I won't let you down.*

Levi closed his eyes, then he bent his head and

nuzzled my bare stomach. I stroked his forehead then tried to touch his fronds again. He jerked away.

Sorry, I said.

Levi narrowed his eyes at me, then he shoved his way between my arms again. I held on, and we darted through the water once more.

We swam for ages until I completely lost track of time. I could have stayed under there with Levi forever. But when his stomach groaned loudly, I chuckled.

Time for lunch? I said. *I saw we have sandwiches again. There's not much to eat in the inlet.*

Don't want to go, he said with downcast eyes. I hugged him around his neck.

We'll swim again soon, I promised. *This was amazing. And maybe next time you can meet Squirter properly.*

Levi nodded with a gleam of interest. Then he nudged me, and I floated into my position on his back. Already, it felt natural to wrap myself around the torso of a sea dragon. From not even knowing that they existed to closely swimming with one was a strange progression in a few days, but I reveled in every minute of our swim back.

Too soon, the water grew shallow, and the mirrored surface jostled above our heads. Levi gently shook me off.

Me first, he said firmly.

I bit my lip to keep myself from smiling. *Sure thing.*

Levi looked a little panicked at that, but his communication skills weren't developed enough to argue with me. He peeked his eyes above water. When the coast was clear, he beached himself with a surge of motion. Halfway out, his tail twisted into bare legs that crawled the rest of the way.

I counted to twenty then swam to shore, too impatient to wait. When I breached the surface, I coughed out water from my lungs then stood and waded onto our tiny beach.

"That was a really quick minute," Levi said with narrowed eyes. He gripped a towel around his waist, rivulets of water running down his bare chest and his hair dripping in waterlogged waves.

I shrugged innocently and gestured at his towel. "Modesty preserved. What are you complaining about?"

I sauntered closer to him and laid my palm on his chest. His breath hitched. I felt emboldened by our swim, when we'd been so close for so long. Vents, I'd wrapped my legs around his body for ages. Just because he'd been in sea dragon form at the time didn't mean he wasn't still Levi.

Okay, it was a little confusing, I would grant him that. But now that he was in human form, all bets were off. From the look that he was giving me, he agreed.

Our lips met. Seconds later, so did the bare skin of our stomachs. I pressed against him and ran my hands over his slick torso until my fingers met the dark downy hairs on his chest. I toyed with them absently, half of my attention fascinated by them, since men at the

Seamount were uniformly hairless there. Most of my focus was on Levi's lips and tongue, and I soon gave myself up to their sensations and the heat of his hands on my back. My fingers found the remnants of smooth scales on Levi's neck, and he gripped me tighter.

A muffled musical ring rose from Levi's backpack. He stiffened and drew away from my lips. I frowned at his backpack as he stooped to pluck out his phone, his hand still clutching the towel around his waist.

"You could have left it," I said, instantly hating my petulant tone. My body ached for more Levi, and its cries for attention made it hard for me to think straight.

"It's not a call." Levi pressed a button and straightened. "It's an alarm. I need to get back to the Lodge soon." His mouth twisted with the same frustration I felt, which mollified me slightly. Pipa probably wished she could make Levi look like that. "I'm sorry. We spent so much time underwater that the morning passed us by."

"That's why we were here, after all." I turned my back to give Levi the privacy he was so adamant about and pulled out my skirt and shirt from under the log where I'd stashed them. After I'd shimmied into my clothes, I said, "Are you decent?"

"Good enough," came the muffled reply. I turned just as Levi's muscled chest disappointingly disappeared under his shirt. He slung his backpack over one shoulder and took my hand. "We'll have to eat our sandwiches in the car."

We had to let go of each other at the skinny trail back to the main path, but I liked how he'd taken my hand despite knowing that we would need to let go soon.

Back at the truck, Levi started the engine and handed me a sandwich.

"I'm starving." He ripped apart the waxed paper holding his sandwich together and tore into his food with his teeth. "Swimming and changing form always gives me a huge appetite."

Levi pulled out of the parking lot and onto the highway with one hand on the wheel and the other holding his food. I unwrapped my sandwich with more composure and examined the contents. The tuna filling made me smile.

"What's this important meeting about?" I said after a few bites. "The Lodge has you wrapped around its tentacle, doesn't it?"

"I know, I'm sorry. I'm just trying so hard to get my footing since taking over management. It should settle down at some point, but most of the time it feels like I'm barely treading water." He chuckled. "Sometimes I say phrases that I've learned from human friends, but they really don't mean much to us, do they?"

"When we can breathe water, there isn't much point in keeping your head above the surface," I agreed.

"This meeting, it's not actually that important. But I said I'd be there, and I like to keep my word. I want my employees to trust me, you know? That matters to me." He took a bite and swallowed it, clearly unable to eat fast enough to satisfy his hunger. "It's training Pipa on the motorboat. I said I'd be there at one o'clock. She's been an excellent employee so far, and it's time to get her to help more, since my head maintenance worker Jess will be on maternity leave in a few months."

A fiery burst of anger flared in my chest at the mention of Pipa's name. We'd halted our intimate moment for *Pipa*, of all people? I squeezed my sandwich, and the wrapping crinkled in my tight fingers.

"Jumping through hoops for the new girl?" I said casually. "She's learning how to get you where she wants you."

"What do you mean?" Levi glanced at me, then his brows raised at once. "Are you jealous of Pipa?"

"No," I said immediately. My traitorous cheeks warmed, and I cursed my unknown human father for the inheritance of blushes. "I just think you should watch out. I'm getting strange vibes from her."

Levi glanced at me sidelong. "Yeah, she's been friendly toward me. It's hard not to notice. But there's nothing to worry about." He leaned over and planted a smacking kiss on my cheek, keeping one hand on the wheel while he drove. "You're the only one I want."

I gripped his offered hand, and we drove in silence back to the Lodge. Levi's declaration only partly convinced me. He meant what he said, of that I had no doubt, but Pipa's intentions were opaque.

It almost felt like Pipa had known what she'd be interrupting this afternoon. Had she set up this training session to bring Levi back from our outing early? Surely not, but the memory of her satisfied face brought doubt to her innocence. Pipa was up to something, and I wouldn't put it past her to try wriggling between Levi and me.

If she thought she would succeed? Well, she didn't know me very well yet.

CHAPTER 13

I wanted to further warn Levi of Pipa's likely goals, but everything I thought to say sounded ridiculous to my ears. I had absolutely nothing to go on, and I knew I would sound jealous at best, paranoid at worst.

But Levi was so sure he couldn't be swayed by Pipa's advances. Part of me was relieved at that. The other part didn't want to underestimate her. I gritted my teeth and held out my sandwich to Levi.

"Want the rest? I'm not hungry."

"Yes, you have no idea." Levi scarfed down the half-sandwich.

We were quiet and lost in our own thoughts for the rest of the journey home. I tried not to think of Pipa, because every time I did, a molten wave of anger coursed through my gut. I wished Byssa was there to talk to about it. She was always so level-headed about stuff like this.

When we pulled into the Lodge parking lot, Levi shut off the engine and turned to me.

"Thanks for swimming with me." His voice was husky with emotion. His eyes, which still glimmered with the glorious colors of his true self, gazed into mine with intensity. "I hadn't realized how much I was missing by swimming alone."

I rested my hand on his cheek. "Thanks for trusting me enough to show me yourself." My earnest reply grew coy. "But I'm still waiting for you to show me more."

As predicted, a rosy hue tinted Levi's cheeks.

"I should go," he said then cleared his throat. "Watch your back for Marina and her shifters. And I'll see you later?"

This last comment was clearly a question. I answered it with a swift kiss on his lips, pulling back before we could get carried away again.

"Later."

I watched him walk into the Lodge—ogling wasn't quite the right word, but it was close enough—and when he disappeared through the double doors, I sighed and stepped out of the truck.

I jumped when my phone rang from my pocket.

"Byssa," I said with feeling when I answered. "I'm glad you called. It's like you knew."

"Knew what?" Byssa said through the speaker. "Are things not going well in Levi-land?"

"Ugh." I leaned against the truck door. "Sort of. No, I mean, Levi's fine. We're good. In fact, he's really opening up." I swallowed back any further words. I wouldn't betray Levi's trust by telling Byssa his secret. Even if I trusted her with my life, it didn't mean that Levi did. "So yeah, he's good. It's this other woman."

"Uh oh. You leave him alone for a few weeks, and there's already another woman?"

"Right?" Talking to Byssa was as relaxing as drifting on a slow current. I adjusted the phone on my ear to get comfortable. "Her name's Pipa, and she's a new employee here. Half-siren, apparently, but definitely takes after her human parent. If she isn't after Levi, I'll eat an urchin spine. The way she looks at him? And her smirking at me when he isn't looking?" I gritted my teeth, a hot flush of anger sweeping over my body. "She wants me out of the way."

"But you said you and Levi are getting along great," Byssa said slowly. "And that things are progressing really well."

"Yes, he doesn't think Pipa is a problem," I blurted out. "But what if she wins him over because he misjudges the situation?"

"I think you need to give Levi a little more credit," Byssa said firmly. "It seems clear to me that he wants you. I haven't seen him with this Pipa person, but you haven't said anything that tells me that Levi is torn between you two. Just relax and trust that your connection is strong. Honestly, he seems pretty smitten."

I sighed. Maybe Byssa was right, although Pipa's smug face floated in my mind's eye. I didn't want to underestimate her, no matter how "smitten" Byssa thought Levi was with me.

"Maybe," I said then changed the subject. "Why did you call? Or was it just to calm me down?"

"Ha, no, although I'm always happy to do that. I'll be at the Lodge tomorrow, actually."

"What? Why?" A glow of happiness at seeing Byssa here warmed my chest.

"It won't be for long, don't get too excited. Jules's friend Zeb is starting his new job up there, the one that Levi offered him. I'm driving him and Jules up in my car."

"So, you're going to drop Zeb off at the Lodge, then

you and Jules will have a cozy road trip back to Vancouver?" I said in a suggestive voice.

Byssa tsked at me. "It's a favor for a friend, nothing more."

"Of course. You're just friends. He's not single, you don't like him like that, and taking a full day off is no big deal to you." Byssa huffed a sigh of exasperation, and I chuckled. "Okay, I'll stop teasing you. Oh, I have other news, but you're not going to like it. Marina is here—in the ocean, anyway—and she almost got me. I managed to escape, but it was a close thing."

I wanted to give Levi credit, but that would involve exposing his secret. I bit my tongue and pondered the difficulty of keeping things from Byssa.

"Lune!" Byssa's shocked voice was loud in my ear. "How did she find out? How did she get up there so fast? What are you going to do?"

"I don't know the answers to any of those questions." My teeth chewed my bottom lip. "But she's upper echelon, so presumably she knows about the Lodge. It was probably a good guess, then she sensed me underwater. Marina can't handle being on land— she can't breathe very well—so I'm not that worried about her catching me, but it does mean I can't swim here. I haven't seen the seal shifters around, so presumably Marina is currently hatching a plan that she's not ready to implement yet. I'm going back to Vancouver in a day or two, and hopefully she doesn't follow me back. I don't know what to do if she does, but I'll have to figure that out in the city."

"Okay." Byssa heaved a breath. "Text me when

you're in Vancouver. I want to hear that you made it back."

I said my goodbyes to Byssa then pushed away from the truck. I felt slightly better about Pipa after speaking with my friend, but the other woman still bore watching. Levi might want me, but I couldn't underestimate Pipa.

I stopped in the staff dining hall to graze on more food, since Levi had eaten most of my lunch, then I wandered down the grassy slope that ran beside the main Lodge building without a destination in mind. I was at loose ends without Levi, and I wasn't sure what to do. Swimming was out, even though I chafed to dive into the water. Was Squirter wondering where I was? How could I contact my squishy friend to let him know I hadn't abandoned him?

As I pondered this dilemma, a familiar figure approached me.

"Hi, Kim," I said. The younger employee's hair was a deep purple today, and it was pulled up in a high ponytail above her round-cheeked face.

She grinned at me. "You look bored. I was about to head in for a swim. Want to join me?"

I glanced at the sea with longing but shook my head. "Thanks for the offer, but not right now."

"Aw, come on," she wheedled. "I found a great cave that I'm pretty sure has a giant Pacific octopus living in it. We could go say hello to our new neighbor."

"Another time," I said.

"Come on. You know you want to."

I frowned. Why was Kim so persistent? I'd already

said no.

"I'm sure Darren will go with you," I said. Kim was usually inseparable from her boyfriend. "I'm going to check on Levi. See you around."

I left Kim looking disgruntled and strode with sure steps to the staff dining hall until she was out of sight. I paused inside the door to collect myself. Why had Kim been so pushy? She was normally bubbly and easy-going, not forceful under a veneer of friendliness.

I shook my head and peeked outside. Kim wasn't around, but a familiar dark head of tousled, touchable hair caught my eye. Levi was on the dock talking to Jess, the head maintenance worker with a growing baby bump. Jess pointed at a piling, and Levi nodded thoughtfully.

Maybe Levi would finish soon. At least his appointment with Pipa had been quick. I wriggled my shoulders in anticipation and pushed the door open, eager to be near him again. Maybe he could take a short break with me. My mind wandered as I imagined what we could do during that break.

Levi bent down at the dock's edge to examine the piling. Jess stood. Then, with a deliberate step forward, she shoved Levi.

I gasped. Levi teetered, his balance broken. For one long moment, he hung over the edge, choppy water splashing below him. If he submersed in the ocean, he would have a hard time explaining his transformation—or his disappearance—to Jess.

I opened my mouth to shout out—to distract Jess, maybe, although I didn't know what good that would do—but Levi wavered, caught himself on the piling, and heaved upright. His chest rose and fell with unsteady breaths that I could even see from my vantage point halfway across the lawn.

Jess placed her hand on Levi's arm, an expression of contrition written across her face. Multiple exclamations of "sorry" drifted through the air. I frowned. If she had deliberately pushed Levi, why was she sorry about it? And why in Ramu's name did she want Levi in the water?

I loitered at the dock's ramp to the beach until Levi and Jess finished their investigation of the piling. Jess strode quickly away, her face concentrated on her destination. Levi followed, and his face lit up when he saw me.

"Lune, hi," he said. "Keeping yourself amused?"

"Sort of," I said with a glance at Jess's retreating back. "What happened out there? Why did Jess try to push you in the water?"

Levi stared at me. "She bumped into me by accident. Don't get me wrong, it freaked me out, but she didn't mean to do it."

"Yeah, she did." I glared at his skepticism. "Look, you didn't see what happened. It was as clear as tropical water that she shoved you on purpose. What I want to know is why."

"Do you think she suspects?" Levi's lips thinned. "I don't see how, but…"

"I don't know. Just, keep an eye out, okay? I mean, Jess clearly isn't a seal shifter, but testing you reeks of Marina's influence. I feel like I'm being too suspicious, but it could be her somehow."

"We'll leave the Lodge tomorrow," Levi promised. He tucked a piece of hair behind my ear, and I leaned into his touch. "Let me wrap up a few things, then we'll be out of here."

I offered to help Levi with his work, and we spent a pleasant hour sorting receipts from the front desk. It was dull, but the company made up for the work. When we'd accounted for all the receipts, we followed our noses to the staff dining hall. The room only had a sprinkling of people seated at the benches.

"That's everyone here, at this time of year," Levi said quietly to me. "Summer season is far busier. Even though pale folk guests come year-round, the human guests slow to a trickle."

We helped ourselves to scallop curry, then I walked toward Echo's waving hand where she sat next to Austin and Henry. I slid in next to her, and Levi sat across from me.

"Don't forget I'm off early tonight," Sandy said to Levi as she passed. "Remember to finish payroll before you leave tomorrow."

She patted his slumped shoulder and left. Levi shoveled his food in faster.

"I guess you're busy tonight," I said with an attempt at a smile.

Levi looked at me with expressive eyes. "I'm sorry.

It's just—leaving tomorrow—"

"I get it." I laid a hand on his warm forearm and gave it a squeeze. "Don't stress. Do what you need to do so we can get away from you know who."

Levi nodded then returned to his dinner. Too soon, he was done and gone after a brush of his hand on my back that made me close my eyes with a shiver of longing.

Echo nudged me. "Are you okay?" she said in Seamount language.

I nodded and tried to pull myself together. "We're leaving tomorrow. Do you still want to come?"

Echo nodded vigorously. I took a bite of my curry, then I tuned into the conversation happening between Henry and Austin.

"You saw a brown catshark up near the shallows?" Henry speared a scallop on his fork. "That's rare they make it up so far. You're lucky."

"It was really friendly, too," said Austin. "Like a slow-moving puppy."

Henry put his palms on the table and leaned forward with an intense gaze at Austin. "Have you felt the long creature swimming around here lately?"

I stiffened. Had Henry sensed Levi? I didn't know how much Levi swam in these waters. I'd received the impression that he tried not to show himself underwater near where sirens swam. But he'd rescued me from Marina. Maybe Henry had felt him then? Austin and I exchanged a nervous glance. Austin knew about his brother's other form, and it looked like he knew that I also knew.

"What kind of long creature?" I asked. "How big?"

Henry huffed a breath out and shook his head. "Enormous. Like something I haven't felt since my Seamount days. If I didn't know better, I'd say it was a ligan."

It was Echo's turn to stiffen beside me. Henry continued to speak to Austin, who did his best to change the subject from long creatures. I turned to Echo with a questioning glance. Her frightened eyes stared at me.

"Marina is still here," she breathed. "The ligan came with her. She rides one. That's how we got to the Lodge so quickly from your city—we hitched a ride on it."

I blinked at Echo. Marina had a ligan under her control? Either the upper echelons secretly raised ligans as pets—I wouldn't put it past them—or Marina's abilities were stronger than I'd given her credit for. Either way, the presence of a ligan under her control wasn't comforting.

"Why didn't you tell me this before?" I hissed, using my gestures as well. Frustration with Echo rose in me in tight waves.

"The ligan might be dangerous," she replied, "but Marina is the greater threat. Everything else fades into the murk next to her."

With that dispiriting notion, I turned back to my dinner, although my appetite had vanished. I poked at a scallop. When there was a break in the conversation between Henry and Austin, I jumped in.

"Have you seen any seal shifters lately? Echo here

was wondering where her companions had got to. They were separated earlier."

That was all true, although I hoped that the others wouldn't try to approach the seal shifters to reunite Echo with them. We'd be gone tomorrow, thankfully.

Henry looked at me with a frown. "Now that you mention it, there have been a couple of seals swimming around that I don't recognize. I saw them this afternoon. So, maybe? They're so similar to regular seals, and I didn't think to check for shifters."

I swallowed my unease and exchanged a glance with Echo. My expression must have translated enough of my meaning because she bit her lip. Marina and her shifters were still here.

CHAPTER 14

I couldn't set aside my worry for Squirter any longer. Entering the sea with Marina and a ligan floating around was beyond dangerous, but I had to know that Squirter was safe. After dinner, I left Echo with the others playing a game of cards and took a direct route to the tiny southern beach that the staff liked to use as a private entry to the ocean. I stripped down to my undergarments and splashed into the dark surf of the windy October evening, my heart pounding. If Marina was close by, I was done for.

Squirter jetted past in my mind's eye, and I squared my shoulders. I had to do this for my friend. I'd do it quickly, that was all.

With a deep breath in, I dived under the surface. Immediately, I sent out a hum of calling for Squirter. If he was nearby, he would recognize my call and come for me.

I didn't dare do it for more than a minute, in case Marina or her seal shifters were nearby. I swam to the shore and pulled myself out of the waves to sit on a driftwood log beside the crashing surf. Would Squirter come? He'd been taking deeper and deeper dives lately. Could he even hear me from wherever he was?

I gave it a few minutes, then I waded into the water again. When I was waist deep, I concentrated on sensing my surroundings through the water. It was difficult with the wave action, but I could feel enough to know that no pale or shifter folk were nearby.

Unfortunately, neither was anything eight-armed.

I ducked down so my head and chest were underwater. Waves pushed me around, but I sent out a desperate call for Squirter again. I didn't dare do it for longer than a few seconds, then I waited in the shallows with my breath held. Would he come? Could he hear? Or was he already food for a ligan?

Something approached me underwater, and my heart leapt in my chest. It settled into an erratic, fast heartbeat when I recognized my octopus friend.

Squirter jetted toward me and wrapped his arms around my middle. I hugged his squishiness gently.

Bad people in water, I said to him. *Ligan, too. I'm leaving soon.*

He made a vibration of distress. *Me too?*

Yes, I replied. *Come on land with me.*

Taking him home on the ferry would be awkward, but I was willing to make it work for his safety's sake.

No, he said firmly. *Swim.*

Was the little cephalopod giving me cheek? I knew he was growing, but I didn't think he'd reached the teenager stage yet.

Too dangerous, I said with finality. *Land.*

His arms drooped. *Land,* he repeated.

My shoulders relaxed with relief. I gathered him in my arms and stood. Squirter hung limply, gripping my shoulders and waist, while I waded onto the beach. He was noticeably heavier than the last time I'd carried him, and his arms reached much farther.

"How fast are you growing?" I muttered to him. The octopus tightened his grip in response to the vibration of my speech through my chest.

It was fully dark at this point, which I was grateful for, considering my state of undress and the sea creature clutched in my arms. I would have nothing helpful to say if any human guests saw me.

I picked up my clothes with a free finger, awkwardly shoved my feet into my boots, and stumbled up the path to the Lodge. Halfway along, laughter floated over the sound of surf.

I crashed into the trees, cursing the dark and my lack of skin sense on land. A bush loomed ahead of me, and I crouched behind it, trying to quiet my breathing.

A couple strolled into view, hand-in-hand. If they were siren, they certainly didn't look like it. Dry folk, by my guess. They whispered and giggled together, the first woman's curls bobbing as she walked, the second woman's short-cropped blond spikes a stark contrast.

I waited until they passed the next bend in the path, then I jogged back to the trail and toward the Lodge. That had been too close. I shuddered to think of Levi's reaction if he heard that I'd revealed Squirter to human guests. Lumping sea creatures around on land drew far too much attention. I didn't want to disappoint him or cause trouble for the Lodge. He'd had enough to deal with already in his short tenure as manager.

I made it to the staff bunkhouse without further incident and deposited a squishy Squirter in the tub. He looked sad and flat, and I grabbed a bucket from under the sink, threw on my clothes, and ran to fetch seawater. A few trips later, he floated contentedly in the tub.

"You're filling that bath up," I said to him, playing with the tip of his arm. He spanned the length of the tub now, and his body was almost the size of my head. I raised my eyebrows in amazement.

I didn't want to leave Squirter alone right now, not so soon after we'd reunited, so I draped myself over the tub's edge and tickled his mantle slowly. My eyelids drooped, and Squirter patted my hand with gentle motions.

My eyes opened hours later, gummy and blinking in the bathroom's light. How long had I slept? My stomach clenched when I thought of Levi. I'd hoped to see him that evening, but now the time had long passed. He was likely asleep in his bed by now.

I amused myself by imagining Levi in bed, his naked chest rising and falling, his serene face illuminated by moonlight. Then, with an exasperated sigh, I pushed upward and stumbled to my own empty bed, leaving a slumbering Squirter floating motionless in the tub full of seawater.

The rest of the night passed in slumber. In the morning, I freshened up in the bathroom, tossed Squirter a scrub brush from under the sink to play with, then wandered to the dining hall for breakfast. A brisk wind whipped over the water and pelted my side with a sprinkling of raindrops from a heavy gray sky. It looked about ready to pour, and I hurried toward my destination. I didn't mind getting soaked, but humans always gave such odd looks if I wandered around in wet clothing.

My chest tightened at the sight of Levi's familiar head bent over a bowl of porridge. I snatched a piece of buttered toast from the buffet table and flopped down beside him.

His face brightened when he saw me. "Lune, there you are. I was worried about you, but then Pipa said she saw a light under your dorm door, so I figured you'd just gone to bed early. I didn't want to disturb you."

You can disturb me anytime, I thought. And what were he and Pipa doing chatting about me? Aloud, I said, "I fetched Squirter last night. Now he's in my tub, and I felt bad leaving him."

"You went in the ocean?" Levi's eyes widened and his brow contracted. "That was too dangerous."

"I know." I traced the edge of my toast with one finger. "I couldn't leave Squirter down there, though. Not with a ligan on the loose. I was quick and careful."

"A ligan?"

"That's how Marina got to the Lodge so quickly. Echo told me."

Levi wrapped his arm around my shoulder and gave it a squeeze. I leaned into his warmth and basked in the comfort of his embrace.

"Oh, did you know Byssa and that guy Zeb are coming this morning?" I said.

"Zeb Artino, that guy starving for Grace? Yeah, I found him a job." Levi removed his arm to continue his breakfast, and I mourned the loss. "It's not at the

Lodge, but at an outpost a little up the coast. We keep some boats there. It's a jumping-off point to get to Desolation Sound, where the fishing and wildlife tours want to go. He's going to work on boat maintenance and dock repairs there for the winter."

"That was kind of you." I stole a hashbrown from Levi's plate and popped it in my mouth, and he grinned. "I wish someone had looked out for my Grace needs like that when I was at the Seamount. I was the provider for my friends there."

Levi's face fell. "I hate to think of you living like that. At least you're here now. Although you're still under Driftwood's thumb. How much more do you owe him? Can I help?"

I shook my head vigorously before the last words came out of his mouth. Things were starting to go well between Levi and me. The last thing I wanted was a debt to muddy the waters.

"I'm getting close," I said, omitting my worries that Branc would find a way to never let me go because I was too valuable to him. "Thanks for the offer, though. As for our plans: let's leave today. Marina is still down there, hatching a plan, and I desperately want another swim. Vancouver is calling."

"Yes, later today will work, if I can get my tasks done."

"Ready or not, we need to leave." How could I explain the urgency to Levi? Every hour we stayed at the Lodge was another hour closer to Marina capturing him. I couldn't let that happen.

"I have a lot of responsibility here. But I'll do my

level best to manage the five o'clock ferry." He bumped my shoulder with his. "I'm looking forward to spending some more time with you."

I bumped him back, pleased at his comment. "Of course you are. I'm amazing." I frowned. "I'm looking forward to leaving Marina behind as soon as possible."

"Don't forget, you said Marina can't breathe well on land. Her seal shifters can, but they can't siren anyone. As long as we stay out of the water and avoid her and her ligan, we're fine."

"I bet she's cleverer than you give her credit for," I warned, then I sighed. "Fine. This afternoon. Echo's coming with us, by the way. Oh, and do you have something we can take Squirter in? A bucket or something? He's getting pretty big these days, and I don't have my special backpack with me."

"Would an old garbage can with a lid work? We have lots of those." Levi put his spoon in his empty bowl and stood. "Let's grab it now."

I followed Levi out the door and into the worsening weather. Behind a maintenance building, Levi unearthed a plastic container with a lid that snapped on. It had a residue of old leaves from yard work, but that was easily washed out.

"I'll wash and fill it before we leave," I promised. "Now, is there anything I can help you with to get us out of here faster?"

Levi grinned and gestured at me to follow him. At his office, he set me in front of a stack of receipts, and I spent a tedious hour flipping papers and slowly typing numbers into a computer while Levi made phone calls to suppliers. When Byssa's text came through saying she was pulling into the Lodge driveway, I leaped up gladly. Helping Levi was good, but a distraction from numbers was better.

"Byssa and the others are here. I'm going to go say hello."

"I'll come too." Levi stretched his arms over his head until a sliver of firm stomach showed under his shirt. "I need to give Zeb instructions on how to access the boathouse at the outpost."

I tore my eyes away from Levi's tempting skin and walked out of the office, eager to see Byssa. I especially wanted to see how she and Jules were getting along.

Byssa pulled into a parking spot just as I exited the Lodge with Levi behind me. I jogged over to her and gave her a tight hug when she emerged from her car door.

"Lune!" Byssa beamed at me when I let go. Her green eyes were bright in her petite, pale face. "What a reception. You'd think you hadn't seen me for months."

I shrugged, a little embarrassed by my display. I'd missed her, though, especially with everything going on with Levi and Marina. Now that I wasn't keeping any secrets from Byssa, I wanted that connection.

"It's good to see you. I see you brought company." I waved across the car's roof, glistening from the earlier rain. "Hi, Jules."

Jules grinned at me, his shaggy hair flopping as he waved back. "Nice to see you again, Lune." He pulled Byssa to the side and pointed at something in the distance, and they moved off to speak together.

"And you must be Zeb," I said to the man unfolding himself from the backseat. He was so clearly of pale folk descent—the white hair and gray eyes gave it away, although his olive skin showed his human heritage—that it was astonishing he'd almost succumbed to land sickness. How had no other pale folk recognized him for what he was before this point?

He looked far better now than he had during the video call when Byssa had diagnosed him with land sickness. Then, he'd been pale and gaunt, trembling with illness. Now, his well-muscled torso and handsome face looked healthy and strong.

Zeb gave a nod, looking uncomfortable with my scrutiny. "It's Lune, right? Byssa mentioned you in the car." He gazed at me with more intensity. "She said you used to live at the underwater city."

"The Seamount, yes." I tapped my fingers on my thigh, wondering what he knew about the place. Not much, I imagined, if he hadn't even known about Grace.

"I wish I could go," he murmured. "My mother never told me anything about it."

"It's not a friendly place if you have human blood. Your mother was a half-siren, right?" I pursed my lips when Zeb nodded. How could I give him a sense of the place so he wouldn't feel badly about never having been? "I wouldn't recommend visiting. Beautiful, yes, but there's lots of prejudice against us. And they wouldn't let you leave again if you went. That's if you can even get close without being attacked by mer folk or a brigar."

He shuddered. "Yeah, I've been on the wrong end of a brigar before. Not a fun time."

"Honestly, hang out at the Lodge here if you want a flavor of pale folk society without the oppression." I smiled at Levi, who grinned back and approached us.

"Zeb, hi. I'm Levi Storm. Come into my office and I'll go over your paperwork."

Zeb followed Levi with a thoughtful expression. Jules sauntered to the edge of the sloped lawn for the view, and I pulled Byssa aside.

"What's the deal here?" I said with a half-glance at Jules's back. "You're dropping Zeb off at his work? That's awfully kind of you."

Byssa crossed her arms and gave me a glare that held no heat. "I can do a favor for a friend if I want to. It doesn't have to mean anything."

"Of course it doesn't have to mean anything." I leaned toward her and waggled my eyebrows. "But it does."

"You're terrible." Byssa lightly pushed my shoulder and giggled. "I'm just being friendly. Honestly. Jules is getting over a break-up. I'm no rebound girl."

"That's fair." I glanced at him again in consideration. "But he could probably use a nudge in the right direction."

I started toward the oblivious Jules, but Byssa caught my arm before I could take two steps.

"What do you think you're doing?" she hissed. "I don't need you to do any 'nudging'."

"I can help," I protested. "Just a quick conversation,

a few subtle hints, and he'd be looking at you in a whole new light. No sirening, I promised, remember?"

"Back off." Byssa crossed her arms and glared at me, for real this time. "I don't need you to fight my battles. I'll decide for myself when to approach Jules."

"Okay, okay." I shrugged, unsure why Byssa was so defensive, but not willing to fight with her on this point. I'd have to think of another way to help her and Jules get along better, because they weren't moving at any great speed. For all Byssa's matchmaking zeal, she was terrible at managing her own love life. But maybe I should take a barnacle off Sandy's rock and do more "suggesting" than downright taking over situations. Her masterful way of handling Levi impressed me. "He's all yours."

Byssa had other things on her mind. "Why are you still here?" she asked with a piercing look. "Marina is after you. Shouldn't you be gone already?"

"We're leaving this afternoon," I assured her. "I haven't gone swimming since she captured me, and Squirter's on land, too. We found him a tank."

"Good." Byssa sighed in relief. "At least in Vancouver we can swim in unpredictable places, and Hades and I can come with you."

Three half-sirens would be no match for Marina and a ligan, but I appreciated Byssa's offer.

We chatted about lighter topics—mainly Byssa prying about me and Levi, and me pretending to be coy in answering while also avoiding Levi's secret—then Levi and Zeb returned. Jules wandered back, and Byssa gave me a swift hug.

"Get out of here soon," she said. "And I'll see you in Vancouver tomorrow, okay?"

"Enjoy your trip," I said with one final eyebrow twitch. Byssa snorted with pursed lips and shut her car door.

Levi joined me as the others drove off. "That was a quick turnaround," he said. "I think Zeb will do well at the outpost, though. He seems like a quiet guy, and it's not exactly hopping there. Plenty of maintenance to do, though, so he'll be busy."

I slipped an arm through his. "Congrats, your good deed is done for the day. Now, can we please get moving?"

"Really soon," he promised. "I'll finish up with Sandy then pack my stuff. Sound good?"

I slipped my arm through his and squeezed against him, enjoying the warmth and closeness of his body. He returned the pressure, and I smiled at him.

"Sounds good."

"Hey, Levi." Liam, a maintenance employee I recognized from my time here in the summer, wandered up to us. His silver eyes fixed on Levi, and he wore an easy smile. "Want to come for a swim with me?"

Levi's brow contracted. I stared at Liam. He'd been here for years. How could he not have known that Levi never swam with anyone?

CHAPTER 15

"Thanks for the offer," Levi said to Liam once he'd recovered from the shock of being asked to swim. "But I'll have to decline. Lune and I are getting ready to leave soon."

"Aw, come on, man." Liam slapped his hand on Levi's shoulder and left it there. "Just a quick one. There's an old wreck I bet you've never seen. Come check it out before you go."

A faint hum traveled through my connection with Levi's body. I stiffened and pulled away. Liam was trying to siren Levi. The secondhand compulsion wasn't strong enough to affect me, especially now that I had eaten the eelgrass concoction, but I didn't want to take any chances.

Levi's eyes widened when he realized what Liam was doing.

"I'm good," he said more forcefully. "I don't swim, remember?"

Liam dropped his hand with an easy grin, and Levi and I exchanged bewildered glances. Something wasn't right here. Why was Liam acting this way?

"No worries," he said. Before I could react, his hand snaked out and grabbed mine in a tight grip. "How about you, Lune?"

"That's enough." Levi swatted Liam's hand away and pushed against his chest. "I don't know what you're playing at, but neither of us wants to go for a swim. And do I have to remind you of the zero tolerance rule the Lodge has for sirening?"

Liam blinked a few times, a slight frown creasing his forehead. I pulled at Levi's arm to whisper in his ear.

"I have a bad feeling Marina is behind this," I murmured. "Don't be too hard on him. He might not be in control of his actions."

Levi's lips tightened at Marina's name. He turned back to Liam. "Aren't you on dock duty today? Maybe you should see what task Jess has for you."

"Yeah, okay." Liam rubbed his forehead and wandered toward the water's edge. My grip on Levi's arm loosened with every step Liam took away from us.

"You really think Marina is sirening people to lure us into the water?" Levi's features were hard with worry.

"Yes, I really do. And I don't know whether she's targeting us, or just getting the people she meets to lure others swimming so she can check them out. She's looking for you, remember." I swallowed, my stomach uneasy. "She wants to punish me, but she needs your healing powers."

"So, we can't trust anyone here." Levi glanced around. Pipa was nearby, sweeping the front step, but we were otherwise alone. "Who else has she compromised?"

"Pack your bag," I said. "I'll do the same. We need to get out of here."

"Levi," Pipa's gratingly sweet voice drifted over to us. When I turned to look at her, she wore a strange expression of anticipation and fear. If I hadn't been so annoyed by her, sympathy might have blossomed in my chest. Pipa gripped her broom tighter in her grip. "Can

I have a private word?"

"We're in a bit of a rush," Levi said. "Can it wait until I get back?"

"It's really important." Pipa glanced at me briefly, but without the smug animosity she often directed my way. "I need to tell you something. Something about yourself that you should know."

Levi frowned. "I don't have any secrets from Lune. You can say whatever it is here."

I almost melted on the spot at Levi's words. Is that truly how he saw us? I leaned into his side.

"Please," Pipa said. "You can tell her whatever you want later, but I need you to hear it first alone."

"You haven't been swimming off this beach recently, have you?" I said with suspicion. Pipa's odd request had the stain of Marina smeared all over it.

"No," she said with pursed lips in my direction.

"Fine." Levi sighed. To me, he said, "I'll be fine, remember?"

Levi's sea dragon qualities would protect him from compulsion, so I nodded and the other two wandered out of earshot. I stayed where I was, watching their interaction without hiding. I didn't trust Pipa in the slightest, and if Levi wanted me to know whatever she was going to talk about, I had no reason to look away.

Pipa's mouth moved with urgent intent, and Levi's frown deepened. Then, his eyes widened, and he stared at Pipa in disbelief. His face paled, and he staggered back a step.

"Are you okay?" I called out.

Levi blinked a few times, then he waved me over. I

jogged toward them, ignoring Pipa's disgruntled expression.

"What's the matter?" I said once within easy speaking distance.

"Pipa," Levi said hoarsely. He cleared his throat. "Pipa says she's a sea dragon too."

I stared at Levi for a long moment, then my head whipped around to look at Pipa. She gazed back, her jaw set and her eyes hard. My eyes raked over her features and wondered how I hadn't noticed the resemblance before. Both she and Levi had the same mahogany tresses, tanned skin tone, and height. At Pipa's neck, a faint glimmer of silvery discoloration showed her scales. Her eyes, now that I looked more closely, were an unusual mixture of green and blue that wasn't as vibrant and mesmerizing as Levi's but was still strange for a human.

"I don't understand," Levi stammered. "What—how—"

Pipa rolled her eyes. "It's not complicated. When I enter the ocean, I shift into a different form, just like you. I'm happy to go for a swim to prove it."

Now that I was looking for it, I noticed the faint accent that clung to Pipa's words.

"Where are you from?" I demanded. If Levi was too shocked for questions, I would have to ask for him. "How many more of you are there? Do you know Levi's family?"

Levi stared at me, then looked at Pipa with increasing hope in his eyes.

Pipa ignored me and spoke to Levi. "Far to the

north," she said with a dismissive wave of her hand. "We have a group of villages on land mostly isolated from the humans. And yes, I know your mother."

Levi's breath sped up until he was almost hyperventilating.

"I—I—what? Really? This is—" He stopped and simply stared at Pipa with hope and a longing that I didn't like to see. I told myself it was simply for Pipa's knowledge, but the suspicious part of my brain warned me of this complication. I pushed it aside as an unworthy thought—Levi needed this information, and I would be the last person to stop him from getting it. Even if Pipa was the delivery source.

I wrinkled my nose.

"This news might be easier to swallow in your other form," Pipa suggested. "We could go for a swim right now."

Levi's face contorted with his warring emotions.

"It's not safe off the Lodge's beach," I blurted out. I'd only swum for the first time with Levi yesterday, and now he was jumping in the water with Pipa? Besides, it wasn't safe for Levi here. Now, I had to protect him from both Pipa and Marina at the same time.

Levi spun toward me. "Maybe Pipa could come with us to Vancouver. Is that okay?"

My stomach clenched. Taking Pipa to Vancouver was the last thing I wanted to do. I'd been looking forward to leaving her behind and consolidating my relationship with Levi without the influence of her and the Lodge. But I couldn't say no to the feverish hope in

Levi's eyes.

"I guess," I said, even as my chest tightened. "But, whatever we do, let's do it soon, before Marina comes after us again."

"Can you come to the city for a few days?" Levi asked Pipa. "I'll keep paying your wages."

"It's fine." Pipa waved her hand again. "I'm only here for you. I don't care about the job."

I bit my tongue so hard it left a dent. No wonder I'd felt strange vibes from her. I hadn't imagined her interest in Levi.

"Okay." Levi shook his head, his expression bewildered. "Okay. Let's get ready to go. Pack your stuff and meet at my truck in half an hour. Lune, can you find Echo?"

I nodded and waited until Pipa turned and walked away. I wasn't going to leave them alone a second more than I had to.

"Be careful," Levi said, although his eyes hardly saw me in his distraction. "Don't let anyone siren you."

"I'll be quick." On impulse, I reached up and kissed him on the cheek. "See you soon."

I left Levi wandering toward the Lodge's front door and strode toward the staff dining hall in search of Echo. Maybe chatting with her would distract me from the gnawing jealousy that threatened to swallow me whole. I needed to remind myself that not everything was about Levi.

When I entered the dining hall, Echo was attempting to play cards with Austin. She brightened when she saw me.

"Hi, Lune," she said in English, then she switched to a mash-up of Seamount language and English. "What's up?"

"We're leaving shortly. Pack your stuff and meet at the parking lot."

"Oh." Echo's eyes went wide, and she gave a half-glance toward Austin. He was shuffling the deck, but he caught her eye.

"Marina?" he said. "Levi told me. You should get moving." He gave me a significant look.

"That's the plan," I assured him.

"You're right to be worried," Echo said. "Marina will never give up if she wants to punish you. I've never met anyone so determined to see justice done. Granted, Shoal is in rough shape, but it's not like killing you will bring him back to health."

I exchanged another glance with Austin.

"That's why we're leaving now," I said. "I'm pretty sure she's been sirening Lodge people to try to get me into the water. It's not safe here."

Henry wandered in, noticed our little group, and headed straight for our table.

"Hey, did you hear?" he said in greeting. "There was an attack up the coast. Someone found an old siren on the highway past Halfmoon Bay, scratched up and bloody. She was in a bad way."

"What?" Austin's eyes were wide. "What happened to her?"

"Police picked her up," Henry said with a shudder. "They were about to take her to the hospital—she wasn't talking sense—but Bob from Gibson's drove by, luckily. Bob managed to convince the police that the woman was his lost aunt and bundled her into his car. I guess he recognized her from somewhere." Henry shook his head. "Crazy how close she was to going to the hospital. I wonder what attacked her. Anyway, I need to grab some food. I'm starving."

Henry wandered toward the kitchen, and I heard him greet the staff inside. I waited until he disappeared before turning to the others.

"That's really close to where I met an old story singer named Marea. Do you think it's her?"

"There aren't a ton of us here." Austin shrugged and started shuffling again. "There's a good chance it was the same person."

"Story singer?" Echo stared at me. "The attack must have been by Marina or the shifters with her."

Austin gave her an incredulous glance. "Why do you say that? I know this siren is bad news, but she doesn't have a monopoly on evil."

"But she saw that strange creature who attacked her during the erasure ceremony for Lune." Echo bit her lip. "Marina is fanatical about knowing everything. She wouldn't let a mystery like that slide by her. And if she knew of a story singer on this coast, that would be the first place she'd go."

Austin and I exchanged worried glances.

"It's not the first time this week I've heard mention of strange creatures," he said. "Henry was talking about another long creature as well as the potential ligan."

I rubbed my leg with an anxious motion. Rumors of sea dragons, and an attack? Now that Echo brought up

Marina's involvement, it seemed obvious. Marina would have had her suspicions about Levi's healing abilities confirmed by the story singer.

My heart sank at the suffering old Marea must have endured. Why hadn't Marina simply asked nicely? Or had she done so, but the story singer's information hadn't been enough to satisfy the frantic Marina?

Either way, we needed to get out of town. Marina was too ruthless to cross paths with again. The only saving grace of the situation was that Marina didn't know who the sea dragon was, but that secret would be revealed soon enough if she continued to compel everyone around us. The safety of Vancouver tugged at me, and I stood.

"Come on, Echo. We need to get out of here."

Echo had nothing to pack, so she agreed to meet me at the truck when I was done. I washed the garbage can for Squirter, put it in the back of Levi's truck, and filled it halfway with seawater. Once my task was complete, I strode purposefully toward the staff bunkhouse to collect my things. My heart ached for the lost opportunities of this trip—somehow, I'd managed to spend every night away from Levi's room—and my fists clenched as I remembered the cause. Marina and her quest for vengeance had shoved a knife in my urchin, and her discovery of the sea dragon had cracked it wide open. I was tired of her chasing after me, but I didn't know what else to do except run. I only hoped Vancouver was large enough to hide us until we came up with a better plan.

It didn't take long to pack my drybag with the few possessions I'd traveled with. All I had to do was grab Squirter, and I could be out of here.

The dorm room door opened with a click. I jumped when I turned around and three people were standing in the room behind me.

"You scared me," I said to Kim, Liam, and a lanky older man I didn't recognize. "What's up?"

They said nothing. For a single, hanging moment, we stood staring at each other. Then, as one, the three leaped toward me.

CHAPTER 16

I screamed, but it ended with a gurgled choking as Liam wrapped his hands around my neck to throttle me. Kim swept out my legs, and I fell back into the arms of the older man. My eyes bulged, and I scrabbled at Liam's hands around my throat. I couldn't compel anyone while choking. Air, I could do without for many minutes, but that wouldn't be much consolation when trussed up like a fish in a net.

I bucked my body back and forth like I was swimming, but my attackers held firm. They carted me to a dorm room on the opposite side of the hallway and threw me on a bed. The lanky guy closed the door then grabbed rope and tied me to the bed. Kim held my twisting body down. Liam kept his hands firmly around my neck.

"You're going to stay here until nobody is watching," he said to me through clenched teeth. "Then you're going underwater where you need to be."

All three were clearly under Marina's compulsion. I despaired at the strength of her sirening ability. I could do nothing against these three.

The lanky guy tightened my bonds with a flourish. At his nod, Liam let go of me then shoved an old sock in my mouth. The three jumped away from me and started singing the birthday song loudly. I coughed, my eyes streaming. Before I could send a compulsion toward them through the floorboards, they ran through the door and disappeared.

When would they be back? I presumed they would create a distraction outside, then come fetch me when the coast was clear. I didn't have long to escape. I strained at the ropes futilely. What could I do? Shouting for help was out with the disgusting sock lying on my tongue, and no one was around to compel.

Wait, that wasn't true. Squirter was in the building. Could he hear me from here? I let a calling hum build in my chest, growing louder and louder to account for the distance. I hoped the mattress wouldn't deaden the sound too much. Would the floorboards carry my vibrations so Squirter could hear me?

I increased my volume as much as it could go. To the hum of calling I added a layer of urgency.

What felt like hours later but was probably only two minutes of nonstop humming, the doorknob turned. With a click, the door swung slowly open. On the other side, Squirter clung to the knob with his suction cups.

I ceased my hum with a huff of relief. Squirter slithered down the door and crawled painstakingly across the floor, leaving a trail of damp behind him. He crawled up a bedpost until his arm plucked the sweaty sock from my mouth.

I gasped fresh air and spat to the side to remove the foul taste. Squirter slunk to the ropes binding my hands and got to work. They were tight, but he snapped at them with his beak and plucked with his arms until they loosened slightly.

With that little leeway, I wriggled my hands free and untied my ankles. I scooped my octopus friend off the bed and stood with wobbly legs.

"Let's go, Squirter," I said quietly. "I'm done with the Lodge for now."

No one was in the hallway when I poked my head out. I dashed across to fetch my drybag. The coast was also clear outside, but my neck prickled with foreboding as I jogged toward the main Lodge building.

"She's escaping," Liam shouted from behind me. "Get her!"

I didn't bother looking at my pursuers. Instead, I sprinted across the rain-soaked lawn, fervently hoping I wouldn't slip in any patches of mud.

Pipa and Echo were already in the backseat of the truck, and Levi was lashing the plastic garbage can to the truck bed.

"Incoming," I shouted at him.

He turned with raised eyebrows, but I shoved past him and dropped Squirter in the container of seawater. I slammed the lid shut and pushed at Levi.

"Get in the truck," I said with a finger pointed behind me. "Marina's goons are after me. Quick!"

Levi, to his credit, flung himself into the driver's seat. His bewildered face turned toward my pursuers even as he put his keys in the ignition. Pipa and Echo made noises of consternation from the back. I ignored them and slammed my door shut.

"Go, go, go," I screeched. Levi shoved the car into drive and roared past Kim, Liam, and the lanky man. All wore expressions of wild-eyed frustration.

"What was all that about?" Pipa yelled from the backseat. Echo said nothing, but she met my gaze with a questioning expression when I looked back, and I nodded.

"A siren from the Seamount named Marina is after Lune," Levi said. He shot out of the Lodge's driveway onto the highway and peeled down the road.

Pipa glared at me. "And why is this Marina after you?"

"We have history." I didn't feel like getting into the details with Pipa, of all people. "But we needed to get away, because she's targeting anyone she can find underwater to bring me under. She can't stay on land for long, so she gets others to do her dirty work."

Levi passed a slow-moving minivan. "Marina is also hunting for anyone who knows something about sea dragons. Marina saw one rescue Lune."

"Why does she care about sea dragons?" If Pipa's eyes had been bone blades, I would have been bleeding from multiple stab wounds at this point. "Aren't they a little-known legend to Seamount dwellers?"

"Marina's lover Shoal is ill," I said heavily. "She wants him healed. She figures a sea dragon is the only way."

"How does she know that this sea dragon she saw can even heal?" Pipa said with a half-glance at Echo. The seal shifter stared out the window, unable to follow our fast-paced conversation. "Not all can, from what I've heard."

Levi swallowed and tightened his jaw. He clearly was desperate to ask more questions, but with Echo in the car, it was too risky to speak more.

Instead, I answered. "Marina wouldn't know that. All pale folk know is that sea dragons can heal all wounds. She'll be single-minded in her desire to find the sea dragon who saved me. I hope whoever it was is far away from the Lodge by now."

Pipa pursed her lips but refrained from replying.

With hard eyes, she stared out her window. The air was heavy with unspoken questions and explanations, and the rest of our ride to the ferry was made in silence.

I ran to pick up my backpack at the beach while the others waited at the ferry terminal to pay. The ferry was busy with busses from an organized trip of some kind, but we managed to snag tickets for the next sailing. After Levi parked the truck in line, we got out to stretch our legs and enjoy the rain-free weather.

Levi's eyebrows raised in recognition. He waved at a woman approaching us with a baby on her hip. Her brown hair was pulled into a ponytail, but her luminescent skin spoke of her pale folk heritage. The baby's tuft of downy hair was pure white, and it gurgled and patted its mother's shoulder.

"Chrissie, hi," Levi said to her. "Heading back to the city?"

"Hi, Levi." She smiled at our group and adjusted the baby. "Yeah, we had a nice time visiting Uncle Liam, didn't we, guppy?" She tickled the baby's stomach, and it chortled. "Are you heading out of town? I didn't think you ever left the Lodge."

She grinned to show that she was teasing, but Levi flicked his eyes downward in embarrassment.

"I seem to have that reputation," he muttered. "Yes, we're going to Vancouver for a few days. Stop on the way for a swim for a couple of us, first."

He jabbed his thumb at me and Echo. I waved my
fingers at the acknowledgement and leaned against the
truck to get comfortable.

Chrissie brightened. "Have you ever swum at
Whytecliff Park? It's a gorgeous spot, with a protected
bay then a bracing current off the point that is just too
fun to get swept around on. Like a waterslide or
something. I totally recommend it."

"Thanks for the advice." Levi looked at me with a
questioning expression. "What do you think?"

"Sounds fun," I said. "I'm always up for a good
time."

Levi's cheeks tinted at my innuendo. Chrissie didn't
seem to notice.

"Enjoy yourselves," she said to us. "I'd better get
Jack ready to board. He needs feeding and changing
and all that. Have a good vacation."

After Levi said his goodbyes, she turned and
sauntered down the line of cars. As the baby watched
us over her shoulder, she pulled out a phone and called
someone.

Levi walked over to my side of the truck and leaned
against it with me. Echo gazed at the ocean from the
edge of the asphalt a few cars away, and Pipa was lying
down in the backseat.

"I want to talk about—you know—but Echo is with
us," he said, his voice strained. "I'm losing my mind
over here."

I slipped my hand into his and squeezed it. "Maybe
we can find a private spot on the ferry."

Levi caught my eye and grinned. "Private enough for

a conversation, maybe, but not private enough for anything else."

I pretended to pout. "You and your human sensibilities. Honestly."

When the ferry finally announced it was ready for boarding, we hopped into the truck and followed the line of cars up a ramp and onto the car deck. On the passenger deck, Pipa glanced at Levi's strained face then at me.

"Are you hungry, Echo?" she asked. "Maybe you and Lune should go find some food."

"I'm not hungry," I said. Quickly, I tore open my wallet and shoved a bill into Echo's hands. "But you must be. Here, you and Pipa find something tasty. Levi and I will be on the outside deck when you're done."

Before the others could protest, I dragged Levi by the arm toward the outer door. I shook my head at Pipa's presumption. She would do anything to get Levi alone. So would I. But as his girlfriend, I was allowed to.

Girlfriend? Was that the right word for what we were? We'd never discussed it, but nothing else seemed to fit. I liked the ring of it.

Since it was a cold day in autumn, the outer deck was deserted. I pushed Levi toward a large, flat-topped container that housed lifejackets and hopped up to join him.

"Okay, we're alone," I said. "No one can hear us talking about sea dragons. Spill."

Levi let out a long sigh that showcased his lung capacity, then he stared at the waves beyond the ferry's railing.

"I don't know," he said at last. "It's all so crazy. I've been alone all my life with no one like me around. My adoptive parents are great, and Austin is a good brother." He eyed me with a wry grin. "Except when he's not."

"I remember." Austin's misguided descent into arson had been a lowlight of my summer. Although, it had brought me closer to Levi, which I could never regret.

Levi gazed outward again. "There's a place filled with people like me. I can't begin to describe how incredible that feels."

"A few small villages, by the sounds of it." At Levi's exasperated glance, I raised my hands. "Just tempering your expectations."

"I wonder what Pipa looks like. Are all sea dragons the same?" His eyes widened. "Do you think there's a dragon language underwater that's different from Seamount language? One I can actually communicate in?"

"Maybe." My chest squeezed at the thought of one more way that Pipa could ingratiate herself with Levi, then I pushed away the unworthy notion. This moment was not about me, nor about me and Levi. This was about Levi discovering the secret of his life, and I wouldn't stand in the way with my petty jealousy. "Maybe she could teach you, so you and I can talk together under there."

"I'd love that."

"Look, I know this is a huge moment for you. But

don't forget that everyone has a motive, and we don't know why Pipa is here, telling you all this."

"Why are you saying this?" Levi frowned at me, exasperation clear in his voice. "Is this the jealousy thing again? I told you, there's nothing between us, at least not on my end. Can't you just be happy for me?"

"I'm sorry." And I was, both for hurting his feelings and for the fact that he was still blind to Pipa's advances. Something was going on with the other sea dragon, but it looked like I would have to keep watch on my own to avoid Levi pulling away from me. "You're right. This is an amazing opportunity for you."

"And Pipa said she knew my mother." Levi said this so quietly I almost missed it. When I heard, I grabbed his hand on impulse. He gripped it tightly. "There's so much I want to ask her, starting with why she left me with Seafoam and Kane. I assumed she'd died. Now, to hear she's alive and living in a sea dragon village? Why didn't I grow up there, with her?"

Levi's voice was filled with so much pain, frustration, and anger. My heart ached for him. I shuffled closer to put my arm around his shoulder. His body was stiff at first, then he relaxed into me.

We sat in silence, staring at the water.

"What are you going to do?" I said after a few minutes.

"I don't know. Find out more from Pipa, for a start. I have a sea dragon with me. I need to know everything she can tell me. Then, I don't know. How can I not go to her village and meet the others? Talk to my mother? I don't know how I can leave the Lodge, but isn't this more important?" He slumped and rubbed his face. "I don't know anything anymore."

I squeezed him tightly, unsure what to say. My gut clenched at the thought of Levi traveling to some northern destination to seek his heritage. What if the sea dragons weren't an accepting bunch? What if they harmed him? What if he was crushed by whatever his mother had to say?

Worse, what if he liked it there and stayed?

CHAPTER 17

Pipa and Echo returned with bags of food, and we shared a meal on the deck. Echo was full of curiosity, and I pointed at our surroundings—islands, sea gulls, railings—to help her learn English.

"But I will be leaving soon," Echo said finally, after chewing and swallowing a fry. "Why do I need to learn your language?"

"Don't you want to explore land a little first?" I asked. "You might not get another chance. And after returning to the Seamount, I guarantee it will feel pretty small and contained. Might as well check out the wider world while you're here."

Echo chewed another fry and gazed at me in thought.

"Maybe you're right," she said. "I should look around before I leave. I'll have good stories to tell my friends, if nothing else."

Levi's phone rang, and he picked it up.

"Hey," he said. "Yeah, we're on the ferry." The other person spoke while Levi narrowed his eyes and nodded. "Okay, good. Call me if anything changes."

"Is everything okay?" I asked when he hung up.

"That was Austin. He said people have stopped trying to get others in the water, so that's good. Marina must have given up."

Echo and I glanced at each other. She had told me that Marina was stubborn. Why would she have given up, unless she knew I wasn't at the Lodge anymore?

I'd hoped to feel safer in Vancouver, but now I wondered if anywhere was out of Marina's reach. Surreptitiously, I reached into my bag and withdrew the package Branc had given me. While Pipa pointed out more things to Echo and Levi munched distractedly on his burger, I withdrew another piece of dried eelgrass paste and bit off a quarter of it. I quickly swallowed before the bitter flavor could linger in my mouth. I returned the rest to the envelope and shoved it deep in my bag. At least Levi was safe from compulsion.

Soon after, the ferry docked and we disembarked. The park that Chrissie had recommended was only a few minutes' drive down the highway, and Levi pulled into the empty parking lot soon after leaving the ferry grounds.

I was eager to go for a swim, but Levi looked as if he couldn't keep still, he was so excited. A wave of jealousy crashed over me. I tried my hardest to paddle out of the wash. I wanted to swim with him, but I knew I had to let him experience this moment with the first sea dragon he could remember meeting.

That didn't mean I liked it, though.

Levi jumped out of the truck as soon as he cranked on the emergency brake. The rest of us followed more sedately. He fidgeted in place.

"Pipa and I will wait on the beach for you two," he said to me and Echo. "Have a good swim."

I bit my lip but couldn't say anything similar back to him, not while Echo was listening.

"See you soon."

I turned to the back of the truck and opened

Squirter's container. His arms emerged as soon as the lid was open, and I carefully pulled him out and draped his new heft over my shoulder. We all walked down a short path until it opened to a pebbly beach, then I stripped off my outer layers without jostling Squirter too much. Echo copied me but removed every stitch of clothing. I glanced around the beach, but the windswept shoreline was empty in the worsening weather. I caught Levi averting his eyes and grinned.

"Next time, keep your underclothes on until we're in the water," I advised Echo. "Dry folk don't do nudity well."

She looked at me in confusion, but I pulled Echo's arm so we could enter the water faster. Levi's impatience was nearly palpable. I didn't want to make him wait, even if it meant him spending time with Pipa.

That grated to my core, but I set my jaw and marched into the gray waves crashing against the pebbly shore. I'd promised myself I wouldn't get in the way of his self-discovery, but vents, it was hard. I'd have to grill him later about their swim so I could monitor Pipa's actions.

I splashed into the water without a backward glance and dived in as soon as the water was deep enough. Echo followed, and Squirter slithered off my shoulders and jetted away once submerged. The poor guy must have felt cramped in that garbage can, and the fresh oxygen probably felt good.

He came back almost instantly and stared past me with interest. I turned, and a seal gazed at me with large brown eyes.

Squirter, this is Echo, I said to him. *Seal shifter. Friend.*

Squirter stayed motionless, watching Echo. In return, Echo did a slow-motion somersault then wiggled her tail fin. Squirter clicked in pleasure and jetted around the seal, and I smiled.

We swam deeper, and Echo and I played tag with Squirter. He was getting faster, and I didn't have to pretend to miss him anymore. Echo fared better, as a speedier swimmer, but even she couldn't always keep up with the little cephalopod.

At the edge of my skin sense, two sinuous figures floated past and out of range. I didn't say anything to Echo. She didn't have a skin sense, not anything like the sensitivity of pale folk, so she didn't notice. I wanted to follow Levi and Pipa so badly, but it was my job to keep Echo from finding out about them.

Something else emerged in my skin sense from the silty seafloor, and I pointed my body in that direction. A shipwreck loomed out of the darkness. Echo clicked with interest.

This wreck is different from the ones at the Seamount. She swam closer to examine the rusting shell of a tugboat.

It's a type of boat that doesn't go into the open ocean, I explained. *Come on, let's explore.*

Squirter was way ahead of us. He landed on the crumbling deck, fanning out his arms and webbing as he landed. The tips of his arms wriggled over the surface in exploration.

Echo followed him and nosed the railing. I joined them and examined an old anchor perched on the edge. I lifted it and was surprised to discover it was heavier than I'd expected.

Something moved in the distance. I stiffened when, instead of the tiny body of a fish, it resolved into something far larger. At this stage, I couldn't even tell where the body ended. It was far too large for a shark, a killer whale, or a sea dragon. A part of me wildly hoped that it was a submarine, but I knew better.

Marina's here, I shouted at the others. *With her ligan!*

Echo and Squirter responded immediately by dashing toward the beach. My relief at their escape was short-lived. When I dropped the anchor to follow them, the pointed end landed on my ankle and pinned me to the shipwreck's rotting deck.

The ligan was too quick. Marina straddled its neck as it shot toward me.

I shoved the anchor off my leg with a grimace of pain as it caught my ankle bone. I darted away, but the ligan was on me, preceded by a rush of current as it pushed through the ocean. My heart pounded in my chest when I turned. A huge maw ringed with long, curved fangs filled my vision.

I threw myself downward. Instead of being crunched in the monster's jaw, it merely snagged my arm. Sensation exploded in a riotous mess of stabbing pain. I pulled wildly then punched the ligan's snout. The ligan released my arm and shot away.

It immediately circled back. I floundered, hazy with pain. I tried to swim with my injured ankle and agonizing arm, but didn't have much luck.

Vibrations shimmered through the water and my torso. Marina was sirening me. I felt it, and for an instant my mind clouded over, then it cleared.

Branc's substance was working. A jab of gratitude and relief pierced me.

I didn't have long to feel it. The ligan was almost on me again.

Ignoring the searing agony from my injury, I dived deeper. I propelled myself feetfirst into a hole in the wreck's decking.

I wasn't fast enough. Pressure on my shoulder gave way to pain as the ligan clamped down. It dragged me out of my hiding place. I screamed.

The ligan released my shoulder, but I was in too much pain to escape. I clutched my arm to my chest and squinted toward my attacker. The monster swayed back and forth, with Marina holding on with grim resolve and confusion. Only I could see the small octopus gripping the ligan's face.

Squirter, no! I shouted in desperation. The monster was magnitudes bigger than the little octopus. How could I keep him safe if he acted like that?

When Squirter released the ligan, blood from the sea serpent's ruined eye flowed out in a cloud of black. The next moment, a much larger thunderstorm of black ink overtook the blood. Squirter jetted away from the cloud that now engulfed the ligan and Marina.

A sleek brown body wriggled between my arms. I gratefully clung to Echo with my good arm. With swift strokes of her tail, she darted toward the beach with me in tow.

CHAPTER 18

My coughs to expel seawater on the shore were interspersed with screams of pain. I was a trembling, bleeding mess, and crashing waves knocked me over with every hit. Echo, now in her human form, lifted me around the torso and dragged me out of the surf. When I looked back, a dark blob with eight arms waved at me from the water. I wanted to scream at the octopus for being so reckless, but I couldn't deny that his quick thinking and brave actions had saved me. That is, if I could stop the bleeding.

Echo propped me against a log out of reach of the waves and knelt beside me. I shuddered uncontrollably from shock. Blood oozed out of the fang wounds with every beat of my heart. The amount of red dripping down my skin terrified me.

"Press on them," I begged Echo. A long stipe of bull kelp on the beach ended in a bunch of leaf-like blades, and I beckoned at it. "Pass me that seaweed."

Echo leaped toward the algae and dragged it over to me. I ripped off a blade and wrapped it around my arm, hissing at the pain. Dots floated in my vision. I swallowed bile.

Echo saw what I was doing and tore off her own piece of kelp to use as a bandage. With both of us pressing on my wounds, there was little more we could do.

"That should help," I panted. I blinked hard to stop my vision from tunneling. "The bleeding will stop soon."

Echo bit her lip but said nothing. She scanned the waves. When her fingers pressed tighter on my shoulder, I glanced up through watering eyes.

Levi and Pipa were running from a rocky outcrop at the far end of the pebbly beach. Both were fully clothed. Pipa looked confused, but Levi's face twisted with fear. For me? My wounds weren't that bad.

I glanced down at blood staining the rocks below me and swallowed again. Okay, maybe they were that bad. Maybe—if I even survived the blood loss—I wouldn't be able to use my arm again. I tried not to think like that, but the notion caught hold in my brain and refused to let go. My breath came faster and faster. Echo looked at me with a creased brow.

"It's okay," she said in English. "You're okay."

"No, no, no." Words forced themselves through my closing throat. "There's too much blood."

Levi crashed to the ground next to me, spraying Echo with pebbles. He leaned over me, his expression tight.

"Lune, hold on," he said. "You're going to be fine. Remember what I can do?"

"Not in front of…" I trailed off. Was he really considering showing Echo his secret?

"It's fine," he said firmly. "Move over, Echo. I've got this."

The seal shifter glanced at me. At my nod, she backed away. Pipa wordlessly handed her clothes from the pile we'd discarded earlier. Her eyes followed Levi's movements with an almost hungry gleam.

I glanced out to sea. "You can't heal me. Marina could pop her head up at any moment. What if she sees you? You can't reveal yourself like that. I won't let you."

"I don't care," he said with a fierce glare at me, although I could tell his ire was directed at the siren in the water. "Your life is far more important than potential danger in the future. We'll figure it out later."

"No," I protested. I leaned away from him, but stopped when pain radiated through my flesh with burning jabs. I needed to stop him for his own good. He clearly didn't know what was best for him.

Levi carefully lifted the kelp from my shoulder. My body throbbed with pain, and I couldn't bring myself to fight anymore. He winced when he saw the damage, then his jaw set with determination. Slowly, he bent his head to my skin and kissed the very top of my wound.

I hissed at his touch, but almost immediately a cool sensation flowed from the spot and numbed the pain. I blinked at the skin knitting together.

"More," I whispered.

Tenderly, Levi kissed the next part down. His lips grew stained with my blood, but as his kisses traveled down my shoulder, the numbness spread until fresh new skin covered my injury.

Levi's mouth continued down my arm to my other injury. His hand cupped my elbow and stroked the skin there gently, comfortingly. When the cool numbness had taken away the rest of my pain, a new sensation grew. Levi's lips on my skin heated me in places other than my arm, despite my wooziness from blood loss.

When Levi raised his head and smiled hopefully at me, I sighed in a mix of relief and disappointment.

"Thanks," I whispered. "You look like you've been nibbling at my arm, not healing it."

He wiped his mouth with his sleeve, his eyes abashed.

"It's weird, I know," he said. "It's the best I've got."

"I think I might have been dead without you," I said. It was the truth. Now that I wasn't at risk of keeling over, I shuddered at how close I'd come to death.

Levi mistook my shiver for remnants of shock, and he scooted up to wrap his arm around me. I wasn't about to deny myself the luxury of his embrace, and I leaned into him. Maybe he had made the right decision. Being released from the jaws of agony was a relief beyond words. He hadn't done what I'd wanted him to do, but maybe his decisions had some merit despite being different from mine. We could deal with the fallout later.

"What just happened?" Echo said. Her eyes were large, and she glanced between Levi and me in bewilderment.

Pipa's look was harder to discern. She gazed at Levi like he was a large cake she wanted to devour, but I couldn't figure out why. Didn't she have her own healing ability?

She muscled her face into an expression of polite concern when she caught me staring. I narrowed my eyes at her, but she ignored me.

"What happened to you?" Levi asked me, ignoring Echo's question.

"Three guesses. Starts with an M."

Levi paled. "Marina got you?"

"Her ligan, specifically." I snuggled closer to Levi. "Marina tried to siren me, but I'm taking something to prevent that now. Due to Squirter's bravery and Echo's quick thinking, we escaped."

"How did she know you were here?" he said, horror infusing his voice. "A few people at the Lodge knew we were going to Vancouver, I guess."

"But to find us so quickly, it's like she knew exactly where we would be." Pipa scowled and crossed her arms over her chest.

"Liam's sister," I said after a moment. "At the ferry. Chrissie, I think her name was? She knew."

"And she called someone right after," Pipa said. "Marina must have got to her, the same way she sirened the other employees. Chrissie probably called her brother at the Lodge, and he passed along the message."

"Let's get out of here," Levi said after a moment digesting the news. "The ocean isn't safe."

I nodded, and Echo helped me up and wrapped a towel around me. Levi tried to stand, but he stumbled on the way up. Pipa narrowed her eyes at him.

"You healed her too much," she chided. "Healing isn't free, you know."

"I know." Levi stretched and yawned. "I'm fine, though. I just need a nap."

Echo splashed into the water and folded at the waist to dunk her face in. A moment later, she reemerged, shaking her head.

"Squirter doesn't want to come," she explained. "I left him in there."

I grimaced but couldn't see another way forward. If Squirter didn't come with us willingly, I couldn't do much about it. I hoped he would stay clear of the ligan.

Pipa led the way to the truck, followed by Echo. I picked my way across the pebbles, wobbly from blood loss but enjoying pain-free steps. Levi glanced back at me with concern.

"Do you need a hand?" he asked. "How are you feeling?"

"So much better." I smiled at him. "Like it never happened. Although that nap sounds good. I might join you."

His mouth twitched, and I gave him an arch look.

"Naughty boy."

A prickle on the back of my neck turned my head to the sea for one last look. Among the frothing waves, a white head bobbed. Marina stared at me with a blank expression before sinking below the surface.

"Vents," I breathed. My stomach plummeted. "Marina saw us."

Levi stared at me. "Why are you so worried? We know she knew you were here. Her ligan attacked you."

"But she saw me healed." My mind churned through the implications, and I didn't like my conclusions. "She knew I was badly wounded. My blood was everywhere down there, and my arm was mauled. I shouldn't even be alive after that, let alone walking around."

Levi blinked slowly as he came to the same conclusion as I had. "You were healed, and there are only the four of us on the beach."

"She knows Echo is a seal shifter, and that I'm pale folk. That leaves you and Pipa as targets."

I wrapped my towel tighter around my shoulders. Before, Levi had been only a sea dragon possibility in Marina's eyes, strictly because he and I were close. Now that she'd seen me healed in his presence, she knew there was a fifty percent chance he was the healer she was desperate for.

The ride home was quiet. I didn't know about the others, but I was overwhelmed with the events of the day. Actually, I was mostly just tired. Bone-tired, deep core-weary tired, more tired than I'd ever remembered being. Maybe it was the result of my injuries and the healing, and now my body wanted to recover in slumber.

Levi wasn't faring much better. Once or twice, I caught his head nodding forward and the truck drifting into the next lane.

"Wake up," I hissed and poked his side.

He jerked upright and blinked furiously.

"I was awake," he said in an indignant tone, but he glanced at me with guilt.

"I'm afraid driving is up to you," I said. "I can't drive, and neither can Echo. Pipa, can you?"

"No," she replied from the back. "No cars in my village."

"I'm fine," Levi said with conviction. "We'll be at

your place soon. Another half-hour, maybe."

I grimaced, but there wasn't much I could do about the distance. I vowed to keep poking Levi every few minutes, despite my desire to lay my head on his shoulder and fall asleep myself.

Finally, after a few more close calls and too much time on the road, Levi pulled the truck into a free parking space a block away from my apartment building. I stumbled ahead to lead the way, my feet dragging with every step. My keys were at the bottom of my drybag, of course. It took me far too long to dig them out and remember which key went in the front door.

The stairs were monumental, and I vehemently wished for water to fill the stairwell so I could simply swim upward. When the door to my apartment swung open, the dingy walls and tatty furniture had never looked so welcoming.

A note lay on the kitchen table, and I wandered over to investigate while the others filed inside. The words were in Seamount-writing:

I'm with Joel for a few days. We're riding the waves on a board on the big island.

I chuckled at Cetus's attempt to describe surfing in our language.

"Cetus isn't here," I informed Levi.

"That works out," he said. "Then there's more room for Pipa and Echo at your place."

I opened my mouth to reply, then snapped it shut again. I hadn't imagined the others would stay with me. I'd had hazy notions of a motel, or staying with friends of Levi. My place was cramped enough with two, let alone four.

But I couldn't let Echo fend for herself, since she had no money and no understanding of a human city. I felt somewhat responsible for her, at least until she swam back to the Seamount.

Pipa could walk out anytime, as far as I was concerned, but it felt churlish to allow Echo to stay and not offer the same courtesy to the sea dragon. Besides, I couldn't bear to see the reproach on Levi's face if I sent away the only link to his past.

"Yeah," I said. "Lucky Cetus isn't here. Echo, Pipa, make yourselves at home. There isn't much in the cupboards for food but eat whatever you can find. Couches will have to do for sleeping." I turned to Levi. "As for you, can we please take that nap now?"

Levi nodded, relief washing over his face. He looked around. "Where?"

"Does a bed sound reasonable to you?" I pushed him toward my bedroom and caught the hint of a grin on his face.

I shut the door behind us, and Levi dropped his bag on the ground then squatted next to it. A contact case appeared in his hand, then he popped out his contacts, closed the case, and flopped onto the bed. I debated getting changed into something more comfortable first, but weariness dragged me down until I was horizontal beside Levi.

"This is nice," he murmured, his eyelids half-closed over his mesmerizing eyes.

I watched them with sleepy fascination. I wanted to

do more than talk right now, but my limbs were as heavy as if gravity had increased to Jupiter-proportions. I longed for the weightlessness of the ocean.

"Thanks for saving me today," I whispered. "Even if it exposed you to Marina."

Levi opened his eyes wider and gazed at me. His hand reached out languidly to brush hair from my face and cup my cheek.

"Of course," he said. "It doesn't matter about her. You needed me."

My eyelids fluttered closed, despite my desire to keep looking at Levi. The warmth of his hand on my cheek lulled me into an ocean of dreamless sleep.

CHAPTER 19

I blinked awake when the bed shook. When I turned my head, Levi smiled sleepily at me.

"Good evening." He glanced at the window, where a sunrise was streaming through an unexpected opening in the clouds. "Whoa, we slept a long time. Good morning, I guess."

I reached my arms above my head and arched my back in a full-body stretch. Levi's eyes traced my curves, and I held the position for longer than I'd been meaning to.

His mouth curved in an appreciative smile. I collapsed then rolled over onto Levi's front.

"Oof."

Levi's arms snaked around my middle, and I tilted my head and gazed into his eyes.

"I like finding you in my bed after waking."

Levi's hands ran down my back, but before they could reach interesting places, voices from the other room paused his motions. He blinked, and an awareness of our situation stole into his eyes.

"I forgot, the others are here too," he said, removing his hand from my back. "Yesterday was intense."

"You can say that again." I wriggled in closer to him, loving his warmth against my front.

"Wait a minute. Marina attacked you yesterday," he said. His sleepy voice grew sharper with anger. "That hagfish sent her ligan after you."

"Yeah, she did." I didn't want to give up our

comfortable position on the bed, but Levi's tensed muscles were difficult to cuddle. He sat up, and I slithered off him and pulled the blanket over my legs more securely.

Levi grabbed my hand with a crushing grip in his intensity. "You could have died. She needs to pay."

"What do you mean by that?" By the set of Levi's shoulders and the crease of his brow, I could tell he was furious. Part of me reveled at his protectiveness over me, but the rest of me grew nervous of what he meant to do. An angry Levi could mean a reckless Levi.

"We keep running, and she keeps finding us. I'm tired of being on the defensive. Let her feel out of control for once." He let go of my hand and mashed his palms together. "If we don't solve this and get her off our tails once and for all, we'll never be free."

"I guess some of us have literal tails," I murmured. I didn't disagree with his sentiment—being chased by Marina was an endless, exhausting affair—but pitting ourselves against a powerful female siren and her pet ligan didn't seem smart. I didn't want to give Marina an opportunity to capture Levi. "What sort of retaliation did you have in mind?"

"Hit her hard, hit her fast," he said promptly, fire lighting his eyes. "Get her off our backs once and for all."

"And how do you propose we fend off a giant sea serpent?" I asked, waving at my shoulder. "Do I need to remind you of what happened the last time I met Marina's ride?"

Levi laid a protective hand on my arm, and I thrilled

at the pressure and heat of his touch through the thin blanket.

"That isn't going to happen again," he said fiercely. "But Marina does need to pay for it."

"Why don't you and Pipa leave for a while?" I hated to say the words aloud—Levi leaving was the last thing I wanted, especially in the company of Pipa—but I couldn't keep quiet in good conscience. "Marina wants you, now that she knows you exist. Not me. I was always the consolation prize."

"I'm not leaving while there's still a chance you're in danger," he countered. "When she can't find a sea dragon, don't you think she'll go back to plan A? No, running isn't the answer. You could come with us to the sea dragon villages, maybe, but if Marina is as stubborn as Echo says, she'll still be waiting for us when we get back. We need to fight."

I ran my hand down his arm, enjoying the hard curve of his bicep even as I tried to calm him. "Slow down. Can we at least agree to make a plan with the others before charging into the waves?"

"Fine. But you have to agree that we can't keep living like this. Something needs to come to a head."

I nodded. My stomach clenched at the danger Levi might put himself in, but a fire kindled in my chest. If I were by his side, leading him down the right paths, he could come out unscathed. "Yes. One way or another, we need to deal with Marina."

When we emerged from the bedroom, Pipa barely gave me a glance before she trained her gaze on Levi. Echo looked up from the couch with bright eyes.

"Pipa told me all about sea dragons," she said in her mix of Seamount language and English. "Her Seamount accent is super thick, but we managed. I had no idea you guys existed. Who else is in this vast ocean we call home? Incredible."

"That's how I felt, too." I perched on the couch's armrest next to Echo, and she twisted to continue our conversation. Levi rummaged in my kitchen and came back with salty crackers, which he munched at the table. I said, "I take it you didn't have a story singer education either."

"Seal shifters rely on pale folk for history," Echo replied. "We live more in the moment. My education was centered around farming and avoiding predators. Maintaining the Grace fields is our top priority, after all."

Pipa rose from her seat on the couch to join Levi at the table. She tried to keep her voice low, but I stopped my conversation with Echo to listen.

"Levi, how long have you been healing people for?"

Levi swallowed his bite and answered at a normal volume. My heart squeezed with gratitude at his inclusion. "Since I was a teenager, I guess. A little after I started shifting. I figured it out after I sucked a cut finger—a vegetable peeler gone rogue—and the gash was gone the next minute."

Pipa nodded. "What have you healed in the past? What sort of injuries?"

"Scrapes and gashes, mainly. My brother Austin smashed his hand between the boat and dock once, that was bad. We were lucky I was around."

"What else do you know about your healing ability?" Pipa pressed.

"I don't know, that something in my saliva heals. It's not like I've had anyone to ask." Levi frowned, clearly done with Pipa's interrogation. "What about you? What sort of wounds have you healed?"

Pipa stared at him for a long moment, her eyes searching.

"Healing is a rare gift," she said at last. "Most sea dragons can't do it. I certainly can't."

"What about the story singer legends from the Seamount?" I asked. "They talk about healing."

"But the story only spoke of one sea dragon," Levi said slowly. "That one must have been a healer, just by chance."

Pipa shrugged. "I don't know this legend, but Levi must be right. Only a very few healers are born each generation." She placed her palms on the table and leaned toward Levi. "Look, there's so much you don't know about your people, about your abilities, about yourself. You would really benefit from coming back to the villages with me. You could learn so much there."

Levi's lips thinned as he gazed at Pipa.

"You could even meet your mother," Pipa pressed. "Meet your family. It sounds like you have a great relationship with your adoptive family, but aren't you curious about your other side?"

Levi's longing was written across his face. I wrinkled my nose. Why was Pipa pushing this so much? Maybe her words on the surface reflected her true goal— wanting Levi to understand himself better—but I couldn't help wondering if she had other intentions. I'd been correct in my vibes earlier, when I'd thought she had been more than a disinterested employee. I didn't want to ignore my intuition.

"Maybe we should both go," I said to Levi. He perked up at the idea. "Like you said earlier. Get out of town for a while to let Marina cool off. Maybe she'll think we left for good, and she'll stop hanging around Vancouver and the Lodge."

"That's not a good idea," Pipa said at once. "My people are not good with outsiders. If you approached in a form other than a sea dragon, they would likely attack you. We have not forgotten our persecution by the other peoples. We're trained to attack first and ask questions later, if at all."

I narrowed my eyes at her. While her words seemed plausible, her explanation also felt a little too convenient in getting Levi to her homeland without me.

"How many sea dragons are there, anyway?" I asked.

"About five hundred," Pipa said, "give or take. Since there aren't many of us, we're very protective of our villages."

I leaned back in my chair to digest this information. Was that why Pipa was vent-bent on taking Levi back with her? Prospects must be thin, and there was no doubt that Levi was a catch.

I scowled then swallowed the catty words that threatened to emerge from my mouth. Was I selfish? Maybe I was holding Levi back from his rightful place with his people. Levi and I were only at the start of a relationship, so it felt far too soon to worry about a future together. But was I dooming a race by even considering it?

"Maybe you should go with Pipa for a bit," I said aloud to Levi, even though the words were bitter on my tongue. But telling him to go to the villages felt like the best way to protect him. He needed me to push him in the safest direction. "At least until Marina gives up and goes away. With you out of the picture, surely she won't hang around forever, no matter how determined she is. It's you and your healing ability she wants."

"That's a great idea," Pipa said quickly. "A little trip to visit the villages and learn about your heritage, and let Marina forget about all this. Double benefits."

I tightened my lips. Pipa was too enthusiastic about my suggestion, which didn't surprise me but still infuriated. I wanted her out of this conversation, but that wasn't going to happen.

Levi crossed his arms. "I'm not going anywhere. Not while Lune's in danger."

"But Marina wants a sea dragon, not her," Pipa protested.

"She'll still try to take revenge," Levi said. "No, there's no way I'm leaving without Lune. We need to meet Marina head on. I'm done running away."

Echo stared at Levi with round eyes after his declaration. "She's too powerful. And her ligan…"

"You're serious?" Pipa said. When Levi nodded, she pursed her lips. "Fine. I'll help. Then we can go to the villages, yes?"

"Yes." Levi nodded with decision. "I'd like that."

My stomach flopped. My mind knew that I had

nothing to worry about—Levi truly hadn't ever looked at Pipa with romantic intentions—but my body hadn't got the memo. Or, rather, it knew more than romance could sway a person.

Pipa would introduce Levi to his past, his people, and possibly his future. What if he found his life at the Lodge inferior compared to a new life among sea dragons? What if the villages beckoned him with purpose and community that he couldn't find on the west coast of Canada? What if sea dragon prospects made more logical sense to him than a burgeoning relationship with a half-siren, despite his feelings?

The crackers Levi had opened didn't look appetizing anymore, and I looked away.

"We still need a plan," I said to the window. "And maybe reinforcements. Byssa and Hades would help, I know, but only you two can decide if you want to let more people into your secret."

While I didn't want to expose Byssa and Hades to danger, they would never forgive me if I kept them in the dark for their protection. If Levi decided he didn't want to share, that was fine, but my conscience demanded that I at least ask to tell my friends and let them help.

And we would need as much help as we could get. Squirter was still down there, and I worried that he would do something reckless to help our cause.

Levi was right: this was our best chance to end the conflict with Marina so we could live without fear again.

After a long pause, during which I imagined with

jealousy the non-verbal communication going on between the two sea dragons, Levi replied.

"I'm okay with telling Byssa and Hades, but it stops with those two. If you trust them, Lune, so do I. And this isn't just about me. Your life is at stake, too."

I sighed, low and slow, and my shoulders dropped with relief.

"I'll call them right now," I said. "In the meantime, start thinking about how to get the better of Marina Highcave."

CHAPTER 20

Byssa texted me back, her frazzled state clear from her sparse words. She was usually verbose via messaging.

Swamped here. Can't meet until later.

We'll come to the Crispy Prawn after the lunch rush, I texted back. Byssa had enough on her plate without me insisting she swing by my apartment after her long day. I wanted her full attention and her agreement to help. She would give me both anyway, I knew, but that didn't mean I couldn't make her life a little easier.

Hades agreed to meet at the restaurant, and I laid down my phone with anticipation. I didn't want to keep things from them, not anymore, and Levi's secret had tested me.

Levi's concern showed in his expression when I told him where we were meeting.

"Should we talk about this in public?" He rubbed one hand on his arm in a subconscious gesture of nerves. "It's hard to keep things secret out in the open."

"Normally, I'd agree with you." I waved at my kitchen. "But we have no more food here, and I'm starving." I smiled at him to show I was joking. "There will be hardly anyone there at two o'clock. They'll all be human, almost guaranteed, and we can speak in code."

"I guess so," Levi said. "This is weird for me. I'm so used to keeping this close to my chest. I've never told anyone before you—my bio parents told Seafoam and

Kane, and Austin grew up with me—and now we have a whole crew in the know."

I laid my hand on his shoulder and squeezed. "I can only imagine how hard it is for you. But if it helps, Pipa keeps the same secret about herself, Echo will leave soon for the Seamount, and I would trust Byssa and Hades with my life. Besides, we're all used to keeping secrets from dry folk."

"That's true." He squeezed my hand then rubbed my knuckles with his thumb, back and forth in a comforting pattern. "I really like you knowing."

We had a little time before we needed to leave for the restaurant. Levi paced, restless as a dolphin in a net, and Echo played with the edge of a couch cushion. Pipa stared with clear boredom out the window from her perch on the sash.

"Okay." I clapped my hands. "We can't just sit here doing nothing. Who's up for a game of strolia secrets?"

Levi grinned, but Pipa frowned in confusion. Echo's eyes widened.

"I've never played," she said in a hushed voice. "It's for pale folk only."

"Really?" I'd had no idea that shifter folk didn't play. They kept to themselves, mostly, and I hadn't known many in my life. "Well, I don't mind. Do you not want to?"

"Oh, I will," she said quickly. Her eyes brightened.

"It will pass the time, I suppose." Pipa followed me to the table where Levi already sat. I opened my odds-and-ends drawer in the kitchen and pulled out a strolia horn mounted on a block of wood and a cloth bag filled with shells and small stones. Cetus had given me the game after he'd won it in some contest between him and a new friend. I hadn't asked questions but instead accepted the gift. I'd played with regularity at the Seamount, and the game brought back happy memories.

"How do we play?" Pipa asked without interest.

"I pass around a selection of shells and stones," I replied. "Keep them hidden. Then, all together, we expose one item at a time. If one of your items matches another's, whoever grabs the horn first wins that round. The winner then chooses someone to ask a question to."

"What kind of question?" Echo stared at me, her breath held.

"Whatever you want."

Levi's eyes flicked to me, and we exchanged a grin. The last time I'd played, he and I had tried to pull out secrets of the arson mystery at the Lodge. We'd also drunk more than we should have, and I'd spilled my own secrets to him.

I passed around the shells and stones, and we started to play. Levi grabbed the strolia shell faster than Echo, who stared at his mussel shell with an open mouth.

"What's your favorite food?" he asked her.

"You're going easy on her?" I said teasingly. "You're lucky, Echo."

"Sea cucumber," she answered promptly. "Let's play again."

Pipa stood up. "I don't feel like playing," she said in a strangled voice. She rubbed her forehead. "You three have fun."

She spread herself out on the couch. I shrugged and gestured to the others to continue playing. Was Pipa not feeling well, or did she have secrets she didn't want to share? I had a feeling it was the latter.

The three of us had an enjoyable time playing the game. We kept the questions light for Echo's sake—she felt too young and innocent for anything more interesting—but it was a good way to pass the time.

We waited until just before two o'clock, then the four of us piled into Levi's truck and drove the short distance to Byssa's work. My mouth salivated when the restaurant's awning appeared from between lampposts and parked vehicles. I'd consumed many delicious meals within its walls, and even the secrets I'd be revealing to my friends failed to dampen my appetite or distract me from thoughts of tasty fish.

I was starving after not eating since the Lodge, and our ordeal with Marina had further sapped my strength. What must Levi have been feeling after both shifting and healing me? His stomach must have been eating itself at this point. A quick glance at his tight jaw told me that either he was digesting his own fat stores—not that he had much to begin with—or he was nervous about telling Byssa and Hades his secret. Probably both.

I touched his thigh in comfort, although my caress enflamed rather than soothed me. We had to find a moment to ourselves sometime soon. Levi's firm muscles under his jeans were too distracting.

"Park here," I directed him instead of acting on my impulses. "It's free."

The hostess looked droopy after the lunch rush, although the few customers still in the dining room were finishing up their tea to prepare for leaving. Hades waved at us from our usual booth, and I darted directly to him, the rest in tow.

"Hi, stranger." He patted the bench seat next to him, and I slid in and nudged his shoulder with mine. "Long time, no see."

"Five whole days," I teased. "What a concept. Glad you could get the afternoon off today."

"I worked overtime a few weeks ago. I earned it." He looked with curiosity at the others.

"Hades, meet Pipa and Echo." I waved at the other two who sat stiffly across from us. Levi tucked in beside me, and his solid warmth was both reassuring and distracting.

"You said you had something to tell us," Hades said with a pointed look at the other two. "I assume they have something to do with it?"

"Sort of," Levi replied. "Is Byssa coming?"

"I'm here, I'm here." Byssa slid in beside Echo, her normally cheerful face frazzled. "What a day, and it's only half done. A tour company dropped off a whole busload of tourists for lunch, and we were run off our feet. Okay, I'm ready. What's the big news?"

Levi and I glanced at each other.

"Maybe I could write it down," he suggested. "In Seamount-script. Seafoam taught Austin and me."

"Sure, that works." I pulled out my phone. "I'll find a picture to help describe. Go on, write it out."

The twins looked mystified, but Byssa tossed Levi a

pencil from her apron and shoved a napkin his way. Levi stuck the tip of his tongue out of the corner of his mouth and painstakingly scratched a message.

Instead of reading along, I searched for an image to illustrate what Levi was writing. When I found the right one, my mouth curved in a smile.

Byssa frowned as she read Levi's message, then she stared at him.

"Are you serious?" She glanced at Hades then back at Levi. "You're a—"

"Tap dancer," I blurted out, then hissed, "Code, people. This is secret, remember?"

"Tap dancer?" Levi muttered under his breath. I grinned.

"I've never heard of—tap dancers," Hades said with hesitation. "Do they really exist?"

"Yeah, they do." Pipa crossed her arms. "I'm a tap dancer too. My village is full of them."

I snickered at the thought of a town full of tap dancers, then I pointed the screen of my phone toward the twins. "Just for an idea. It's not an exact representation, of course, but you get the concept."

"That's not right at all," Levi said indignantly, then he looked at me. "Is it?"

I shrugged. "How many mirrors have you looked in while you were dancing, twinkle toes? This is close enough for a general idea of what your 'costume' looks like."

"Amazing," Hades breathed. He looked back and forth between Levi and Pipa with shining eyes. "Man, I want to see you two dance. That would be incredible. I had no idea."

"Did you read the second part?" Levi said. "About Marina and what she wants?"

Byssa's face fell, and she bit her lip. "That's not good. What do we have to do to get her to leave you alone? She keeps cropping up like sand in an oyster."

"That's what we're here for," I said with a glance at Levi's tight mouth. "We want to fend her off for good, but we'll need help. Levi hasn't told anybody about his tap dancing before, but the threat from Marina is too great to ignore, and it's too much for us to handle alone. That's why he's telling you about it."

Byssa's eyes moistened. "That's such an honor, Levi. I promise you won't regret trusting us."

Levi nodded. "I know I won't. If Lune trusts you, then so do I."

"We're on board, always," Hades said. "But what's the plan? Isn't Marina an upper echelon female?"

"And don't forget her ligan," Echo reminded us. She eyed the sushi platter, and Byssa waved at it in distraction. Echo dived in with her fingers, and I followed with more dainty movements of my chopsticks.

"And two shifter folk are with her," I said. "We don't have a plan yet. I was hoping we could brainstorm together."

"I don't know how we're going to get past the ligan," Pipa said. She fidgeted with a chopstick wrapper. "That will be tricky. But tap dancers are immune to pale folk charms. Get Levi and me in, and we can deal with her."

"Noted," I said. "But what do we do with her once we have her?"

"Kill her," Pipa said with a shrug. "It's the simplest solution."

"Hush," Byssa said with a glance around the room. "You can't say stuff like that aloud. Call it 'stomping' or something. And we're not stomping on anyone. Right, Lune?"

"I hadn't thought that far ahead," I hedged. At Byssa's frown, I said, "But I had no plans to do any stomping."

"It's tidy and solves our problems." Pipa winced and pressed a hand to her temple as if a headache formed there. "It's the tap dancer way. I don't see the issue."

Levi swallowed as he contemplated Pipa's words. He didn't look any more pleased by her comments than I did. We knew very little about sea dragon habits. After Pipa's comment, were they something that Levi wanted to learn?

"No stomping," Byssa said firmly. "Not if you want my help. What about compelling her so she's confused about the whole situation?"

"Marina is super strong," I said. "She's an upper echelon female and incredibly well-trained. She's cornered me a few times, and I didn't have a herring's chance in a school of tuna at escaping. I have some product that helps us resist her compelling, but I don't know that even if you, me, and Hades teamed up on her, whether we could subdue her."

"What's this product?" Byssa asked.

"Branc Driftwood gave it to me. Upper echelon

males use it at the Seamount."

"Driftwood 'gave' it to you?" Levi raised an incredulous eyebrow.

I shrugged. "I bought it. It works great. But still, I think compelling Marina is out. Unless we ask that old story singer Marea for ideas."

"I heard she's too hurt after the attack to tell us much," Levi said quietly.

I grimaced and took a sip of my water to give me space to think. I hadn't expected Marina's attack on the story singer. It showed me exactly how desperate she was, and how carefully we would have to swim around her.

Hades spoke into the tense silence. "Maybe I missed something, but why don't you heal Marina's guy? It sounds like that's all she wants. Maybe she'll go away after that. She might even forgive and forget her issues with Lune."

"No," Pipa said at once. "By the sounds of it, this Shoal is far too injured to heal without severe repercussions on Levi's own health. Levi might even die, especially since he isn't an experienced healer. It's very easy to overdo it, which is why healers spend years practicing on small wounds before healing larger injuries. It's too risky."

"Everything is risky at this point," Levi said. "But I don't particularly want to risk death for the man who tried to hurt Lune. And I don't owe Marina anything, not after her attacks on us and the story singer. Lune nearly died after her ligan attack."

Levi crossed his arms and breathed heavily, his face

stormy.

"I have to agree," I said after a glance at Pipa's smug face. I hated to back anything Pipa said, but she had a good point. "I don't trust that Marina will stop at this healing. You should have seen the greedy look on her face when she first saw Levi. She knows exactly what tap dancers are capable of, and the tremendous good the previous tap dancer did for the Seamount. She'll want to bring Levi back and keep him locked up forever. And let's not forget, Marina is upper echelon, and we all know how much they care about social standing. Bringing back a healer would only elevate her further. She might even use Levi as a bargaining chip to force the Protectorate's hands when it comes to the rogue faction's goals."

"Why don't you hide somewhere?" Echo said in her mash-up of Seamount-speak and English. I translated the occasional word for Pipa's benefit, because the sea dragon had some trouble with Echo's dialect. Echo waved around the room. "There are other dry folk cities, right? Can you move and not come back here? Marina is stubborn, but if you never return, she can't wait you out in these waters forever."

"You wouldn't leave, would you?" Byssa said in horror. "You belong here with us. You can't let Marina run you out of town."

"I have the Lodge to think about, too," Levi said. "And I don't want to run, not really. Marina needs to be dealt with. Unless we leave for a short bit. I wish Lune could come with us to the sea dragon villages for a visit."

"Definitely not," Pipa said immediately. "Tap dancers are fiercely protective of their villages. Lune would be no safer arriving there than she would be if she stayed here."

Levi's face darkened, but I laid a hand on his arm.

"Running is a short-term measure that won't solve our problems. You're right, we need to deal with Marina once and for all."

"She'll never stop," Echo said in a solemn tone.

"If we can't stomp on her, and we can't compel her, then we capture her," Hades said.

"What do we do with her after that?" Byssa said, although she looked relieved that killing was off the table.

"That's a problem for another day," Hades said. "Maybe we can talk to her, reason with her. Maybe we can work things out like sensible people if we're not focused on attacking and defending all the time."

"I like it," I said. Maybe I could convince Branc to store Marina, for a large enough fee. And that would give us a chance to work out a compromise with the exasperating siren. "But we still need a way to capture her safely, not to mention the ligan and seal shifters with her."

"Even if we set a trap, how do we draw her in?" Byssa asked.

Pipa huffed. "It's obvious, isn't it? Dangle what she wants in front of her. She wants a tap dancer, so we'll give her one." She leaned back and crossed her arms. "I'll do it."

Levi frowned at her. "We can't ask you to do that."

"You didn't. I want this dealt with, same as you. Then you can come back with me to the villages for a visit without worrying about this ridiculous business." Pipa rubbed her forehead with a wince then smoothed her features with effort.

"Okay, great," I said. Hopefully the peppiness I felt at Pipa acting as bait hadn't shown in my voice. "Pipa leads Marina to the trap. How are we going to capture her? And how can we avoid the ligan in the process?"

"Capturing Marina will be the easy part," Byssa said with confidence. "I still have that net contraption from the battle a few weeks ago. If you can get a few stinger prods from Driftwood, and we use the anti-compelling substance, we'll have Marina no problem."

"Same goes for the seal shifters," Levi said. "But that still leaves us with the ligan."

"We need somewhere the ligan can't go, but Pipa and Marina can." I twirled my chopstick absently. "Somewhere small, like a cave opening or a tight lagoon."

"Ligans hate moving, enclosed situations," Echo said. "They're always out in the open. I've seen Marina's ligan avoid kelp forests because it refused to go in. Marina couldn't convince it to enter."

"It's late in the season, and they'll be dying off soon for the winter," Byssa said. "Are there any forests still around?"

"There's one nearby." My heart thumped harder as our plan coalesced. Levi and I exchanged a hopeful glance. "We can hide in the forest where Marina won't be able to sense us. At high tide, so we can hide in the kelp blades. Pipa can show herself then swim into the kelp forest. Marina will have to dismount the ligan when it refuses to follow. The rest of us can pick off the shifters and capture Marina within the forest."

"That might work." Byssa's eyes were bright. "Lune, try to get more weapons from Driftwood, if you can. High tide is at five o'clock. Can we do this today?"

"Yes," Levi said firmly. "The sooner, the better. I'm tired of looking over my shoulder. I want to move on."

A whale call moaned mournfully from under the table. Levi and Echo looked startled, but I grinned as Hades pulled out his phone and answered his unusual ringtone.

"Hi, Rachel," he said in a guarded yet hopeful voice. He listened for a few beats. "I'm actually heading to the beach at five, but I really do want to talk—" His mouth twisted as he listened. "Okay, sure. Five o'clock at Spanish Banks."

"Rachel's coming to our trap mission?" Byssa said incredulously once Hades had hung up. "Is that smart?"

"Maybe not, but she wants to talk, and she can't meet earlier." Hades heaved a sigh and stirred his soy sauce with a chopstick. "If she wants to meet, I can't say no. I really want to hear what she thinks of all this, whether we have a chance or not."

"It'll all work out," I said with a confident smile. "Rachel will accept you, we'll capture Marina, and the ligan will swim back to the Seamount."

"Right." Byssa stood up. "I need to prep what I can for the dinner rush then plead illness."

"And I have to get more weapons," I said. Levi

scooted off the bench, and I stood up after him. "Pipa, Echo, and Levi, let's leave my apartment at four forty-five. Hades and Byssa, we'll see you at the beach."

CHAPTER 21

When I passed the kitchen, Byssa was deep in conversation with Jules. She waved her hands at the counter. Jules gripped her flailing wrist with gentle fingers, and Byssa looked at him with such an expression of open hope that my jaded heart melted a little.

"It's fine." Jules's lower voice carried further than Byssa's. "You don't need to explain. We'll call Tim, and I'll take over what I can. You've been teaching me for ages now. I can handle it."

"Are you sure?" Byssa said.

"Whatever you're dealing with looks important." Jules smiled and slowly let go of Byssa's wrist. "Just—be safe, okay?"

I left before the pair noticed me, but I couldn't suppress the grin that stole over my face. Maybe I didn't need to intervene in their burgeoning romance, after all. If I got a chance, though, I might take it. Just to make sure they were on track.

Levi caught up with me at the front door just in time, because I stumbled over the threshold and only avoided falling flat on my face through his quick actions.

"That ligan attack took it out of me," I murmured. I peered at Levi, whose eyes were bordered by black rings of tiredness. "How are you holding up?"

"I've been better," he admitted, "but it's fine. I'm fueled by the promise of finishing Marina's influence on our lives. She has far too much sway right now."

"It will be good to get her off our backs," I said. Levi held the door open for Pipa and Echo. "I need to get to Branc's. Will you drop me off?"

"Of course." We walked down the street, the other two following us. Levi released a heavy breath. "Maybe I should come in with you."

"Not a good idea." At Levi's frown, I raised my eyebrow. "The last thing I need is you two posturing at each other. Branc is far more likely to give me what I want if you aren't breathing down his neck. And I'm perfectly safe. Branc has too many uses for me to wish me harm."

"That's what I'm afraid of," Levi muttered, but he let the matter go.

I dragged myself out of the truck at Abyss's door and waved away Levi and the others despite Levi's frowns. When the truck turned past a gaggle of walkers on the street corner, I walked down the shaded alley to get to Abyss's back door.

"Branc's not here right now," the bouncer Reef said when he answered the door. The pearl stud in his earlobe gleamed, and I stared at it in weary fascination.

"I'll wait," I said. "I'll need a chair, though. I'm exhausted."

Reef waved the way to the main bar area and left me to wander across the dance floor. I climbed up to a bar stool, hating more than ever the gravity that dragged at my body until I wanted to slide down to the sticky floor and sleep for a week. My head couldn't stay upright, and I rested it on my folded arms against the bar.

"I'll close my eyes for a minute," I whispered to myself. "Just a minute."

I awoke to the sound of ice clinking in a glass. My eyes blinked until Branc's profile emerged from my fog of sleep.

"What are you doing here, Lune?" He sipped a whiskey clasped between long white fingers. "I didn't call you."

I pushed myself upright and attempted to straighten my hair. It was a lost cause, and I gave up eventually.

"Do you have any of those weapons left?" I asked. "The stinger prods would be great, or spear guns. I'd like to buy some off you, or at least borrow them." I pulled my wallet out of my pocket, which Levi had filled with bills before we'd parted. He'd anticipated a steep fee from Branc, as had I. "I can pay."

"I don't want your money." Branc took another sip of his drink without looking at me.

"You won't sell them?" My shoulders slumped. The weapons were a vital part of the plan. How would we incapacitate the seal shifters and Marina without them?

Branc gave me a sidelong glance. "I didn't say that. I said I wouldn't take your money. What else can you offer me?"

I sighed. I'd been afraid it would come to this, from the moment Levi had given me the cash.

"A favor," I said heavily. "Like before."

"It's a start." Branc finished his drink and pushed the glass down the counter away from us. "But not enough. You put stipulations on the last favor. I want those removed."

"I'll have absolutely no veto rights?" I stared with an open mouth at Branc, hating him more than ever. "You're crazy."

"What if I promise I won't make you kill anyone, nor use your body against your will?" He turned and his black eyes skewered me. "Then I'll give you the weapons that will change the course of whatever battle is coming up for you. You want to protect yourself, don't you? Or maybe keep your friends safe?"

My lips grew tight. Of course I wanted Byssa, Hades, and the others safe, and these weapons would go a long way toward that goal. But could I promise such an open-ended favor?

Dread pooled in my stomach, but I nodded. We needed the help Branc could provide. I would have to pay the price another day and hope that I wouldn't regret it.

"I accept."

"Good." Branc slipped off his chair and beckoned me to follow him. "Come get what you want."

I followed Branc into the back hallway and tried to ignore the churning of my gut that told me I'd made a foolish decision. We walked past his office and around a corner then stopped in front of a room I'd never entered. Branc drew a keychain from his pocket and unlocked the door with a practiced motion. He swept inside.

"How many do you need?" he asked.

My jaw dropped at the arsenal before me. Modified spearguns lined the left wall, illuminated by track lighting from the ceiling so they gleamed dully. Stinger prods perched on racks against the back. A shelf above that held a pile of nets. Along the right wall, a variety of land weapons were arrayed, most of which I'd only seen on television at Byssa's place.

"Are you allowed all those?" I pointed at the land weapons—guns and rifles and who knew what—and frowned at Branc. "I thought you needed special licenses or something."

"Surely you know by now that I have resources." Branc stared at me without expression.

I shrugged and turned to the water weapons. Branc and his illicit affairs didn't concern me. I needed to focus on the upcoming mission.

"I'll take three spearguns, three stinger prods, and two nets," I decided. "That will be all we can handle."

"What are you doing with them, may I ask?" Branc lifted a speargun from the rack and examined it before handing it to me and selecting another.

"I don't know that it's any of your business, but I don't keep secrets like you do, not anymore. We're going to capture Marina Highcave."

Branc coughed. When he turned to me, he'd already mastered his expression, but something in his eyes showed his surprise.

"Is that wise?" he asked.

"No, definitely not," I replied. "But what else are we supposed to do? She won't stop coming after us—me, and I want her off my back." I winced internally at my slip. The last thing I wanted was for Branc to know about Levi. Marina would most likely exploit him, but Branc absolutely would.

A thought occurred to me. "Wait, do you know Marina? Did you tell her I was leaving for the Lodge last week?"

"What makes you think I would tell her anything? Marina and I aren't friends." Branc walked to the nets and pulled down two of the small packages. "Here are the nets."

Branc hadn't really answered my question, but the mystery would have to wait until after our battle with Marina. And if Branc didn't want to tell me something, I couldn't force him.

"I don't know who else would have told her," I answered honestly. "But you can't say anything to her about our plans for tonight."

"How can I tell her details I don't know?" He raised his eyebrow at me.

I stamped my foot, frustrated at him. "Promise me you won't tell Marina anything about me, okay?"

"I promise."

His sincerity surprised me, and I blinked.

"Okay, good."

"Why do you want to capture her? Why not deal with her for good?"

Branc meant killing Marina, and I pursed my lips. "It did occur to me," I admitted, "but I don't want to be that person. Besides, my friend Byssa wouldn't help if that was the plan, and we need her. We're hoping to talk to Marina without the threat of compulsion. And without her ligan skewering me again."

Branc's already pale face turned even whiter. "You encountered her ligan? And you're still here?"

"Lucky break." I shrugged, annoyed with myself for mentioning it. Branc was too astute. If he even had the slightest suspicion about Levi, he wouldn't stop investigating, and then we'd have two problems on our hands. Marina was enough.

"What about the rogue faction?" I asked to change the subject. One arm gripped the spearguns tightly while I accepted a stinger prod from Branc. "Any news on that front?"

"Nothing lately, but that doesn't mean it's over. I've been discussing the situation with other distribution centers in the States and up the coast, and we're staying alert and prepared." He passed me the final stinger prod with an arrested, inward-gazing look. "I wonder if Marina could be convinced to abandon her faction values. She would be a powerful ally in our cause, given her position as the Siren Protector's daughter."

I stared at Branc, disbelief mixing with resignation in my mind. "You want to make friends with Marina Highcave? The murderous siren after my blood? Whose side are you on, anyway?"

Branc pushed the stinger prod's rack clip back into place. Without looking at me, he said, "I'm on my own side. Always."

I shivered and turned to go. "Thanks for the weapons."

CHAPTER 22

I strode into Abyss's back hallway clutching my awkward bundle of weapons. Reef narrowed his eyes at me when he wandered out of a break room with a yogurt cup in his hand.

"Hold on," he said and disappeared.

I balanced the weapons in my hands until he returned with a large black duffel bag. He opened it for me, and I gratefully dropped the tools inside.

"Thanks, Reef," I said. "I'll bring it back later."

He shrugged. "Whenever. I know you come around."

The bus ride home was long and slow to my tired mind. I was intensely relieved that I didn't have to explain my odd weaponry to my fellow passengers. I dragged my ungainly bag off the bus at my stop and stumbled the last block to my apartment building.

I opened the door to my place, and Levi's relieved smile made my heart squeeze.

"You made it." He leaped forward to take the duffel bag off my weary shoulder. "And it looks like Branc was willing to sell."

"Looks like it," I agreed, wondering whether it would be better to keep Levi's money and allow him to think Branc took it, or to tell the truth about how I paid. I couldn't deal with Levi's concern at the moment, so I pushed the decision aside for another day. I sniffed the air, which was filled with the scent of hearty soup. "What do I smell?"

"Dinner." Levi ushered me into the room and sat me at my table. "We stopped at the grocery store on the way home. I know we ate recently, but we all need fuel for the evening ahead, and Pipa and I will be starving if we have to transform on empty stomachs."

"Bring it on," I said, rubbing my hands.

Pipa and Echo joined me at the table. Pipa gave me a chilly nod, which I returned with a slight tilt of my head. Echo patted my shoulder.

"You look tired," she said. "Still feeling rough from your last ligan encounter?"

I gave her a smile to hide the bone-deep exhaustion I felt. "I'm fine. A lot better than when I had fang wounds, that's for sure."

Levi placed a saucepan on a folded tea towel on the table and sat with a sigh. He didn't look much better than I felt. How long would it take for him to recover from healing me? Suddenly, I felt confident in his decision to not heal Shoal.

"It should be simple tonight," I said as Levi dished clam chowder into our bowls. "We'll be able to pick them off one by one in the kelp forest, and the ligan won't be an issue. We'll be back here celebrating before long."

The others nodded, and I ate some bread. It was true. With Branc's weapons, the substance that protected us from compulsion, and two sea dragons on our side, we would prevail quickly and easily. I wished we'd thought of this earlier and saved me the stress of the past week.

"Where are we going to keep Marina?" Echo said. She swallowed a spoonful of chowder with a twist of her mouth at the unfamiliar flavors. "She can't really breathe on land."

"Right." I drummed my fingers on the table. "Tie her up underwater, I guess. We can take turns guarding her to make sure she doesn't compel any passing pale folk. Hopefully, she comes to her senses sooner rather than later."

Thinking about the aftermath of our upcoming trap felt overwhelming to my tired brain, so I didn't think about it anymore. Our hastily sketched-out plan would have to do.

"What do you have in your bag?" Echo pointed at the duffel bag.

I dragged it over to the table and unzipped it. "Weapons. Spear guns, stinger prods—these make the victim unconscious—and expandable nets to entrap opponents. They all work great."

"I'm sure they do." Echo bit her lip and twisted her hands together. "But they won't work against compulsion. I know you have that eelgrass stuff I can take, but are you sure it works on shifters? What if Marina overpowers me? Then you'll have three seal shifters to deal with instead of two."

"And that's why you're not coming." I gave her a reassuring smile. "For exactly that reason." The eelgrass likely worked on shifters, but Echo was a timid seal with only sixteen sunsweeps behind her. She'd proven her bravery to me already, but I didn't want to worry about her under the water. The eelgrass was as good an excuse as any to keep her safe on land.

"Time's getting on," Levi said. "We should eat up and go."

We enjoyed the rest of our meal in silence. The food went a long way toward my weariness—helped by the delicious flavors Levi had coaxed out of the clams—but a nap would have perked me right up. Unfortunately, we had no time for sleep. High tide was almost upon us.

In the truck, Pipa rubbed her temple again with a wince, but she desisted when I glanced at her. I considered asking her what was wrong, but I shrugged and turned toward the windshield instead. Pipa was a big girl. If she needed a painkiller, she could ask for one. Until then, her headache wasn't mine to worry about.

With Pipa looking coolly unconcerned and Levi drumming his fingers on the steering wheel, I gave up all attempts at conversation and focused instead on resting for the duration of the trip. I would need all the strength I could get.

Byssa and Hades were already at the beach when we arrived. The evening was darkening, and a stiff wind whipped the waves into a frothy churn. Despite the popularity of this beach, nobody was out in this chilly weather in the gathering dusk. Byssa gave me a hug after I stepped out of the truck.

"You look rough." Worry laced her voice. "Are you

sure you're up for this?"

"I want Marina out of the picture," I said quietly. "And I'm fine. Nothing a solid sleep tonight won't cure. Let's get this done and go home."

Byssa nodded, even as her expression was unconvinced. I dug in my pocket for the envelope I'd stashed in there before we'd left my apartment.

"Here," I said. "Eat a piece of this. It will stop Marina compelling you."

Byssa took the eelgrass concoction without question and chewed it down. I gave another piece to Hades, and I tore off a small chunk for myself. I didn't want to take any chances today.

I passed around spearguns, stinger prods, and nets, then stripped down to my undergarments. The speargun strapped tightly to my back, the net tucked into my bra, and the stinger prod rested comfortably in my hand. I clipped the dive knife that Levi had bought me onto my calf in its holster.

"You look ready for war," Hades said. He hoisted the stinger prod onto his shoulder then ran a hand over his close-cropped orange hair on the sides. The longer black locks on top were spiked. Hades must have been feeling positive again.

"That's going to get messed up as soon as we get in the water," I warned him. "I hope you brought extra gel."

"I always do." He gave me an impish grin which slid off his face at the sound of his name.

"Hades?"

A short woman with shoulder-length black hair and

large silver hoop earrings stood on the beach, her arms crossed over her generous curves. I recognized her from work. This was Rachel, Hades's pined-after human and the one who recently found out about his ocean heritage.

"Give me a minute," Hades murmured to us, his face more solemn than I'd seen it for a while. "I need to talk to her."

Before I could respond, he'd strode toward Rachel and waved her further away from our interested ears. I sighed and fidgeted with my stinger prod. The wind tossed my loose hair around my face, and I pushed it back impatiently.

"We'll be in the water soon," Byssa said to me. "It's still a few minutes until high tide."

I stilled my hands and gripped the weapon more securely. Byssa was right. Hades was risking his life to help me deal with my enemy. The least I could do was allow him a minute to deal with his love life, which was hanging by a finger in the current.

Byssa approached Levi. "I have to say, I'm so excited to see you underwater," she said in a low voice so her words wouldn't carry to Rachel. "You too, Pipa. It's my hobby to photograph sea creatures. Obviously, I would never take a picture of you, but I still like to document the sight in my mind."

Byssa's longing for a photo was clear in her voice, and Levi shifted uncomfortably.

"Yeah, I'm not too keen on photography. Although I would like a mirror. I've never seen myself."

Byssa breathed in quickly with an arrested look.

"A mirror," she murmured. "How could we do that?"

"Everyone," Hades called out to us. He walked hand-in-hand with Rachel, his smile wide. "Meet Rachel. Rachel, these are my friends Lune and Levi, my new acquaintance Pipa, and my sister Byssa."

I blinked. Just like that, Rachel had forgiven Hades for his secrets and accepted his strange life? I'd scoffed at Hades's decision to not siren her, but now I wondered if he'd been wiser than I'd given him credit for. He'd let Rachel decide her path for herself, and it had paid off for Hades.

"Pleased to meet you," she said in a sweet voice and gave a shy wave. "Are you all—" She shook her head. "Never mind, you don't have to tell me anything."

"We are," Byssa said warmly. "And I can't wait to get to know you better, Rachel. But unfortunately, we have something we need to do first. Hades?"

"I'll wait on the beach," Rachel said to Hades with determination. "If that's okay with you."

"Totally and absolutely okay," Hades said with fervor. "We'll deal with this pesky problem, then I'll come back up and I can tell you all about it."

Rachel smiled and walked back to a wooden shelter above the hightide line. She wrapped her coat more securely around herself to keep out the cold wind pouring off the ocean. I walked closer to Hades as we approached the waves.

"I hope you won't tell Rachel everything," I whispered to him. "Levi is off limits."

"Of course."

"I wanted to make sure. There's no knowing what you'll say in your lovey-dovey bliss."

Hades rolled his eyes. "I'm not that far gone. I recognize the need for Levi's secrecy as much as you do. Now, come on. What are you waiting for?"

Hades shot me a cheeky grin and splashed into the crashing waves. I glanced at Levi and Pipa, who were walking toward a cement pier down the shore to shift out of sight of Rachel. Levi waved to me. I suppressed my jealousy of Pipa getting naked with Levi before their shift. Why should she get to do that and not me? I hoped he made her get in the water first.

The water closed over me once I entered, cool and welcoming, and I sucked it into my lungs gladly. I needed the flexibility of remaining underwater undetected. It was enough that Byssa would have to dart to the surface on occasion. We didn't need another person grabbing breaths of air as well. I hoped the blades of the kelp forest would flutter to the surface to cover Byssa's ascents. Luckily, with the high tide, there would be plenty of shifting fronds to distract Marina's skin sense.

I followed Hades, who had struck out to the north with renewed vigor after his reunion with Rachel. He led us unerringly to a large kelp forest. I felt it before I saw it: a shifting mass of confusion anchored by long, naked cords that attached to the rocky seafloor below. When I was close enough to see, the brown blades of kelp tossed in the stormy waves, and every long stipe angled in the same direction as the current. Fish darted in and around the kelp, further adding to the confusion.

I smiled grimly. Marina would have a tough time sensing us in this mess.

The fish reminded me of Squirter. I really wanted to see him and make sure he was safe. Besides, he'd proven time and again that he was a worthy companion in a tight spot. I wanted him by my side.

Cautiously, I sent out a call that he would recognize. We were almost at the kelp forest and could hide in there if Marina came early.

Two approaching figures cut long, sinuous paths through the water toward us. When skin sense gave way to vision, I blinked at the beautiful silvery-blue of Levi. Then I saw Pipa. Her scales were black tinged with gold edges, and her fronds and spines were a slightly lighter shade of gray. Would they be red in surface light?

Byssa and I exchanged a glance. Her eyes were wide and impressed.

Amazing, she said. *I had no idea they existed. I wish I had my camera. The photos would be gorgeous, especially with a flash.* At my frown, she rolled her eyes. *Obviously, I'm not going to take a picture. I get the need for secrecy. But you have to admit, they're amazing.*

I couldn't deny it. The sea dragons' graceful forms weaved around each other in a mesmerizing pattern of silvery-blue and black with gold. I could watch them all day.

But we didn't have all day. I poked Byssa in the arm.

Come on, I said. *Let's get into position.*

Byssa jolted, and a split second later I felt the wash of pressure on my skin sense that must have triggered her reaction. My entire body tensed. Was Marina here already?

The motion resolved into a much smaller form than a ligan, and my muscles melted in relief.

Hi, Squirter, I said to my octopus friend when he floated in front of me. *Happy to see you.*

His green eye with its rectangular pupil stared at me for a moment. Then he reached out an arm and tickled my shoulder.

Hide with me? I asked him. *We're trapping bad siren today.*

Yes, he replied, and he crawled over my body until he suctioned onto my back like a backpack. I hummed a call toward the other four. They gathered around me at the seafloor, out of the choppy wave action.

Time to get into position, I said once they were paying attention. Levi's beautiful, striated eyes looked at me, and I hastily turned my gaze to Byssa, who was far less mesmerizing. *Does everyone remember their roles?*

We have this, Hades said with pep. He patted his stinger prod and the net half-tucked into his swimsuit waistband. *Marina will be in our custody within the hour.*

We know what to do. Pipa's eyes didn't roll, but the exasperation was clear in her voice. Her accent was so thick I barely understood her, and she used the crest around her face to help communicate. My natural curiosity wanted to understand her speech technique, but I reminded myself that we were on a mission. Besides, did I really want to spend extra time with Pipa?

Good, I said. *Then let's roll.*

Everyone except for Pipa melted into the thick kelp forest and was lost in the murk and shifting blades until neither my eyes nor skin sense could find them. Pipa swam away, out to sea. Her black and gold tail disappeared into the gloom. I joined the others hiding in the forest.

I settled amid swaying blades and held onto the stipe of a bull kelp to anchor myself against the current. Rolling waves pulled and pushed me in a circular motion. I gritted my teeth and gripped the kelp harder. A moment passed.

An unearthly call filled my ears. Haunting and totally foreign, the sound dipped and soared like a whale call, but the tone was unlike any whale I'd ever heard. Trills mingled with deeper long tones that rippled up to piercing heights before plunging into rich bass once again.

I held my breath, spellbound, not wanting to miss a moment of this call. It had to be Pipa. Could Levi sound like this? Did he even know how? The melancholy melody brought the heat of tears to my eyes as I thought of everything Levi had missed growing up among humans and pale folk.

Pipa's call flowed through the water column. If Marina was anywhere nearby, the call would draw her to the sound like a shark to blood. She could never mistake that melody for anything else, especially if she'd been paying attention to Marea's stories.

I waited, kelp tickling my bare skin with its movements in the wash, while Pipa's song transfixed me. I didn't know how long I waited there, basking in the glorious call.

It grew strident then stopped altogether. My body

tensed and I strained toward Pipa with eyes and skin sense alert, even though I could hardly see or feel through the kelp.

I needed to know what was going on. Carefully, I swam through the blades until I reached the edge of the forest. I peered out from the shifting blades and looked.

My skin sense told me what was happening before my eyes did. The sinuous form of Pipa darted toward me. The larger, longer form of the ligan followed close behind. My fingernails dug into my palms. I held my breath again. Was Pipa quick enough?

Her black and gold body shot into view and darted into the long stipes of kelp that anchored them to the rocky seafloor. My eyes trained on her pursuers. Would the ligan follow?

The sea serpent's massive head emerged in the gloom. It was gargantuan and vicious with fangs visible through a half-open mouth. I shrank back. My previous encounter with this ligan had left mental as well as physical scars. My hands trembled. I gripped the kelp and my stinger prod more firmly in my grasp.

The ligan's yellow eyes fixed on the kelp forest, and it swam forward. My heart lodged in my throat.

CHAPTER 23

Just before the ligan touched kelp, it stopped and reared its head back. Marina clung to its neck, her flowing white dress billowing in the stormy waves. She sent out a call of command to the creature.

It ignored her and turned its head to the side. It was clearly ill at ease with entering the forest. Would its will prevail, or Marina's?

Marina increased her command, but the ligan twisted its head as if to dislodge its rider. Marina gripped the ligan and shouted a new command.

Shifters, she called. *Follow the sea dragon.*

Two sleek brown figures shot past the writhing sea serpent. They darted into the kelp forest without hesitation. I let them go. Levi and the others were ready for action and would deal with the seals in short order. I wanted to keep tabs on Marina.

Marina struggled with the ligan for a full minute more. No sounds emerged from behind me, so either the seal shifters were too far away for their noises to carry, or the others had dispatched them with swift stinger prod action. Either way, my true quarry was ahead.

Finally, with a growl of frustration, Marina pushed off the ligan and swam toward the kelp forest. She didn't give the sea serpent a backward glance. It gratefully twisted its massive body to swim out to sea. Marina undulated forward, her face set in an expression of fierce determination.

She entered the forest below the shifting layer of blades to swim between the bare stipes. I followed cautiously among the chaotic blades, painfully aware that she might feel my motions if I moved too quickly.

I could have raised my speargun in her direction, but I wanted to follow the plan. Let Marina swim to the center of the forest, then we could surround her. If my shot missed and alerted her to my presence, she might escape our trap.

I kept Marina in my sight and moved forward, attempting to sway my body in time to the movement of the kelp blades. She slowed in a clear space where the kelp didn't grow on a patch of sand. Her head darted around to search for Pipa.

Were the others in position? I didn't know how to decide when to make my move.

Squirter detached from my back and jetted slowly through the blades toward my left. In a moment, he was back.

Byssa there, he said.

My shoulders relaxed fractionally.

Thanks, Squirter.

I pulled out the net tucked into my shoulder strap and readied both it and the stinger prod. I hoped the others were watching as intently as I was. They would wait for my first move, I knew, but that would only help if they noticed it.

At least Byssa was there. Emboldened by that thought, I gripped the net tightly. With a burst of speed, I swam directly toward Marina.

She spun around as soon as I descended from the

blades. Her face contorted in fury.

You, she snarled.

I threw the net at her and darted forward with my stinger prod. From my right, my skin sense told me that Byssa and Hades approached with weapons at the ready.

Marina dived down and missed my net. My heart dropped to my stomach. I grabbed my speargun and aimed it at her.

She sent out a howl of compulsion strong enough to turn us all into mindless drones. But aside from a faint buzzing in my ears and a slight weakening of my limbs, nothing happened.

I pulled the trigger, and the speargun's harpoon sliced through the water. Marina twisted aside, her eyes wide with surprise and rage. I sent a silent message of thanks to Branc and his eelgrass concoction.

Byssa threw her net at Marina, but the slippery siren dived under my friend. She grasped Byssa's leg with long, white fingers then sent a vibration so strong I could feel it from my vantage point. With the skin contact, it must have felt like a shock wave to Byssa.

My friend's eyes rolled back in her head, and I despaired. Would Branc's substance be enough to withstand a direct attack of Marina's strength?

Marina grinned. She had a wild light in her eyes as she placed one hand farther up Byssa's leg as if she was climbing her. Hades yelled, and a harpoon shot toward the pair from his direction.

No, I screamed, but it was too late. The harpoon did little more than graze Marina's side, but it planted itself in Byssa's thigh. I shouted wordlessly at Hades, but he only stared in horror at his sister.

The only silver lining of Hades's disastrous mistake was that Byssa wasn't compelled anymore. She screamed in pain, but she also pushed Marina away with what little strength she still had. Marina clung to her.

Squirter detached from my back, jetting toward the struggling pair. I wanted to grab at him, hold him back, maybe compel him to stay safe, but I didn't. Time and again, he'd proven himself brave and capable in a tight spot.

But I still needed to help. After shaking off my shock, I chased after him with Hades close behind me. Squirter had already reached the others. His eight legs fanned out, and a black cloud ballooned from his siphon.

Within seconds, the ink enveloped Byssa and Marina. It drifted rapidly outward, obscuring everything in its path. Since Squirter was from the Seamount and had evolved alongside pale folk, his ink had the properties of obscuring skin sense as well as vision. The cloud in front of me was void of information, including Byssa's whereabouts.

To me! Marina called out from the blackness. *Shifters, help!*

They're busy, Hades shouted with satisfaction. Levi and Pipa must have been dealing with the two seal shifters. *Now, get away from my sister.*

Marina emerged from the inky cloud. Hades darted into the blackness to help Byssa, leaving me and Squirter to handle the irate siren. I reminded myself to stay outside Marina's reach, since Branc's substance apparently had limits. Already, Squirter was floating motionless—the result of a disorienting blast from Marina—and my stomach knotted. Luckily, Marina ignored the little octopus and focused her attention on me.

I could do this. All I needed to do was poke her once with my stinger prod, and she'd be as limp as a dead squid.

I shoved the now useless speargun to my back and readied my net and stinger prod. Marina bared her teeth at me. Then she brandished a bone spear in my direction.

Come get me, scum, she snarled. *I wanted a sea dragon, but killing you will be an acceptable consolation prize.*

I swam toward her. At the last moment, I tossed the net, trying hard not to telegraph my actions. Her eyes flicked to my wrist before I acted.

She darted to the left. I'd lost the element of surprise. One corner of the net landed on her foot, and she kicked it away with a furious expression.

No matter. I still had my stinger prod, and Marina wasn't running away. I held the weapon up and kicked toward Marina.

She met me with an outstretched bone spear. The two weapons clashed with a parry that jolted my arms. I came back quickly. Marina's spear was already in place to counter my move. Again and again, we parried in an absurd parody of a land-based sword fight. Her spear nicked my skin three times—on the forearm, against my bare stomach, along my thigh—while the needle of my stinger prod never once touched her.

I gritted my teeth and pushed harder. The weariness that had plagued me all day threatened to overwhelm me. Adrenaline coursed through my body, and I dug deeper and pulled on my last reserves. Surely, I had to get lucky at some point. She couldn't avoid my prod forever, could she?

Marina jolted back with a look of surprised pain on her face. Squirter dodged into the gloom, and I nearly laughed aloud. My little friend had snuck up on the siren and nipped her calf with his sharp beak.

Before I could press my advantage, Marina jabbed her spear forward. Another gash to my other thigh, and I bit my tongue to avoid groaning aloud. I didn't want to give Marina the satisfaction of knowing how much it hurt, but her gloating face told me she knew.

Two sleek brown bodies darted between us in a frenzy of brown flippers. The seal shifters left a trail of blood behind them. One swam in a drunken motion from teeth marks on a flipper, and the other oozed black clouds from gashes in his flank.

I fell back, relieved for the interruption from Marina's relentless attack. Marina tried to swim toward me, but the two sea dragons were close on the tails of the shifters. They bowled Marina over in their wake.

Hades darted forward to take my place fighting Marina, and I gladly relinquished my role. He would be able to press the needle of his stinger prod into Marina's skin. He was fresher than I was. Surely Marina was growing tired by now.

I turned instead to the seal shifters, now encircled by

a writhing ball of sea dragon bodies. I stifled a hysterical giggle at the sight then pinched myself to focus. Levi and Pipa could have killed the seal shifters without much trouble, I was sure, but instead they were trapping them while we dealt with Marina. Levi must have convinced Pipa not to follow her murderous inclinations.

The seal shifters were contained, so I took a deep breath and turned to enter the fray with Hades and Marina.

Hades floated motionless midwater. Marina clutched a stinger prod in one hand and her bone spear in the other.

She looked at the ball of sea dragons surrounding her seal shifters, then at me with my weapon raised. Doubt flickered in her eyes. Her flowing white dress swirled around her, and she swam away.

She's escaping! I shouted at the sea dragons. They could swim much faster than me. *Help!*

Pipa untangled herself from Levi and undulated after Marina while Levi contained the shifters on his own. Her black body overtook the pale woman easily, and I breathed a sigh of relief.

Marina's spear jabbed into Pipa and sliced across her shoulders. An oozing black gash appeared in her gold-edged scales.

Pipa reared back, vocalizing her pain in an eerie call. I swam through the kelp stipes to help, but the others were still full seconds away. Marina yanked on Pipa's frill until the sea dragon's head bent down, then she wrapped her legs around Pipa's neck. The sea dragon writhed in pain and confusion.

Marina took a small seaweed bag from a pouch on her side. She reached around and pulled hard at the corner of Pipa's mouth, then shoved the bag inside. With a squeeze, she pressed the fingers of her other hand against Pipa's cheek and mouth.

Pipa wriggled furiously, and Marina unwrapped her legs and pushed off. When Pipa opened her mouth and snapped at her, Marina jabbed her spear one last time at the beleaguered sea dragon and darted away.

I gave chase, but Marina's powerful body undulated far faster than I could manage in my current state of weariness. Still, I followed her. This was our one chance to capture her.

Marina exited the kelp forest, and I burst out after her. A sense of something ahead made me stop short. The ligan was waiting for Marina. It swam into view, eyeing me with a hungry yellow gaze.

I backpedaled swiftly into the forest. Marina swam onto the ligan's back and held up the seaweed bag in salute. Then the ligan swam away with its rider on board.

One brown body shot out from the forest after Marina and disappeared into the gloom. I didn't bother chasing the seal shifter. Marina was our true prize. Now that she was gone, I didn't have the energy to care about the wayward shifter.

I stared at the darkness where Marina and the others had disappeared, my chest hollow with disappointment. Capturing Marina should have been simple. We'd had a good plan, but somehow it had all gone sideways. Now

Marina was more determined than ever, and she wouldn't be fooled by a trap again.

I swam back to the others. When they came into view, I assessed the situation. Hades was unconscious but otherwise unhurt. Pipa had a gash on her shoulder and cheek. Byssa still had a harpoon sticking out of her thigh, but since she hadn't yet removed it, her blood loss was minimal. Levi had one or two small bite marks from the seal shifters, and my slices from Marina's bone spear throbbed angrily now that I had time to consider them.

Levi had his mouth clamped lightly around the seal shifter's tail. The shifter was finally motionless, presumably to avoid retaliation from the sea dragon. I swam quickly over to them.

I'll hold him for a minute, I said to Levi. *Can you heal Byssa in the meantime?*

Levi nodded. I took my dive knife out of its sheath, gripped the seal's flipper, and pressed the blade of my knife against his throat.

Don't move, I warned him. *Or you'll regret it.*

The seal gazed at me with a baleful expression in his big brown eyes, but he remained quiet and still. With my hand firmly gripping his flipper, I watched Levi approach Byssa. He clicked *come* to Pipa, who slowly made her way over to the pair.

With head motions, he indicated that Pipa should grip the harpoon with her mouth and yank it out. Byssa blanched at the charade, but she was made of stern stuff and held still when Pipa placed her jaws around the shaft of the harpoon.

Without warning, Pipa jerked her head. Byssa's scream was terrible to hear, and my hands clenched convulsively until the shifter squirmed.

Stay still. I pressed my blade against his flesh. The seal's motions subsided.

I wished I could have sirened Byssa's pain away, but with Branc's substance in her veins, my half-human efforts wouldn't have worked. Byssa coughed and choked as water flooded her lungs. Her eyes grew wide with panic. When she'd expelled all the air from her chest, she heaved for breath.

Hurry, I said to Levi. *We need to get Byssa to the surface. She can't breathe well underwater.*

Byssa's choking sobs filled my ears, but Levi was already at work. With swift motions, he licked Byssa's wound. He was much quicker and more efficient with his movements than he had been with me, and my jealous heart relaxed.

Byssa hiccupped into silence when Levi finished, although her breath was still labored. Levi turned to Pipa next. Pipa shook her head.

Don't waste your strength, she said in her thick accent.

Levi frowned at her—at least I thought it was a frown, but I hadn't entirely learned to read sea dragon features yet—and swam over to me. His movements were slow, and I wondered how much truth Pipa was telling. Had healing Byssa, especially on the tail of healing me the other day, drained him of too much energy?

I'm fine, I said to him, ignoring the clouds of blood that seeped from my gashes. We needed to get moving to avoid drawing predators to us, and Byssa needed air. *Let's get back to shore.*

Levi nudged my hand out of the way and licked the wound on my thigh.

No, seriously, I said, alarmed. How much juice did he have left? *They're all minor scrapes. Save your strength.*

Levi butted my hand away again as I fended him off and licked my forearm.

Okay, okay, I'm good. I turned to the seal shifter and considered him. What were we going to do with him? I had no interest in keeping him captive, but I didn't want him going back to Marina and helping her.

You will swim to the Seamount, I said to him, infusing a powerful compulsion into my words. The vibrations traveled through my hand into his flippers with their pale patches, and his eyes glazed over. *You will avoid Marina on the way.*

I released the seal shifter. He shook his head. Then, without a backward glance, he swam westward instead of north toward Marina and the ligan.

Levi followed him. I frowned at his glazed eyes, then my eyes widened in horror. When his tail whipped past me, I grabbed it and held on tight.

Stop, I said with compulsion. *Ignore my last instructions.*

Levi turned his long body around and blinked at me in confusion. When he was close enough, I stroked his nose.

I guess you're susceptible to sirening when you're tired, I told him. *Good to remember.*

CHAPTER 24

The swim back was slow. Levi's snake-like motions were laborious and ungraceful with his weariness, and Pipa dragged Hades's limp body in her mouth using a gentle grip. Byssa glanced at them in consternation when she wasn't slumping over with her own tiredness. Squirter pushed Byssa from time to time, which she responded to with a grateful hum. In the shallows, he said goodbye to me and darted away. A lump formed in my throat as his arms disappeared into the gloom. Would he ever come home with me again?

I put on a burst of speed which almost finished me, but I managed to pop my head out of the water before anyone else. The dark and windswept shoreline was deserted except for a cold-looking Rachel huddled in the shelter. She leaped up when she saw me.

After I coughed out the water in my lungs, I called out to her. "We could use your help, Rachel."

She ran to me and splashed into the crashing waves without hesitation. Inwardly, I marveled at the change in Rachel, from overwrought denial of our world to complete acceptance. Had Hades known that this would happen? Maybe allowing Rachel to make up her own mind, to choose her own way, had made her eventual decision a stronger one.

I waved my hand underwater, and Byssa's head emerged. She hauled on Hades's unresponsive body until it breached the surface.

Rachel gasped and splashed forward. "What's wrong

with him? What happened?" She took his arm and pulled him closer to shore.

"He'll be fine." I stood and swayed until my balance came back. "He got on the wrong end of some knockout juice, but it will wear off shortly. Look, he might even be stirring now."

Hades's pale face twisted under his soaked black and orange locks. Then he coughed water while Rachel held his shoulders from behind. He lay back and blinked upward, then he gave her a goofy smile.

"You're here," he rasped out. "I'm so glad you found out."

Rachel bit her lip and shook him gently. "Don't scare me like that. You promised to take me out to the best fish tacos in town, and I'm holding you to that."

Levi and Pipa emerged from behind the pier, fully clothed but limping. Pipa still had bleeding cuts that smeared her clothes with red, but she waved Levi away when he pointed at them. When they got closer, the exhaustion on Levi's face was obvious. His skin was unusually pale, dark circles gathered under his eyes, and he walked too slowly and carefully for a young man.

I ran up to them, leaving Rachel, Hades, and Byssa to wander to their towels.

"You look terrible," I said to Levi.

"Thanks." He rubbed his chest. "I feel terrible."

"You did a lot of healing today." Pipa crossed her arms. "Too much, especially on the tail of Lune's healing. Plus, you don't know what you're doing and how far you can go without severe repercussions."

Levi kicked a stone into the ocean. "I can't believe

Marina slipped through our fingers. She'll never fall for a trap again. How can we possibly capture her now? Maybe I should heal Shoal, if only to get her off our backs for good."

"But it won't be for good," I reminded him. "She'll keep you, I have no doubt."

"And did you not hear anything I just said?" Pipa sounded exasperated. "No one's trained you to use your healing abilities. Given how hurt Marina's man is, you would almost certainly overextend yourself and probably die."

"How would I even heal someone's brain injuries?" Levi wondered. "There are no wounds to lick."

"The properties of your saliva will travel through skin and help even internal injuries," Pipa said.

Levi's gaze turned inward. "Could I heal my adoptive father's heart condition? Would that work?"

"Only once you've been trained," Pipa repeated with a frown. "Which is why you need to come to the villages with me. You have so much to learn."

"Wait," I said. "Marina did something to you, Pipa. What happened there?"

"She took a sample of my saliva," Pipa said heavily. "I assume she'll use it to try to heal her lover. It won't work, of course. She doesn't realize that not every sea dragon can heal."

"So now she'll know." I stared at Levi, who blinked at me with growing horror. "She'll know it's you."

"You have to come with me to the villages," Pipa urged. She rubbed her forehead with a pained expression. "Forget Marina for now. Maybe if you learn what you need to in the villages, you can come back and safely heal her man. Bargain with her to let you go in exchange for the healing." She stamped her foot. "Or just kill the wretched siren. No one in the villages would blame you, that's for sure."

Levi grew paler. "No. I don't want to kill her. Not unless I have no other choice."

"She's not leaving you with much of one." Pipa stalked toward the truck. Levi stared after her until I took his hand.

"I wouldn't recommend murder quite yet," I said. "But if she comes after you again, fight with everything you've got."

"Same with you," he said with intensity. His eyes bored into mine, and he gripped my hand in his. "And if she ever gets me, promise me you won't rescue me. I'm a big boy, I can figure things out on my own. I would never forgive myself if you got hurt trying to save me."

"I don't think I can make that kind of promise," I said, startled. How could Levi ask something like that of me? Of course I would do everything I could to protect him.

"Promise me." He shook my hand for emphasis.

"I'll think about it," I said at last, unwilling to make promises I couldn't keep, even if it was what Levi wanted. His intentions were good, but I'd have to ignore them if it was for his own safety.

"Maybe Pipa's right," he said at last. At my startled expression, he grimaced. "Not about killing Marina. About going to the sea dragon villages. There is so much I want to learn, need to learn. If I can heal Kane without fearing for my own life, how amazing would that be? And to meet others like me, and my birth mother…" He swallowed. "But I can't leave you to face Marina alone. What if you came partway with us, took a holiday nearby while Pipa and I carried on?"

"Yeah, maybe," I said. "Or we could sneak into the villages over land, talk to the other sea dragons before they realize I'm not one of them. You need to understand your healing ability before you get yourself into trouble."

It hurt, deep in my chest, to tell him to go. I truly wanted him to know his heritage—I'd certainly benefited from reconnecting with mine—but it might come at a steep cost. Pipa would do her best to keep him at her home, I knew. And once he found his people, would he even want to come back with me? Would I be relegated to a mildly regretful episode of his past?

Levi could barely stay awake on the ride home, and I turned the radio up loudly and poked him to keep him on track. Finally, he jerked his head to get me closer.

"Could you siren me awake?" he whispered.

I stared at him with wide eyes. He'd made such a big deal the last time I'd compelled him. Why would he ask now?

"You made your strong feelings on the subject clear

last time," I reminded him under the cover of the music.

"There's a huge difference between asking and having it forced on you against your will. I'm so tired that I'm in serious danger of crashing the truck." He glanced at me. "Please, help a guy out, here. I don't want to be responsible for everyone's injuries later."

"I'll gladly siren you. I just wanted to make sure you knew what you were asking."

I placed my hand on Levi's chest and gently hummed. Forcing someone to stay awake wouldn't work for long—the body needed what it needed—but for the next few minutes, I could keep Levi's eyes open and his brain in a conscious state.

Levi looked more alert than before, but his shoulders also relaxed and he sighed.

"That feels good," he murmured. "Are you also turning me on with your sirening?"

I chuckled. "That's all you, baby."

At the apartment, we all stumbled to our respective beds after giving Echo a brief rundown of our disappointing venture. I must have fallen asleep instantly, because I had no memory beyond kicking off my boots and falling backward on the bed.

I finally awoke in the early afternoon light, feeling sleepy but not bone-tired like the day before. Soft breathing reminded me of who lay in my bed. I rolled over to look at Levi's sleeping profile and mentally traced the curve of his cheeks, the plane of his nose, and the deliciously tousled hair that drifted over his forehead.

Nature called, but I snuck back into bed as softly as I could to not disturb his healing sleep. Despite my efforts, he shifted and rolled onto his side. His beautiful eyes blinked open then focused on me. His smile crept over his face like a rising sun.

"Back in bed with a beauty," he murmured. "How did I get so lucky?"

I smiled back. "Eh, I took pity on you."

He chuckled and reached out to caress my hip. I wriggled closer and tucked my leg against his, craving contact with his warmth. I ran a light finger over his jawline. Unexpected moistness gathered in my eyes. Levi was going to leave, and I didn't know if he would ever come back. I wanted to believe he would return with me, but I knew that the draw of belonging might ensnare him fully. Could I convince him otherwise if I came with him?

Levi's smile faltered when he noticed my damp eyes. "What's wrong?"

Words wouldn't help the situation, not when I knew the best thing for Levi was to go. He might stay out of guilt, but I didn't want to be the source of a deep regret.

I leaned forward and kissed him lightly. We had other ways of speaking, after all. Ones that didn't involve words.

Levi responded eagerly. He pulled me closer until our bodies pressed tightly together. His hand rubbed my back and then cupped me lower down. I pushed into him, not willing to wait any longer, not caring that others were in the next room. Levi was leaving me soon, and I didn't want to part without knowing him like this.

I slid my leg over his until I straddled him. He continued to kiss and caress me, his motions growing more urgent. I closed my eyes, and tears leaked out and dripped onto his cheeks.

He pushed me upright and stared with concern. "Lune, what's wrong? Tell me."

I wiped my cheeks with the back of my hand and gave him a tremulous smile.

"I don't want to talk. I just want you."

Levi stared at me for a moment longer, but when I started moving my hips against him, his eyelids lowered. He pulled my head back down to greet his questing lips.

CHAPTER 25

Coupling with Levi was currents better than with anyone else. Not that I'd had many lovers, but still, his attention to my desires joined with his passionate eagerness to possess me left me shuddering with pleasure.

When we were done, we drifted into another light sleep. Finally, I yawned and stretched.

"We should get up," I said.

"Why?" Levi snaked an arm around me and pulled me closer. "That sounds like a terrible idea."

"Because I'm hungry." On cue, Levi's stomach rumbled, and I laughed. "And so are you. Pipa said healing takes lots of extra energy, plus your shifting yesterday."

"Pipa." Levi draped an arm over his eyes and groaned. "And Echo. They were both out there, weren't they? This is going to be so awkward."

"You're such a human sometimes," I teased him. "All about privacy. So, we coupled. Big deal."

"It was a big deal to me." He gazed at me with his mesmerizing eyes, and I swallowed.

"For me, too. But you know what I mean. It's natural. There's no need to feel shame in front of the others."

"I suppose. I know Echo will feel like you do. I wonder what sea dragon culture is like for that." He sighed. "Yet another thing I don't know."

"But you'll be finding out soon." I wrinkled my

nose. "Hopefully not with firsthand experience."

Levi rolled on top of me and kissed me fiercely. "Never," he whispered, gazing at me without a trace of teasing or mirth. "I'm coming back with you after our visit, and this will be a regular occurrence."

I ran a hand through his soft hair and tried for a smile, although it came out sadder than I intended. "I'm looking forward to it."

When I finally coaxed Levi out of the bedroom, he avoided eye contact with the other two and shuffled to the kitchen to bury his head in the fridge. Echo gave me a knowing grin, and I returned it.

Pipa slammed the window shut, her face thunderous.

"It stinks out there," she said. "I don't know what it is."

I was certain her foul mood had less to do with the smell outside and more to do with the sounds she'd heard from the bedroom, but I peered out the window anyway.

"Garbage day," I explained. "That was a truck to take away refuse."

"Disgusting dry folk," she murmured to herself. "Wasteful and stinky, all at the same time."

My lips thinned, but I didn't bother defending humans. Pipa would be gone soon, and her opinion wouldn't matter to me anymore. A sharp pain lanced through my chest at the thought of Levi staying in the villages, but I pushed it down and the evidence off my face. Pipa didn't need to know how much I hurt. Maybe if I came with them to start, I could make sure the villages treated him well. The thought boosted my mood considerably.

We ate a patched together lunch of buttered bread and leftovers. We lounged around the apartment for a few hours, then ate another meal. By the end of it, Levi, Pipa, and I were all yawning. Echo shook her head at us.

"Back to sleep." She pointed at the bedroom and couch. "If I hear one more jaw crack, I'm going to scream."

My weariness from the healing made my sleep dreamless. In the morning, I slipped out of bed without waking Levi. Echo was out somewhere, but Pipa glowered in an annoyingly pretty way at the table over a glass of water. By the time I'd showered, Levi was up and speaking with Pipa.

"Have you decided on whether you're coming back to the villages with me?" she asked with a pointed glance at me. "I need to head back soon."

"You're sure Lune can't swim with us?" he said with a wave in my direction.

"Positive," she replied. "She'll be ripped apart."

Levi swallowed at the reminder of how vicious his people could be. I took pity on him.

"I'll come by land." I grabbed a banana and started peeling it. "Where are the villages, anyway?"

Pipa's mouth twisted, but she answered, "We're based on the west coast of Greenland. Nice and solitary."

"Oh." That was further away than I'd expected. "Okay, I'll take a leave of absence from the Aquarium, fly to Greenland," with what money, I didn't know, "and find my way there. You can meet me once you've settled in."

"I don't like it," Pipa said. I rolled my eyes at my banana. "Lune won't be welcome no matter how she arrives."

"But will she be ripped apart right away by land?" Levi crossed his arms.

"No," Pipa admitted, then she sighed and laid her palms down on the table. "Do as you will. When do we leave?"

Levi's eyes widened. "Oh, right. Yes. Soon, I guess."

Pipa rubbed her forehead, her face twisted in pain. I narrowed my eyes. What was wrong with her?

"Does your head hurt?" Levi said with concern. "I can go buy you some painkillers if you want."

Pipa leaned back in her chair with a sigh. "No, it's fine. Let's just go back soon. That will help."

Levi frowned but didn't push the matter. I took a thoughtful bite of my banana. Did the dry air not agree with Pipa, or maybe she had some sea dragon-specific pain medication back in Greenland she could take? I shrugged and swallowed my bite. Soon, Pipa and her maddening ways would be out of my life, and I could forget about her.

Along with Levi, once he'd decided he wanted to stay in Greenland. Would I be successful in convincing him to return? My siren abilities crossed my mind, but I banished the thought quickly. I wanted to be more like Hades, but vents, it was hard. I turned to the kitchen so no one could see my face. I wished Byssa were here to talk to.

Luckily, dry folk had invented the phone. I picked mine up from the counter and walked to the window while I dialed. It wasn't privacy, but I could pretend.

"Morning," Byssa said sleepily when she answered.

"How are you doing after your healing?"

"Mmm, good. Tired, but good." She yawned. "Hey, I was thinking about Marina. Maybe you should ask Branc Driftwood for help with her. He seems to have plenty of resources. Maybe he would have a way to capture her, something that we can't manage and he can."

I sighed. "It's not a bad idea, but I can't imagine being even deeper in debt than I already am. I'd merely be trading Marina the threat for Branc the tyrant. Well," I amended, "even more of a tyrant than usual."

"I can help pay," Byssa protested. "And I'm sure Hades and Levi would chip in. Nobody wants to see you under Driftwood's thumb."

My heart squeezed at Byssa's generous offer. I lowered my voice so Levi wouldn't hear. "I wish I could take you up on that. But Branc isn't interested in money anymore, not from me. Now he asks for favors, and I don't want to promise him any more than I already have."

"What will you do?" Byssa asked.

"Levi and Pipa are going to the sea dragon villages shortly." I swallowed past the lump in my throat. "And I'll join them on the land side. I want to make sure he's in a safe place."

"Ah." Byssa considered this for a moment. "Are you sure that's a good idea? The sea dragons don't sound very hospitable. And this is probably something that Levi needs to do on his own."

I lowered my voice even further, although the others were on the far side of the room. "I don't trust Pipa. She's up to something. I want to make sure Levi is safe over there."

Byssa sighed deeply. "Yeah, I get it. But think about your own safety too, okay?"

We hung up, and I clutched my phone to my chest, staring with unseeing eyes out the rain-lashed window. Talk of swimming had reminded me of Squirter. I missed him terribly, and I didn't know how to contact him without exposing myself to Marina and her ligan. I hoped he wasn't worrying about me. How long would he wait in these waters before he gave up on me and found new currents to follow?

I could have used a good swim right then. With great effort, I pulled my mind out of the ocean and back into my cramped apartment. Levi and Pipa were talking, and I concentrated on catching the drift of their conversation.

"We'll get there by swimming, of course," Pipa said with decision. "That's how I got here."

"But how long did it take you to swim from Greenland to the west coast?" Levi countered. "It's a long way, all the way through the Arctic, under the North Pole ice. I don't want to be away for months. I'm thinking weeks, at the most."

I didn't miss the thinning of Pipa's lips. She didn't believe Levi would be coming back, no more than I did. It didn't make me feel any better about my decision to help Levi travel to the villages.

"What if we fly to Newfoundland?" Levi said. "It'll be a little cheaper than flying to Greenland, but it will cut so much time off our journey."

"Fly?" Pipa's face was filled with horror. "I'm no bird. Don't make me get in one of those metal flying things. That's insane."

"They're perfectly safe." Levi pulled his phone out of his pocket and stood. "And Marina won't be able to follow us that way. I can look for flights in a minute. But first, I'll phone Sandy, see what she thinks of running the Lodge for a couple of weeks while I'm gone."

Levi took my place at the window, and I half-heartedly tidied the room to avoid conversation with Pipa. I needn't have bothered. Pipa laid her head on her folded arms and closed her eyes, apparently too pained to pretend she was fine when Levi wasn't looking.

I sighed in exasperation and marched to the fridge. From the freezer, I pulled out a few pieces of ice, threw them in a tea towel, and dropped it on the table in front of Pipa.

"Here," I said. "Press this on your head. It should help with the headache."

Pipa looked with bleary eyes at the tea towel, then at me.

"Thanks, but it won't help," she said. "Not with what I've got."

"Take it or leave it, I don't care." I strode the three steps back to the kitchen for somewhere to go. Pipa gingerly lifted the bundle of ice to her head when she thought I wasn't looking.

Echo arrived back, her cheeks rosy from being outside. She held up a bag of fast food with pride.

"Look," she said. "I bought food. All by myself. Well, Pipa gave me the money."

"Good timing," I said to her with a smile. "I'm hungry."

"It's all arranged," Levi announced to the room. He slipped his phone back in his pocket and walked over to the table, where he leaned his hands on the top bar of a chair. "Sandy and Austin are going to run the Lodge for a few weeks, consulting Seafoam and Kane if they need to. Luckily, traffic is slow this time of year. Hopefully they can handle it. I'll have to drive back to deliver the Gracehouse keys to the Lodge." Levi's face fell slightly at the thought of someone else running the Lodge.

I frowned at the extra delays. "Do you know anyone in Vancouver who could deliver the keys for you? It seems silly to take the trip just for that."

"My friend Bay will be going up shortly," Levi said after a moment's pause to think. "I guess I could drop them off with him."

"Perfect," I said firmly. "Then we won't have to delay our departure. Drop them off tonight."

Echo wandered into the kitchen and opened her bag to dish out our burgers.

"I still wish we'd dealt with Marina for good," Levi said. "It feels like we're only delaying the inevitable. When we get back, she'll probably still be there, waiting for us. The trap didn't work. How else can we handle her?"

I drummed my fingers on the counter. "I escaped her for a year when I left the Seamount by faking my own death. Can we do something similar with you?"

"If you've already done it, then she'll be expecting it," Pipa snapped. "And we can't set up another trap, either. We can't pull the same tricks twice on her."

"What about—not a death, exactly—but what about telling her that the three of us are leaving for good?" Levi's eyes widened with hope. "To the hidden sea dragon lair? She doesn't know where it is, and the ocean is a big place. Surely, she would then give up. She won't have any sea dragons to capture, and no revenge to take on you, Lune."

I couldn't help glancing at Pipa to see how she reacted to Levi's continued assertion that he was returning. Her face was stoic.

"It could work," she responded. "It's a likely scenario, after all. But how could we tell her without risking capture ourselves?"

Silence fell while we pondered Pipa's question. My gaze fell on Echo.

"What if Echo told her?" I said slowly.

Echo blinked at me. As my words filtered through her mind, her mouth dropped open. "Go back to Marina?" she sputtered.

"Marina thinks I kidnapped you, doesn't she?" I said, warming up to my idea. "You could say you escaped from me and swam directly to her. Then you can tell her the news that all three of us are leaving forever."

"That's dangerous for Echo," Levi said with misgiving.

"I don't see how," I said. "Why would Marina doubt her? As long as Echo sticks to her story, everything should be fine. She can eat some of the eelgrass stuff so that Marina can't siren the truth out of her. Then Echo can go back to the Seamount with a protective escort of siren and ligan, which would be helpful across the ocean. Predators lurk out there."

Echo blanched, then she hung her head. "I guess I could," she said in a small voice. "You're probably right that Marina would think you kidnapped me. It does make sense. And it'll be easy to find Marina. There are only two places that she'll be, either at the caves near a long wooden wreck or at the edge of a cove south of the closest island."

"I know that wreck," I said to Levi. "And the island is probably Bowen. But are you up for this, Echo?" I stared at Echo intently. She shuffled her feet, then her spine straightened, and she looked me directly in the eye.

"You've been so good to me. I want to pay you back for your kindness. And once Marina realizes there's no point in waiting here for you two, she'll take me back to the Seamount."

Levi and I exchanged a look. He shrugged.

"It's a good plan," he said. "Let's do it today."

CHAPTER 26

Echo's tanned skin grew paler the closer leaving time grew. To her credit, she didn't once mention any misgivings. I fervently hoped that Marina would buy her story of kidnapping. Despite my assurances that Echo would be fine, a knot of apprehension lodged in my stomach. I didn't want Echo to get on the wrong side of the siren and her pet ligan. All of us had felt enough of her wrath so far.

At least Echo didn't know where the sea dragon villages were. We'd been careful not to mention Greenland in front of her. The fewer people who knew, the easier secrecy could be maintained. Now, we had protection in case Marina decided to siren the truth out of our young seal shifter after the eelgrass paste wore off.

Levi insisted on purchasing plane tickets to Newfoundland for him and Pipa and to Nuuk in Greenland for me, despite Pipa's misgivings.

"It's not natural," she repeated, hands on her hips. She glanced at Echo on the other side of the room and lowered her voice. "We aren't supposed to fly."

"We're not supposed to barrel down the road at sixty clicks, either," Levi said absently, his eyes trained on his phone where the ticketing app blinked at him. "Cars aren't natural, yet you travel in my truck just fine. Trust me, you'll appreciate how quick the plane will get us there."

Pipa rubbed her head and didn't argue further. She

must have been looking forward to whatever painkillers the sea dragon village had waiting for her. I brought crackers and cheese to the table where Echo sat, looking queasy.

"Eat," I urged her. "You'll want your strength for the journey home, and to face whatever tantrums Marina will throw once you tell her the news."

Echo blanched and shook her head. "I'm not hungry."

I tried to push food on her a little more then gave up and crunched the crackers myself. When dusk fell, Levi stood.

"We should get moving," he said with a gentle look at Echo. "Let's get this show on the road. Remember what you're going to tell Marina?"

"You, Lune, and Pipa are flying to the sea dragon lair tonight," Echo said. "I don't know where it is, you wouldn't say the location out loud to me, although it sounded somewhere tropical from the little I overheard. You're planning to live there permanently."

"Good." Levi gave her a warm smile. "Thanks, Echo. Come on, let's get you to the beach."

"Can I come?" I said spontaneously. I wanted Echo to know how much I appreciated her risk, and seeing her to the beach felt like a gesture I needed to make. "I know you're heading to a friend's afterward to drop off those keys for Sandy. I can take the bus home."

"It's fine," he assured me. "He lives just beside the defunct lighthouse at Samson Point, so it's not that far away. I can drop you off at your apartment after we say goodbye to Echo."

We were quiet in the truck. Echo stared out the window at passing cars in the dusky light, rain drizzling down the glass in erratic rivulets. I glanced at Levi from time to time and was occasionally rewarded with a crinkly eyed smile that made herring jump in my stomach.

Levi pulled the truck into an empty spot along a sidewalk a block away from a beach access point. Echo drew in a deep, shuddering breath.

"You'll do great," I said firmly. "Soon you'll be back with your family at the Seamount. Marina will be a distant memory. And you'll have some stories to tell of your time on dry land."

That drew a wobbly smile from Echo's lips. I handed her a small piece of the eelgrass paste, one of the few I had left. She took it and nodded at us both.

"May the currents flow with you and your nights forever sparkle with phosphorescence," she said in a farewell I recognized as one seal shifters often said.

"May storms be gentle and schools of fish follow you always," I replied in a traditional siren greeting, my throat thick.

Echo opened the door, took another deep breath, then hopped out and slammed it shut. She strode toward the beach access path, barefoot and wearing only a long tee shirt in the cold rainy dusk. Levi and I watched her walk until she disappeared around the corner of a house. I released my breath in a long sigh.

"That's it," I said. "Once Echo tells Marina our story, we're finally free."

Levi grabbed my hand, and I tore my eyes away

from the empty path where Echo had disappeared to meet his intense gaze. He hadn't put in his contacts yet today, since he'd only been at home with people who knew about him. I lost myself in those swirling depths.

"We're free," he repeated. "You've been worried about Marina for over a year and hiding with me for the past week. This means we can swim freely, go where we want, talk to anyone we choose. The world has opened for us again."

I swallowed past my thickening throat. I wanted to swim freely with Levi, go places with him, talk to him, but that wasn't going to happen anymore. We were leaving tomorrow for Greenland, and I didn't expect him to return with me. If I couldn't convince him to come home after, how would I heal the raw wounds in my heart?

"We're free," I whispered. I rested my head on his shoulder so I didn't expose the tears threatening to fall from my eyes. He didn't need my emotions to mar the excitement of our upcoming journey.

At my apartment building, Levi pulled over to the curb, and I opened the door.

"I might be back late," he said with an apologetic look. "My friend is a big talker, and it's hard to get away sometimes."

"It's fine. Have fun. I'll leave the door unlocked for you."

I leaned in to give him a spontaneous kiss, which he returned eagerly. Then, I pulled away and walked backward with a wave. I couldn't extend our touch for any longer. It was too painful.

My heart sank when I opened the door of my apartment and realized that only Pipa remained. She was the last person I wanted to spend my evening with. I briefly considered going to Byssa's, but she worked late tonight.

Pipa hardly looked up from her book when I entered, and I didn't bother greeting her. We didn't have anything to say to each other, not really. I knew everything I needed to about her, and she only wanted Levi, not me.

A fervent prayer to Ramu arose in my mind that, if Levi stayed in Greenland and formed a relationship with someone else in the future, it wouldn't be with Pipa. I wanted to pray that he would return home with me, but that felt like too much to ask. I would have to do the heavy lifting on that end, convincing him to return home.

I grabbed some seaweed crackers from the kitchen and barricaded myself in my bedroom for the evening. Best possible scenario, Levi came home shortly, and I could fall asleep in his arms. The more likely situation would be me staring at the ceiling for a few hours, my mind whirling with everything I couldn't change.

I flopped onto my bed and tried not to cry. I sniffed hard and stared fiercely at a stain on the ceiling drywall. It was time to focus on the good things. After tonight, I could swim with Squirter again. A smile cracked my frozen face at the thought of my octopus friend. I missed him.

I pulled a blanket over my legs. Swimming with Squirter and Levi would have been better, but Squirter and I had fun before Levi. We would have fun again. I would survive without the sea dragon in my life, if I wasn't successful at getting him home.

Not that I would fail. I could be very persuasive when needed, and that was without compulsion. Levi would be back shortly, as long as I stayed with him to remind him of what he would miss if he didn't return.

But if he didn't… maybe Hades had some friends he could introduce me to again. The last time I'd met them, I hadn't been in the mood to be building a life. Now that things were different, I could view them with fresh eyes and act far more sociable than I had before. And Byssa would revel in the opportunity to play matchmaker.

My entire body clenched when I thought of moving on from Levi, and I curled it protectively. I couldn't think like that. Levi would come back with me, and that was that. I could convince him. Going to visit the sea dragons was essential to him, I knew, but his life here was important, too. If he lost sight of that, I would remind him.

Odd dreams of dry deserts and glowing eyes troubled my sleep. I awoke with a start sometime in the night, and my phone's display read five o'clock.

Beside me, my bed was empty.

Where was Levi? He'd said his friend was a talker, but this was excessive. He had a flight later today. And didn't he care about seeing me?

I dialed his number, ready to tell him what I thought of his late arrival. The phone rang until voicemail picked up. Undeterred, I rang again, with the same result.

My stomach churned. I called again, and again, hoping he had passed out on his friend's couch and the ringing would wake him up. He didn't answer.

I clenched the phone in my hands and stared unseeing at the wall. Something was wrong. Levi would have texted me if he hadn't come back that night. He wouldn't be ignoring my calls.

"Marina," I breathed. The moment I said her name aloud, certainty crystalized in my mind. Marina must have forced the truth out of Echo. The shifter knew exactly where Levi had been planning to go that evening, since he'd described it precisely to me while Echo was present. Had she told Marina, on purpose or under duress? Sirening wasn't possible, but pain was a powerful motivator.

I tried not to think about sweet Echo under Marina's tyrannical thumb, but no other explanations came to mind. I threw on my clothes and burst out of my bedroom.

"Pipa," I shouted. "Pipa, wake up."

"What's going on?" she said in a groggy voice. "Why the shouting?"

"Levi didn't come home, and he's not answering his phone," I said in a rush. "Something happened to him."

"How can you be sure?" Pipa said, so reasonably that I wanted to scream. "He's probably sleeping at his friend's house."

She put just enough emphasis on the word "friend" to insinuate that Levi wasn't wholly mine. I gritted my teeth.

"I'm sure," I said. "I'm going there now to check. You can come or stay as you like."

That got her off the couch in a hurry. Pipa didn't want to relinquish her claim on Levi, and having me dash off to rescue him didn't sit well with her.

By the time we raced out the door, a dribble of early-morning commuters were driving on the main streets. I ran for a bus trundling along the road, with Pipa chasing after me. Sleepy people heading for work gazed blearily at us until we found our seats.

We didn't speak during the ride, and it was with relief that I pressed the button to signal our stop. Once off the bus, I strode with quick steps toward the lighthouse Levi had mentioned. I didn't care if Pipa was following me, but her footsteps tapped along behind with a regular rhythm.

I broke into a run when Levi's truck with its Lodge insignia glinted from under a streetlight. I dived to the driver's side.

The door was half-open. Levi's phone lay on the seat, and a torn piece of his red shirt lay on the ground. With shaking fingers, I picked a tuft of brown hair off the edge of the door.

"It's the color of seal shifter hair," I said in a hoarse voice. "Levi struggled and lost."

CHAPTER 27

Pipa hissed some expletive that I didn't recognize then kicked the truck's tire. I watched her tantrum through a fog of numb disbelief. We'd tried so hard. How could Marina have won? How could Levi be gone?

He was supposed to be happily meeting his people, with me at his side, not dragged to the Seamount to perform healings at the whim of Marina and the Protectorate until he died of over-healing. My breath could hardly reach my lungs through the constriction in my chest.

"I need him." Pipa gasped and dropped to her knees on the sidewalk. She gripped her head like it was about to explode. "He has to come back to the villages with me."

"Why?" I asked dully. I didn't really care—Pipa's concerns were nothing to me, not in the face of Levi's kidnapping—but the words crawled out of my mouth despite my disinterest. "What do you want with him so badly? Are prospects so limited at home? I know he's a catch, but this is extreme."

"I'm not trying to date him." Pipa glared at me through eyes watering from pain. "He's a healer. My people need a healer every generation, and none have been born in the past forty years. Well, except for Levi. They've chosen me to be the sacrifice to our god Hermo this year, in the hope that Hermo will grant us a healer. If I can bring Levi back, they won't have to sacrifice me at the vents."

I stared in horror at the writhing woman at my feet. Every interaction with Pipa was suddenly illuminated from another angle. Her dislike of me wasn't as a romantic rival, it was rooted in fear that I would keep him on this coast. Her advances to Levi weren't a ploy to show her attractiveness, but an illustration of what heritage he could discover in Greenland to convince him to return with her.

"Why didn't you just say so?" I demanded. "Levi would have bent over backwards to avoid your death. Vents, I would have packed his bag for him."

"Don't you see? Once they have their healer, they won't let him go." Pipa's face was agonized, and she gasped with pain. "They need him. Look what I'm going through. We call it the pull. It's put on every baby born in the villages, and it acts as a tether to our people. We're allowed to travel the world, but only for a while. Before long, the pull starts, and if you don't obey, the mental pain only grows worse. Levi escaped it because he wasn't born in Greenland. But as soon as he returns and they find out he's a healer, they will put it on him immediately. He'll never come back."

I stared at Pipa, my mind a mess of emotions. Fury and hatred swelled in my chest, but horror and pity tempered them. I could imagine Pipa's thought process leading to this moment. A stranger would be forced to spend his life in the villages. What of it? It was Pipa's home, after all. And the strange sea dragon would be among his people. His life would be fine, and then Pipa would live. What else was there to think about?

A tiny thread of relief snaked through my mind. Pipa didn't want to steal Levi's affections away from me. She only wanted him to save her from being sacrificed, and I couldn't find it in my heart to blame her much for that. Sure, I was furious that she'd lied, but I understood why.

"Urgh," I grunted, unable to articulate my frustration. "What the vents am I supposed to do with you now?"

Whatever agony gripped Pipa seemed to increase, because she released a pitiful, gasping cry and curled into a ball on the beach.

"I can't fight against it for much longer," she panted. Her eyes were screwed tight, and her long, dark hair draped over her face. When the latest bout passed, she squinted up at me.

"It comes and goes," she explained. "Well, it never fully goes—I feel the pull constantly—but some times are more bearable than others. I've been away for too long, though. The elders are desperate to move forward with the sacrifice to gain our new healer. They must have increased the pull. I need to find Levi, but I don't know if I can force myself to travel southwards. I can't fight it any longer."

I stared at Pipa. Every minute that ticked by was another minute that Marina could force Levi to heal Shoal and others at the Seamount. Levi would eventually die. I had to rescue him.

But if I left Pipa, the pull would take her back to Greenland. There, she would die.

It was an impossible decision. The only way both sea

dragons had a chance at living was if I dragged Pipa along with me to rescue Levi. Assuming I was successful, then Levi could go with Pipa to Greenland.

He would never come home, but both he and Pipa would live.

I groaned my frustration to the sky. I wanted to save Levi and ignore Pipa to her lost cause, even though her predicament tugged at my conscience. But what would Levi want?

I held his life in my hands, and that wasn't right. He had to make the decision for himself. I needed to trust that he would do what was right for him.

Even if it meant I might lose him forever.

"Get in the water," I snarled. "You're coming with me."

"But Levi's gone." Pipa hung her head like a wrung-out dishrag. "Marina has him."

"Yes, and we have to get him back." I crossed my arms, unwilling to give up like Pipa. Sure, Marina was a powerful siren with a gigantic sea monster at her beck and call, but Levi was too important to me to leave at the mercy of her whims. I might lose him to his sea dragon heritage, but I was venting sure not letting him suffer at Marina's hands.

Pipa pushed herself off the ground and slowly rose on shaking legs. We faced each other. She clutched her head, but her expression held a sliver of hope. "Do you think we can get him back?"

"I think we need to try." I pushed aside Levi's earlier words, and I was glad I'd made him no promises. He faced imprisonment and death at the Seamount, and he needed to be saved from Marina. I would ignore his wishes for his own good.

Guilt wriggled in my stomach. If I hadn't pushed Echo into acting as our informant, Marina wouldn't have known where to capture Levi. Vents, if I hadn't insisted on Levi dropping the keys off at his friend's house, he would be safe. My fingerprints were all over this kidnapping, even if Marina had been the one to achieve it.

If I'd let the others choose their own paths, would we be in this predicament? I bit my tongue hard. Was my meddling the cause of Levi's capture? But I couldn't leave him down there.

"Whatever we do," I said, "we need to do it quickly. I have no idea what Marina is doing to him. Presumably, if the seal shifter was able to capture him, they have some level of control. And once they wear down his strength, he won't be able to resist compulsion. He was pretty tired anyway, so it won't take much. Marina will force Levi to heal Shoal then take him to the Seamount, and there won't be anything he can do about it."

"He'll probably kill himself when he tries to heal Shoal," Pipa said darkly. "You won't have to worry about imprisonment. Time is of the essence. But I can't promise I'll be able to swim in that direction."

"We'll figure it out. Let me call someone first." I held my finger in the air for Pipa to wait. I pulled my phone out of my pocket and dialed Branc's number.

"This had better be important." Branc's words were thick with sleep once he answered after the third ring, and the growl in his voice was unmistakable.

I grimaced. Hopefully I wouldn't regret this phone call. "It is. Marina Highcave took one of my friends captive, and I'm worried for his life." I didn't mention it was Levi, partly because I didn't want to explain why she'd taken him, but also because I didn't trust that Branc would put aside his dislike of Levi to help him. "I need to know where she is underwater. Have you heard anything?"

I waited for the silence to coalesce into something physical before I opened my mouth to ask again, but Branc beat me to it.

"No," he said. "I haven't."

I frowned in disbelief and growing anger. The lie in Branc's words was clear, even over the phone.

"You know," I accused him. "You know exactly where she is. Why aren't you telling me?"

"Nobody has told me where Marina is," he said more strongly. "I have nothing to say."

"Fine." I huffed a breath through my nose. "I'll find her without your help."

Protestations drifted out of the speaker as I pulled it from my ear. I jammed my finger on the hang-up button with more force than necessary. Pipa looked at me in question, and I shook my head.

"It was worth a try," I said. "Onto plan B."

"Which is?"

"Swim around until we find Levi. Echo gave me two locations to try."

Pipa squinted at me. I grabbed her elbow and marched us to the beach. My hand found two packages that I'd stuffed in my pocket before we'd left, and I drew them out. The first package contained the eelgrass substance that prevented compulsion, and I bit off a large piece and swallowed it down. I didn't want to leave my freedom to chance. If we tried to take Levi from Marina, she would do everything in her power to stop us, including sirening me with all her strength.

The other package held regular Grace, and I allowed myself a healthy dose. I wanted to be ready for anything. Pipa watched my throes of ecstasy with amused puzzlement even as she pressed white-knuckled fingers to her forehead.

"That looks like good stuff," she said. "Got any to spare?"

"I doubt it works on sea dragons," I said. "I've never seen Levi take any, and I'm sure he's tried, living with pale folk all his life. And no, I don't have any to spare. I pay through the gills for it."

Pipa grimaced and rubbed her temple. She must have wanted some relief from the pain, but I doubted Grace would give it to her. I wasn't willing to give her any on the insanely slim hope it would help. Besides, it would only feel good for a minute, then she'd likely be back to her usual self.

No one was on the beach at this early hour—the sun was paling the sky to the east—so I didn't bother hiding my entry. I stripped off my outer clothes and tucked them under a driftwood log.

Pipa stripped entirely naked but waited on the shore with eyes watering from her pain. I took her elbow again.

"I'll drag you into the water," I said. "Hey, can I watch you transform? Levi was shy the last time we swam, and we haven't had a chance to get in the water together since."

Pipa shrugged tightly. "If you like. I don't care."

We splashed into the shallows. I ignored Pipa's cries of distress. When we were deep enough, she immersed herself, and I quickly followed. When she disappeared into the choppy waves under a shark-gray sky, I held my breath and dunked my head under. I would breathe water soon, but I didn't want to miss Pipa's transformation while I was hacking up a lung.

Her human body writhed along the seafloor. I could hardly see anything in the darkness and the silt that churned up with wave action, but my skin sense was crystal clear after the Grace I'd ingested.

Pipa twitched and wriggled. Fascinated, I sensed her body lengthen, her legs fuse, her head enlarge, and her skin burst out in scales that I knew rather than felt were black and gold.

The entire transformation took less than ten seconds. When it was complete, Pipa swam over to me with jerky motions and pushed her face close to mine.

I'm okay for the moment. Now, where do we go?

Her dialect was incredibly old-fashioned. Luckily, communication was my forte as a siren.

Echo mentioned two places where they stayed. We'll check those out first.

The first site wasn't far from the lighthouse. I exchanged air for water in my lungs then struck out in a southwesterly direction. Pipa followed me, her body unfurling with sinuous grace that my traitorous heart still wondered if Levi admired. I found it attractive, and I wasn't even a sea dragon.

I shook my head. None of that mattered while Levi was a prisoner of Marina. I could deal with my jealousy when he was safely in my arms again.

The water was blissfully cool and welcoming after too many fraught days of dry land. Before I could second-guess myself, I sent out a call for Squirter. I had to know if he was all right. It had been too long, and I was worried about him. He was probably worried about me, too.

Pipa's smooth motions grew jerky and ragged behind me. She coiled around herself until she was a ball of scales. Her face contorted in pain.

I waited for her attack to subside. When it didn't after a few seconds, I got behind her and pushed against scales that were starting to show gray and gold in the growing brightness of dawn. It was hard work, and I despaired for our loss of speed. Was bringing Pipa along worth giving Levi a choice?

I hoped so.

Pipa finally unfurled and limped along beside me again, although her dragon face contorted in pain constantly. I felt bad for her pain, but I felt worse for whatever Levi was going through. We needed to keep moving. I was nervous that Pipa was more of a liability than a help as she was. Hopefully, the threat of her teeth and size would help us when we met resistance.

A welcome figure jetted into the reaches of my skin sense.

Squirter! I opened my arms for the little cephalopod and nearly got bowled over from the force of his greeting. His long arms wrapped around my torso, then he crawled onto my back and stuck there.

You're enormous, I said in amazement. He'd grown in the day or two since I'd seen him last. His body was larger than my head, and his arms longer than my legs. There was no way he would fit in his backpack anymore. The thought gave me mixed feelings. I was happy for him, growing up big and strong, but sad that our days of playing in the tub were at an end.

I could ruminate later. For now, we had a sea dragon to save.

New friend captured, I told Squirter. "New friend" was how the octopus referred to Levi. *By bad siren and ligan. We're helping.*

Squirter squeezed my shoulders. When I started forward again, he lifted from my back and hovered in a different direction.

This way, he said.

I frowned at him. *You know where bad siren is?*

He wiggled the tip of an arm at me and jetted away. I glanced at Pipa, who gazed at me with confusion.

You trust this octopus?

Absolutely. I undulated after Squirter to show my solidarity, annoyed by Pipa's skepticism. Squirter had never misled me before. Just because he wasn't a type of human didn't mean he didn't know things. Pipa had the typical disdain shown by those who couldn't communicate like pale folk. They didn't understand the intricate lives of other creatures unlike themselves.

We swam midwater for a while, the seafloor far below us only a faint impression in my skin sense. Light from the brightening sky illuminated our featureless path, sprinkled only with invisible phytoplankton and the occasional haggard-looking jellyfish. The further we got, the more frequently Pipa curled into a scaly ball. Once, she even started to swim back the way we'd come. I panicked and pinched her frond to snap her out of it. She desisted after a yelp and a glare at me.

She couldn't swim south on her own after that. Squirter was strong enough to help, and together we pushed her along toward Levi.

I wished I'd called Byssa and Hades to come help before we'd leaped into the water. I hadn't been thinking straight while Levi was in danger. Now, I was on my own, caring for an overgrown lizard while trying to rescue Levi.

Squirter's arm brushed mine as we pushed Pipa, and I amended my annoyed thoughts. Squirter was with me, and he was growing stronger and braver by the day. He was transforming from a friendly companion into a capable ally.

A school of fish lazily swam at the periphery of my skin sense. I ignored them and focused on pushing Pipa. A larger body joined the fish, but it wasn't until Squirter prodded me in the back that I paid attention.

The scarred seal shifter barreled toward us, his intent clear.

I quickly scanned the area for the presence of a giant sea serpent, but the seal was alone. I was pleased that Echo wasn't attacking us, but what had Marina done to her instead?

Seal incoming, I warned Pipa and Squirter. I moved to put myself between the seal and the curled-up sea dragon.

Squirter floated at my side. I readied a hum to compel the shifter, but the seal zigzagged toward me. The jerky movement distracted me, then he was on us.

The seal's mouth opened wide. I dodged and released a hum of distress and disorientation. A convulsion in my chest interrupted it. Vents, was I still not over my dust-lung?

The seal twisted and opened his mouth again. Squirter wasn't quick enough to avoid the seal's teeth. With a sickening chomp, the seal's jaw latched onto Squirter's arm.

CHAPTER 28

Squirter's entire body spasmed. A rainbow of colors rippled over his skin. I screamed in anger and pushed the seal as hard as I could, accompanied by a blast of vibration. My sound stunned the seal, and he released the poor octopus from his jaws.

Squirter drifted away, motionless in shock. Seeing him like that hurt like a knife to my heart.

Go! I shouted and pushed his mantle gently.

The combination of my touch and voice spurred my friend into action. With a slow jet from his funnel, Squirter propelled himself behind the curled-up Pipa. He trailed a stream of blood as he went. The heat of anger filled my head until my ears rang with it.

I readied a hum, but the shifter was too quick. A scream ripped through me as the seal's teeth sank into my leg. Stabbing pain lanced up my calf. I kicked instinctively. The seal held on, and the pain intensified.

Dimly, I registered movement behind me. Had the ligan come? The seal released me with a yelp. He swam away, a wound in his side leaking black blood behind him.

I spun and looked at Pipa, who had finally unfurled and now floated beside me, blood drifting from her mouth.

That was you? I asked.

You're welcome, she replied.

I rolled my eyes. *I'll consider it payment for pushing your scaly hide halfway across the ocean.*

Pipa looked where the seal shifter had disappeared. *Should we chase him?*

I don't know where he went. I was too busy looking for my friend to care about the seal shifter. *Squirter, where are you?*

A very sad little octopus jetted slowly into view from behind Pipa's back. He crawled onto my back and draped himself over my shoulders like a squishy scarf.

I'm glad you're okay, I said with a careful tickle of an uninjured arm. His wounded arm hung limply at my side. The bleeding had mostly stopped, which relieved me.

With Squirter accounted for—and not injured badly enough to warrant immediate safety measures—I turned my thoughts to the escaped seal shifter and looked at Pipa.

Did you see where the seal went? I asked her.

No, but I can follow him. At my raised eyebrow, she huffed. *I have a nose. Clearly a more sensitive one than yours. The seal was leaking blood all over the place. He'll be easy to track.*

Point me the right way, I said.

It's eastward, Pipa said. *I can manage that direction.*

Without another comment, she surged forward and took the lead. I was tempted to grab hold of her tail as it whipped past, but we weren't on good enough terms for her to appreciate it. Besides, I'd be pushing her soon enough, and I wanted to make some distance before that inevitable time.

Pipa led us unerringly forward until the unmistakable form of the seal shifter appeared in my skin sense. He wasn't hurrying. Did he think he'd lost us, or was he too injured from Pipa's bite to move any faster?

He couldn't sense us, not in the same way I could sense him, so I remained silent and swam beside Pipa in the dawn light that sent shafts of sunbeams through the water in shimmering columns. The seafloor below us was covered with fronds of seaweed clinging to jagged rocks. Crabs scuttled between the cover of boulders, and a lazy school of perch floated underneath us.

We were closer to the seal now, and at the very edge of my skin sense loomed a kelp forest swaying in the current. I sped up to join the seal shifter so my vibrations could reach him, but my movement alerted him to our presence. He darted toward the forest and disappeared between stipes and blades.

I can't track him in there, Pipa said with a shake of her large head. Her fronds followed along with her motion. *The kelp messes up the blood trail.*

What if we circle around the forest, one a side? I pointed to the right. *You go northeast, I'll go around the other side. Try to catch him but not kill him, if you can manage it. I'll compel him once he's in our grasp.*

Pipa looked skeptical about my plan. *One quick bite and he'd be done with,* she argued.

I wrinkled my nose. Byssa would have my skin if I condoned murder. Besides, the thought didn't sit well with me, either. *I'd rather not. Is capturing him too difficult a task for you? I understand if grabbing hold without excessive force is too delicate a maneuver.*

Pipa snorted and didn't bother to reply. She turned and swam off. I swam in the opposite direction. With luck, we would intercept the seal as he emerged from the shelter of the forest.

Squirter clung to me as I swam and scanned the forest to my right. Glints of silver fish caught my eye from time to time, but no dark shadows of a sleek seal met my searching gaze.

It was a decently large forest, and I'd only reached halfway along its length when I heard a muffled, haunting call. Had Pipa found the seal shifter, or had her headache returned with a vengeance? I dithered for a moment then plunged into the kelp forest toward the call.

I swam below the kelp blades and wove between skinny stipes that anchored the blades to the rocky seafloor. When I emerged from the forest, my skin sense immediately grasped the scene.

Pipa held a squirming seal in her wide mouth. She bit firmly but only punctured skin when the shifter wriggled too hard. I raced forward and cleared my throat in readiness.

Stop moving, I commanded.

The seal suddenly hung limp from Pipa's jaws. The sea dragon gave an audible sigh of relief. I swam closer and laid my hands on the seal's sleek hide.

Swim back to the Seamount, I hummed. *Avoid Marina.*

I propelled myself away from the seal and nodded at Pipa. She frowned, but carefully opened her mouth. The seal slid out, rolled over once, then took off westward.

You're sure he's not going to Marina? Pipa said, skepticism dripping from her voice.

I'm sure. You clearly haven't met many sirens. I tickled an arm floating past my face. *Where is new friend, Squirter?*

His arm pointed forward, and I set off. Pipa followed but soon curled up in a ball. I grimaced and pushed her from behind. She groaned quietly, her eyes shut tight.

Squirter kept us on track by pointing in the right direction from his position on my back. Before long, we approached a rocky cliff face. He indicated we should slow down. I touched Pipa's shoulder, and she held steady while I reached out with my skin sense.

At the base of the cliff, in the clear dimness below the phytoplankton layer, was a wide cave mouth. A long body at the entrance made my heart leap, then it pounded with relief. Levi was at the cave's mouth, not the ligan. I bit my tongue to stop a glad cry that threatened to escape.

My relief was short-lived. Levi sported cuts all over his body. I swallowed and carefully swam closer until my vision took over. Bruising showed up even through his silvery-blue scales. He looked rough, and his eyes were closed. A kelp rope tethered him to the rocks at numerous points along his serpentine body.

The water was warmer in this area, with remnants of cloudy ink swirling in the currents. I wondered if Marina had learned the hard way how hot Levi's breath could be.

My hands shook with fury. I knew Marina had planned to capture Levi and restrain him for the rest of his life, but why torture him?

He probably refused to heal Shoal, Pipa murmured in my

270

ear, *so she punished him*. Her voice held repressed anger.

I shook my head as the reason dawned on me. *Not punishment. She's trying to weaken him so she can compel him to heal Shoal. He's susceptible to compulsion when he's weak.*

Squirter hugged my neck tighter. *New friend hurt*, he said.

I peeked further into the cave. It was a risk to show myself to Marina, but I needed to know what was happening. Besides, I couldn't be compelled, and neither could Pipa, so we could handle Marina. The ligan wasn't in sight, which emboldened me.

My fists clenched when Echo appeared in my vision. She was festooned with her own cuts and also restrained by kelp ropes to the rocks. A little further, and Marina came into view. Her back was to me, her white hair drifting around her head. Grim satisfaction gripped me at the patches of reddened skin where Levi's breath must have caught her.

She floated before a pale, emaciated man whose eyes were half-closed. Shoal looked so different from when I'd confronted him in his cave last year. Then, he'd been full of life and anger. Now, his expression was blank in his half-starved face.

Marina put a piece of sea cucumber in her mouth and chewed then pressed her lips to Shoal's. When she had transferred the mashed food into his mouth, she held his nose and jaw closed until he swallowed.

She raised another piece to her mouth but paused. She whirled around and stared right at me.

You, she snarled. *How did you find me? Have you come so I can get my vengeance?*

Don't be ridiculous. I floated down so we could speak more easily. *I've come for the sea dragon. Let him go. He isn't yours to restrain and use as your personal healer.*

Marina swam over to Levi, who had raised his head with fear and hope dancing in his swirling eyes.

Never, she hissed. *He stays until he's healed Shoal. Then, he's coming back to the Seamount. Think of all the good he can do there. If we'd had a sea dragon present last year, Shoal would never have suffered like he did. And think of what the dragon can do for the movement. How can anyone not join us if we have him on our side? Our numbers for the next push will swell, and we'll have certain victory for what is coming.*

What was coming? I shivered at Marina's ominous words, then I pushed them aside. The rogue faction and their unknown plans could wait. Right now, I had to focus on freeing Levi.

He's a person, too, I said. *What gives you the right to decide his fate and lock him up for the rest of his life?*

It's hard, I understand. But so much good will come out of this that his imprisonment will be a worthwhile sacrifice. Besides, as soon as he heals of his own free will, he'll be treated well. I only hurt him because he refused to heal on his own.

Let him go, I shouted, but Marina tightened her lips and swam over to Levi. She raised her bone knife. Before I could protest, her hand darted out.

The bone knife slashed against Levi's flank. He roared in pain, a rumbling sound that ended in a haunting yelp that tore apart my insides. Marina slashed down again. Blood erupted in clouds from Levi's side. He writhed and roared, but his bonds held fast.

I darted forward instinctively to help. Marina held

her bone knife to Levi's neck and stared at me until I halted in place, my chest heaving.

That's better, she said. *Stay where you are unless you want the sea dragon even more wounded than he already is.*

Let me take his place, I pleaded without hope. Marina wanted a healer, and I wasn't it, but I had to try something.

Levi's eyes had been squeezed shut in pain, but they popped open at my offer.

No, he shouted in his garbled speech. *No!*

I don't care about justice now, said Marina with an incredulous shake of her head. *Not when I have the answer to my prayers in my grasp. Why would I care about you when this sea dragon is about to heal Shoal?*

A surge of current alerted me to Pipa's presence. She shot forward, undulating with graceful curves toward Levi and Marina. Marina jerked her knife against Levi's throat in startlement, and he roared as the blade dug into his skin.

I had no idea what Pipa was hoping to accomplish with her rush, but I didn't have a chance to find out. Halfway to the others, her black body froze, spasmed, then coiled into a ball.

My heart rose into my throat. I surged forward and yanked at her protruding tail to haul the agonized sea dragon out of reach.

I glanced toward Echo in hopeless appeal, but the terrified seal was still bound tightly to the rocks.

Marina bristled. *Don't expect help from that traitor. She's coming back to the Seamount with me. Her family will suffer for her treachery.*

I pulled Pipa further out of the cave mouth, too distracted by my task to answer Marina.

Why don't you take the other sea dragon? Marina yelled. Her eyes grew wider with her mania. *Come on, try to take me out. I'd love to see that. Even the eelgrass root in your veins can't compete with my sirening strength if I touch you. Come on, try to get me. It'll be fun.*

Marina laughed then, a high-pitched cackle that frightened me more than her threats. The strain of the past year—secretly caring for her lover, plus the highs and lows of discovering sea dragons in the past few weeks—must have been pushing her into the abyss. And if I couldn't count on Marina acting rationally, how could I predict her next move?

One thing was sure. Levi was injured, Echo was trapped, and Pipa was useless. Squirter and I were on our own.

CHAPTER 29

I swam behind Pipa and pushed her out of the cave and away from the laughing Marina. I only stopped when we were out of range of my skin sense.

Squirter rejoined us, flushing yellow with shame that he hadn't joined us in the cave.

It's okay, I told him with a tickle on his mantle. *Marina can compel you. It was dangerous.*

Squirter stroked my shoulder in apology. Pipa unfurled from her tense position and gazed at me with sorrowful eyes.

I tried, she said. *I'm sorry I was too weak.*

It's not like you can help it, I said. I wanted to lash out at Pipa—Levi was still trapped, and his suffering was making me frantic—but I knew a little something about mind control. Pipa couldn't fight the pull. Indeed, she was still wincing continually, although she had mostly straightened her body. She started to swim northwards, and I tugged her frond again.

Just let me go, Pipa said. Her eyes closed as another shudder wracked her body. *Save Levi. I'll meet my fate.*

Pipa didn't know how sorely she was tempting me.

Stop talking like that, I snarled. *We just need a new plan. What if—*

The half-formed notion in my mind fluttered away when something hit the edge of my skin sense. My stomach dropped.

The ligan, I choked out. *It's coming.*

Pipa spasmed, but I wasn't sure if that was from my

terrible news or from the pain that wracked her body. Squirter jetted to my side and latched onto my back, flattening his body so we were streamlined.

I froze with no idea what to do. The nearest cave held Marina, who could still compel me if we touched, and no kelp forests were near enough to lose ourselves in. There was nothing except open ocean, and the ligan would track us down easily there.

But we had to do something. I darted downward, trusting Pipa to follow me. We swam to the base of the rocky cliff, deep in the gloom of the depths. I hunted for a crack, any opening where we could take refuge. Squirter understood my intention and left my back to search frantically beside me. He crawled over the rocks with his seven uninjured arms exploring every crevasse.

But we were too slow. With a whoosh of displaced water, the ligan came into view. Its ugly head nosed toward us, and its single pitiless eye fixed on our fleeing bodies. The other eye was a nasty gash only partially healed from Squirter's earlier attack.

Marina sat astride the ligan's neck. She leaned forward.

I didn't say you could leave, she screamed wildly. *You're supposed to attack me, Lune. Then I'll have the pleasure of eradicating your half-blood menace from the ocean as well as keep the sea dragon for healing Shoal. Come on, show me what you've got!*

I backed away involuntarily, and Pipa tensed. Squirter hummed behind me, and a powerful sucker latched onto my ankle.

Ow, I said. Squirter's grip was stronger than usual.

When I glanced at him, Squirter frantically pointed at a dark crack in the rocks a few kicks away. Would it be big enough for all of us?

There was only one way to find out. I surged toward the crack. The ligan's head crashed into the rock a split second after I left, and Marina's scream of anger trailed after.

My heart pounded, and my memory conjured up phantom pain from the last ligan bites I'd sustained. I kicked forward, desperate to reach the crack before imaginary bites turned into real ones.

Pipa growled beside me. The sound made my skin crawl. I glanced sideways while continuing to flee. Her coiled body sprang open and shot toward the ligan. Before it could react, she chomped down on the flank below its neck, near Marina's foot.

Marina screamed, and the ligan twisted in pain. Pipa swiftly retreated, but her efforts had clearly cost her. Her body spasmed once again. She curled up next to me in a protective ball.

A sleek brown body swam toward us. My heart leaped at the familiar sight.

Echo, no! I shouted, terrified for the young shifter who must have wriggled free of her bonds. I pushed Pipa in front of me, Squirter at my side, trying to get us all to the crack before the ligan recovered from its wounds. Marina shouted and hummed at the monster. Echo ignored us all and swam straight for the ligan's throat. With an open mouth, she tore a piece of skin off the ligan's neck.

The monster roared, but it must have been used to

injury by now, because it didn't take any time to recover from Echo's attack. It twisted its head in the seal shifter's direction. Marina clutched its neck spikes to avoid being thrown off. Echo surged forward, but she was too late.

The ligan opened its mouth and prepared to bite down. I released a screaming vibration of rage and distraction. It wasn't enough to stop the sea serpent's motion, but it was enough to lessen the blow. The ligan's fangs slowly sank into Echo's tail instead of plunging into the meat of her back.

With a jerk, the ligan pulled. Echo's skin resisted for a moment then ripped. She let out a cry of distress, but then she was free to limp away, bleeding as she went.

The ligan twisted to give chase.

Ignore the seal, Marina shouted at it. *Get the others.*

Dutifully, the monster turned back to us. I pushed the incapacitated Pipa harder. Squirter quivered by my side but used his own force to propel the large ball of sea dragon forward with me.

A rush of current signaled the ligan's approach. The crack was near. I pushed Pipa harder than I'd ever pushed anything before. Squirter clicked in distress.

Finally, we were above the crack. A wolf eel slithered away in fright as I shoved Pipa inside and dived to the right to avoid the ligan's mouth behind me. It whooshed past. I clawed my way into the crack after Squirter, heedless of the gashes the rocks inflicted on my legs and arms.

I shoved Pipa's inert body deeper into the hole. She was aware enough to loosen her muscles so that her long body could coil into the deep, dark crack in the rock. Squirter scooted under her and farther into the crevasse.

BAM. The rock shook, and a forceful pressure wave slammed into my back. I gripped Pipa's body to avoid being grated against the sharp rocks.

Since the ligan was too large to enter the crevasse, it had bashed its hard nose against the cave entrance. Pieces of rock tumbled slowly down the cliff face. I wriggled into Pipa to get away from the horrific sight of the ligan charging toward us. *BAM,* the ligan's nose smashed on the stone wall again. More rocks rolled down into blackness.

Squirter hummed at me from behind Pipa. *Small exit,* he said. *You and me. No dragon.*

I bit my tongue until it bled. The crevasse wasn't big, and with nowhere to go, we were clams in a moonsnail's grip. The ligan would bash its way into the crack until it tore us out one by one and swallowed our bodies whole.

I squeezed my eyes shut, but the terrible vision of the ligan rearing back for another hit played out in my skin sense. My heart thumped wildly. I didn't want to die, not like this. And what about Squirter?

He and I could escape. The insidious thought latched onto my mind. We could squeeze out the small exit. We could grab Levi while the ligan was busy. This was my one chance to rescue Levi and keep him in my life.

I squeezed my eyes shut. As much as the notion tempted me, I couldn't do it.

Pipa tensed behind me again. She must have been in the throes of another pull-induced spasm. The mental control the other sea dragons had on her must have been incredibly strong. I desperately wished she was at full strength. As much as I hated to admit it, I really needed her right now.

My mind latched onto Pipa's predicament. Her brain was being controlled. While I knew nothing about sea dragons, I knew plenty about compulsion of the mind. Feverishly, one thought followed another. If she was being compelled, how strong was the compulsion? With pale folk, the stronger siren could always cancel any previous compulsion set on another. Could I siren Pipa to release her of her mental bonds?

As much as I wanted to dislike the other woman, she'd only done exactly what I would have in her situation. Now, she needed me, and I needed her. If I had even a slight chance of getting us both out alive from our predicament, I had to try.

I hugged Pipa tightly to press my chest against her skin for maximal contact. The ligan bashed at the rocks again, although Marina had disappeared somewhere. My hair swept forward with the shock wave. I cleared my mind and hummed.

Clear, I sang to her in words and in the deeper understanding between a siren and her target. *Clear your mind, release your bonds, remove your controls. Be free.*

Pipa tensed again. Then, as my hum vibrated her body, her muscles slowly relaxed. She uncoiled as much as she could in the tight space. We both flinched when the ligan hit the crack again, then she turned her head to face mine.

What did you do? she asked in wonderment. *The pain is gone.*

The 'pull' was mind control, I said. *That's what I'm good at. Now that you're feeling better, any ideas about getting rid of this monster behind us?*

Pipa blinked at me, clearly still caught in her amazement at being free. Then, her eyes focused on the ligan outside.

I'll distract it, she said with confidence. *I've got this. You get Levi out of there.*

Pipa slithered out of the crack when the ligan geared up for another hit. Squirter followed her, and I swallowed the protest that fought to emerge. He wanted to help, and who was I to tell him no? I hoped he would be smart about it.

Pipa opened her mouth and blasted the ligan's face with a scalding wash of black fire that glittered with disorienting lights. The ligan roared. I didn't waste my opportunity and kicked quickly to the left, away from the mangled crevasse's entrance. The cave where Levi was being held was hardly any distance away. The ligan's movements wriggled on the edge of my skin sense when I reached the cave.

Levi was still there, but Marina hovered over him with her bone knife in hand. I swallowed again, this time against the bile that threatened to rise in my throat. Clouds of blood drifted from Levi's wounds. His expression was a constant grimace of pain. He must be close to his threshold. Marina would be able to compel him soon if she couldn't already.

The siren considered Levi carefully, like a fishmonger deciding where to start descaling her catch. I surged forward, intent on taking Marina by surprise while her task distracted her.

But she was too aware. Her skin sense must have alerted her to my presence, because she spun around when I was almost on top of her. Quicker than a swordfish, she sliced her bone knife across my bare stomach.

I jerked backward as stinging fire ripped across my skin. I was lucky that she'd only managed a glancing blow, but I didn't feel lucky. Blood blossomed in a painful stream from the wound, black and billowing, mingling with Levi's diffuse cloud.

I pulled out my own knife from my calf holster and brandished it in Marina's direction. It was solid steel and boasted one sharp side while the other held wicked-looking serrations. Marina glanced at it, unimpressed.

Cute, she said. *Now come at me. I have a year's worth of justice to deliver to you.*

I gritted my teeth and lunged at the other woman. She shifted neatly to the side and plunged her dagger at my stomach. I only dodged it by a hair then twisted away to give myself some breathing room. I couldn't let Marina touch me. The eelgrass concoction wouldn't help if she contacted my skin. She was too powerful for that.

Marina followed closely behind me. I lashed out at her outstretched arm. She yanked it back, but not before I caught her finger on the serrations of my knife.

She yowled and stuck the finger in her mouth.

Hagfish, she spat. *I can't wait to see you sink into the abyss.*

She lunged at me and lanced the flesh of my upper forearm. I screamed and clutched the spot when she pulled the knife free. In my distraction, blood leaking from between my fingers, I let Marina's hand wrap around my biceps.

Immediately, I relaxed. A hum of compliance washed through me. Even my death-grip on my bleeding arm wasn't as desperately tight. Marina had me now, and that was fine.

Good, actually. Now she could get justice for my part in Shoal's illness, and that was fair. The two of them had suffered a lot over the past year. It was only right that I paid for what I'd done. Death was a reasonable option.

Marina's hand clenched on my arm, then she released me. Feelings flooded back into my brain. I kicked away from the other woman with a gasp. She'd sirened me, but why had she stopped?

A glance at the scene told me everything. We'd floated close to Levi. Despite his bonds and injuries, his mouth apparently still worked fine. He'd bitten Marina's foot when it had drifted close to his head.

Although the bite had been painful enough to jolt Marina, Levi's hold wasn't firm. Marina yelled and kicked at Levi's head with her other foot to dislodge his teeth from her flesh. He released her with a wince.

I looked around wildly for something, anything, that would give me an edge. While I backed away and tried to gather myself, Marina swooped down on Levi and grabbed his fronds. He roared with pain.

A wave of compulsion slammed into Levi, strong enough that I felt the wash of it from my vantage. His eyes rolled in his head, and he let out a pitiful whimper.

Stop it, I yelled at Marina. *You're hurting him.*

It's a test, she yelled back, a look of triumph in her eyes. *To see if he's ready to be forced to heal. And what do you know? He is.*

Marina let go of Levi's fronds. He slumped limply in his ropes. I took out my dive knife, but Marina ignored me. She swam toward Shoal, who watched us with bleary, wandering, half-lidded eyes but made no move. Marina took his hand and dragged him toward Levi.

I lunged at her. Quicker than I could react, Marina had her bone knife out. She hit aside my dive knife so hard that it flew out of my hands and drifted to the cave's floor.

Stay back, she said, her teeth bared. *And out of my way.*

I looked at Levi in despair. He panted for breath, but his eyes beseeched mine to understand. He flicked his eyes toward Marina, then made a tiny bite with his teeth. When I understood, I shook my head.

Levi wanted me to get Marina in a position so he could bite her. It was a terrible idea. Now that he wasn't immune to compulsion, any contact they made could be exploited by Marina.

But did I have anything better? And what gave me the right to choose which ideas were the best? Shouldn't Levi have a say in how he defended himself?

I swallowed, bit my lip, then nodded. Levi's face relaxed marginally. I retrieved my dive knife from the cave floor. Marina had almost reached Levi with her cargo, and Shoal gazed at me without interest as she pulled him along.

Don't touch him, I screamed, trying to distract Marina

while keeping her close to Levi. Marina slashed at me again. More blood billowed out from my new wound. I sucked in a breath.

Marina laughed. *Pitiful,* she crowed and floated backward. *You're a lumpfish pretending to be a shark. Give it up. I've won.*

I glanced at Levi once more. His plan would unravel as soon as Marina compelled him. He nodded at me, and I gritted my teeth. This was his decision, and I needed to support him.

With a yell, I rushed forward. Marina jerked back, shocked by my sudden movement. Her foot once again drifted close to Levi's face. With a mighty snap of his tooth-filled mouth, he clamped his jaw on her ankle.

Marina screamed and writhed, her free foot kicking wildly. Levi didn't let go despite the battering his head was taking.

If Levi's plan were to have a chance at succeeding, I needed to remove Marina's ability to siren.

The kelp rope that had held Echo captive drifted in the currents. I grabbed the end and pulled hard. It didn't dislodge from the rock. With the serrations of my knife, I quickly sawed through the pliant rope. It broke apart, then I sheathed my knife and approached the struggling pair.

Levi's eyes were closed to protect himself from Marina's kicks, but he still held on with all the strength in his mighty jaws. Marina screamed in frustration and thrashed wildly. She blasted an untargeted hum, but Levi jerked his head to interrupt her song.

I snuck up behind while he distracted her. With one

hand on each end of the kelp rope, I swung it over her neck and pulled hard.

Marina's back slammed into my chest. Her hands groped at the kelp, but she didn't have leverage. I held firm. Without her throat, singing her siren song would be next to impossible. I wasn't killing her—she could survive without air for a good ten minutes—but I was preventing her from compelling me.

Levi kept his hold on Marina's foot, but he squinted up at us once Marina stopped trying to kick him away. His eyes grew wide, but he couldn't communicate with his mouth full and his body constrained by rope.

I've got her, I said to him. My heart pounded, and I let out a huff of disbelieving laughter. We'd trapped Marina. *You can let go now.*

What I was going to do with her now that we held her captive, I didn't know. Byssa's hope of a peaceful negotiation melted away when I recalled Marina's manic expression as she directed the ligan to kill us.

Levi opened his mouth, and Marina retracted her foot closer to her body. Levi floated back, with his eyes half-closed. His efforts had clearly cost him. I pulled harder at the rope in my anger. Marina's protection of Shoal had wounded others, and Shoal hadn't even wanted it.

A sinuous form moved closer in my skin sense. I twisted toward the cave mouth, my heart pounding, but it was only Pipa. Squirter accompanied the sea dragon, and he hummed with pride. In the distance, the ligan thrashed in pain.

Squirter got the ligan's other eye, Pipa explained. She

moved to Levi's side and nibbled at his ropes to release him. *It can't attack when it can't see.*

Good work, Squirter, I said to my friend. *I got Marina. Now what?*

Levi rose from his bonds once Pipa finished and laboriously drifted over to Marina. He stared at her with his blue-green eyes.

I'll heal Shoal, he said slowly in his garbled tongue. *You will keep my secret.*

I didn't want Levi to risk himself healing Shoal, but I felt a little bad about Shoal drifting unaware in the corner. If Levi could push Shoal over the obstacle that prevented him from healing, maybe that would be enough.

We can't trust her, I said to Levi. *She'll be back with an army of pale folk in a few weeks. And I can't confuse her by sirening because she's too strong for me.*

I'll kill her, Pipa said. *It's the only way Levi will be safe.*

I glanced at Levi. His expression mirrored my own uncertainty. How could we resolve this? Was Pipa right?

There is another way, Marina said haltingly using hand signals. Her eyes were wide. *Let me talk properly. I promise I won't siren you.*

I glanced at Levi, who nodded. My eyes narrowed. He wasn't in any position to defend himself. I glanced at Pipa, who moved closer and gave me a firmer nod. With a sigh, I released my white-knuckled grip on the kelp rope.

Marina drifted away from my body, although I kept the rope loosely around her throat. She rubbed her neck with a grimace.

Talk, I said. *And make it quick. Our other option is the black sea dragon happily ripping out your throat.* I pointed at Pipa, who bared her teeth. The siren's eyes twitched in her direction.

One of my roles at the Seamount is Chief Influencer, Marina said quickly. *If upper echelon citizens step out of line, they can choose to be either punished or influenced. If done voluntarily, I can reach deep inside their minds and change their values, personalities, whatever is required in the situation. It goes much deeper than sirening, because I am invited in.*

Was this what Branc had meant when he'd said Marina could get deep in my head if I let her? I'd never heard of this ability, but I used to live among the scum of siren society. We didn't get fancy choices when we fell out of line, only punishment.

Get to the point, I snarled.

I've never influenced myself, but it's theoretically possible. I could influence myself to forgive you and think of you with kindness instead of vengeance. I could even convince myself that the sea dragon should be kept a secret.

Levi and I exchanged an incredulous glance. Marina was willing to reprogram her brain? Assuming it worked on herself.

Marina pursed her lips. *I'd need you as a conduit.*

I didn't like the sound of this, but it was the best chance we had at escaping Marina's clutches for good, while still being able to look Byssa in the eye.

Okay, try healing him, I said to Levi. *I'll turn Marina into my best friend. Pipa, help Levi figure out how far to go. Keep him safe.*

I didn't want to rely on Pipa, but Levi needed a sea dragon to guide him. I had to fix Marina's brain.

Levi swam over to Shoal, his movements jerky with pain. Pipa shadowed him. When they reached Shoal, she spoke quietly to Levi. Marina's eyes were fixed on the floating man.

Pipa opened her mouth and hovered it over Shoal's body from foot to head, then invited Levi to do the same. He cautiously tasted the water around Shoal. When he reached the man's temple, his head jerked back. Pipa nodded with enthusiasm and spoke further.

I let go of the rope and yanked Marina's arm so she faced me. *Time to do your part. I don't want you swimming off with a healed Shoal before we've influenced you.*

Marina's lips thinned. She gripped my hands in her own so we were linked.

I will use you to enter my own head, she said. *The sensation will be strange and intimate. Relax and allow me in fully.*

I didn't like the sound of that. I glanced at Levi. He bent his open mouth to Shoal, and his long tongue reached out to give Shoal's forehead a lick. He paused, waiting for Marina to begin her task.

I needed to do this, for Levi and for myself. I gripped Marina's hands firmly and closed my eyes.

A foreign presence entered my mind. My shoulders tensed. Marina squeezed my hands, and I relaxed my body. My mind took a little more convincing.

Let me in, Marina both hummed and said in my mind. *This is the only way.*

With a huge sigh, I allowed my thoughts to empty. Marina dived in when my defenses were down. Even if

I'd wanted to, I couldn't have stopped her, but she ignored whatever was in my brain. Instead, a river of consciousness streamed through my head and back into Marina.

Unwelcome images flickered across my mind's eye of Marina's life. Nothing was clear, but I recognized Shoal in many of the dizzying thoughts. Emotions accompanied the images, with love and fear dominant. When Marina focused on Levi and me, hatred and greed rose to the surface. Slowly, painstakingly, the emotions morphed into indifference and a need for secrecy.

Finally, the stream of consciousness slithered away from Marina and out of my mind. I gasped and opened my eyes. Marina blinked at me.

Where's Shoal? she said.

I pointed behind her. Marina flung around in a swirl of white dress. Levi licked Shoal's forehead. When he retreated to watch for signs of life, Shoal stirred and moaned.

Marina gasped with her hand over her mouth. Levi looked in question at Pipa. She nodded once more toward Shoal. Levi licked his forehead again before he and Pipa retreated to the cave mouth.

Shoal's eyes flickered open. He gazed at the roof with true observation, then he looked at Marina.

Marina? he said. *What's happening?*

Before Shoal could spot the sea dragons lurking nearby, I swam over to him and clutched his arm. With a burst of compulsion, I said to Shoal, *You need sleep. Rest, now.*

He yawned, stretched his arms above his head, then turned in midwater and fell asleep. Levi limped over to us.

Are you okay? I asked Levi.

Tired, he said with a grimace. *But okay. Let's go.*

I'll be right behind you, I said.

He turned and swam with labored movements beside Pipa. I looked at Marina, who stared at Shoal with love and hope.

Marina? I asked. *What will you do now?*

Take my love home to the Seamount, she said in a blissful tone. *He's finally healed. I will pray my thanks to Ramu.*

And the sea dragons? I prompted. *What about them?*

Shh. She shook her head at me, although her eyes never left Shoal's sleeping form. *We don't talk about them. Dr. Mazzaella healed Shoal, remember?*

That's right. I shivered at the power Marina wielded. *What about the seal shifter Echo? Will you treat her kindly back at the Seamount?*

If you wish it. She finally looked at me. She shrugged. *I don't care about her. She can do what she wants.*

I could accept that. I slowly maneuvered out of the cave. *Goodbye, Marina. Safe travels back to the Seamount.*

The other woman didn't even bother to watch me go. She floated to the sleeping Shoal and curled up with her hand on his chest.

My heart squeezed at the sight of my enemy showing such vulnerability. Then I sighed and swam out of the cave. Hopefully, that was the last time I would see Marina. She'd plagued me for over a year, and I was happy to see the back of her.

I clutched my various wounds as they throbbed with insistent pain and rejoined the two sea dragons outside. Squirter jetted beside me as I raced toward Levi. My arms wrapped around an unharmed central section of his body and squeezed tightly. His smooth scales pressed into my cheek as my eyes warmed with tears.

That was too close, I said.

His long body curled around so his beautiful eyes were gazing at me among cuts that marred his face. He tried to say something, but it was too garbled to understand. He gave a grunt of annoyance then nuzzled my hair with his nose and cheek. I closed my eyes and squeezed him tighter, overwhelmed by relief and adrenaline and Levi's warm body in mine, even if he was currently covered in scales.

Another figure approached us in my skin sense, and my body tensed until I recognized Echo. Her swimming was jerky and pained-looking, but she continued until she was close enough to speak.

You're okay, she said to everyone. *I thought you were goners for sure. I'm sorry I couldn't help more.*

Your poor tail. I released Levi and waved at Echo's mutilated appendage. *You're so badly hurt. Trust me, you did more than I could ever have hoped for.*

Echo ducked her head at my praise. I put my hand on Levi's flank again, not willing to let go even for a minute.

Pipa glanced at the cave mouth. *We should go. We don't want Shoal seeing us.*

Good point. I turned toward the beach. *Let's get out of the water until they've left for the Seamount.*

It was a slow, arduous journey back to the shoreline where we'd entered the ocean. Levi's sinuous movements weren't nearly as graceful as usual, and Echo had to be nudged along by Pipa. Squirter clung to my back, his hurt arm dangling behind me like a streamer of seaweed.

As we rose from the shallows, Squirter detached himself and scooted around to reach my face. I stopped to speak with him.

You were amazing, I said. *Thank you.*

Staying in ocean now. He touched my cheek with the tip of one arm. My little octopus friend was rapidly becoming not so little. I swallowed back my sadness at the change and tried to be happy for Squirter as he grew up.

What about your arm? I pointed at his injury. We both stared at it for a moment, then a large head circled around. Levi stuck out his tongue at Squirter and waited. I held my breath. Did Squirter understand what was going on? Did Levi have enough energy to fix him?

After a moment's hesitation, the octopus reached out his hurt arm and touched the sea dragon's tongue. Levi licked it gently. Squirter twitched, and his skin rippled with color. Then he darted off with far more vigor than he'd shown on the swim to shore.

Levi's head drooped. I put my hands on my hips.

You're using too much healing, I scolded. *Don't push yourself too far.*

His head straightened in defiance of my words, and he swam over to Echo. With a swift lick of his tongue on her tail, the seal's bleeding stopped.

That's enough, Pipa said to him. *She's not bleeding out. Anything else you can heal another day if you must.*

Levi sagged and didn't try to heal Echo again. I got behind him and pushed like I had with Pipa.

I'm getting good at hauling around sea dragons, I joked to Levi. *That's all I've done today.*

Heal you, he murmured.

Don't even think about it. My wounds throbbed horribly at the suggestion of healing, but I gritted my teeth and kept pushing. My injuries weren't life-threatening, but Levi healing me might push him over the edge. I had no intention of letting him do that. *I'm not bleeding anymore. I'll be fine.*

Once we reached the shallows, I exited the water first. The October beach was deserted, and the sky was as bright as the patchy clouds would allow it. When I waved a hand under the water for the others to join me, the human-formed Echo crawled up first. Her left leg was a hideous purple-black, and puncture wounds were barely healed over. She couldn't put any weight on it, so I hauled her to a nearby log. I hoped nobody would come to the beach in the next few minutes. A naked girl would be sure to draw stares, especially in this weather.

Levi and Pipa poked their heads out of the water and laid them on the rocky shore. I watched, fascinated, as they shrank, changed shape, and bled free of color, until their human forms sprawled on the beach. I ran to Levi and dragged him upright. He could barely stand, and we hobbled together to Echo's log. A small part of me noticed Levi's nakedness and tucked that sight away for later, but most of me was overwhelmed with concern for his bedraggled state. Cuts and bruises proliferated on his beautiful face and body, and he sank onto the log with a tremendous sigh.

"Stay there," I told him. "I'll be back with towels from the truck."

I jogged up the sandy embankment to the nearby residential road. Levi had left the truck unlocked, so I yanked open the back door and grabbed a few towels. On the way back, I found Pipa's and my clothes where we'd discarded them on a patch of soggy grass, and Levi's torn clothes where the shifter must have ripped them off for Levi's transformation. When I returned to the beach, Pipa had joined the others on the log. I stifled a giggle at the three naked people in a row, then I dropped towels in each person's lap.

"There we are. Modesty preservers all around." I winced at the sight of everyone's wounds. My own throbbed harder now that I wasn't fighting for my life. I sat next to Levi at the end of the log and leaned my head on his shoulder. He rested his own on mine.

We sat in silence for a long time, accompanied only by the sound of crashing waves on the rocky beach. A sliver of weak sunlight shafted through a break in the clouds and turned the frothing waves into dazzling white confectionary. Finally, I spoke.

"Pipa? I think you have something to tell Levi."

CHAPTER 31

When I glanced at Pipa, her expression was tight. She didn't look at Levi, not even when he gazed at her curiously.

"I guess so." She drew in a shuddering breath. "Levi, I have something to apologize for."

She briefly outlined the status of healers in the sea dragon community, and the plans to sacrifice her to their hydrothermal vent god. She explained the pull, and how the other sea dragons would never let Levi leave once he entered the villages. She mentioned my release of her mind control, and Levi wrapped an arm around my shoulders at the news.

"You lied to me," Levi said once Pipa's words had subsided into silence. His arm was tense around me. "You were going to trap me in the villages forever."

Pipa said nothing, although her face was expressive with guilt and defiance.

"But you did it to save yourself." Levi sighed hugely. "I get it. It doesn't mean I forgive you—I mean, you knew how important it was for me to return here—but I get why you did it. What bothers me more is that now I can't visit, not ever."

His fingers clenched my upper arm until pain sparked. I lifted my hand to his and stroked the fingers until the pressure relented.

I hated that Levi's dreams of knowing himself better were dashed. Anger fizzled in me at these villages of unknown sea dragons and their backward ways. Why couldn't they use medicine like the rest of us? Why enslave the healer of each generation? Now Levi had to stay in the dark about his heritage. Pipa could tell him some things, I supposed, but visiting his homeland would have been even better.

I frowned. Maybe there was a way.

"Pipa, can you tell Levi is a healer from his looks?"

Pipa stared at me. "No," she said slowly. "I didn't know until he healed you."

"Then what if he goes to visit, but without telling them about his healing abilities?" I warmed up to the idea. "He could go, visit, learn, then come home after a couple of weeks, no harm done."

Levi's back straightened. "Would that work?" he said hoarsely.

"Maybe." Pipa's mouth twisted. "You'd have to make sure they don't put the pull on you. There's a ceremony, I can describe it for you so you can avoid it. I've never seen them do it on anyone who wasn't a baby, so I don't know if they would try. Still, you don't want that on you."

"Although Lune could remove it." Levi kissed the top of my head, and I snuggled closer to him. "Like she did to you."

I looked at Pipa, whose face had brightened at Levi's words. "Pipa, what are you going to do now?"

"I can't go home," she said matter-of-factly. "They'll kill me as soon as I arrive, for the sacrifice. Maybe when they birth a new healer, I can go back. I guess I'll travel, see the rest of the ocean and dry folk land. I've lived in the villages my whole life. It's time I stretched my tail.

Maybe I could accompany Echo back to the Seamount."

"What if you meet Marina again?" Echo's eyes were huge at the thought, although she'd shown relief at first when she thought she wouldn't have to travel alone.

"I wouldn't come all the way, of course. I've had enough of sirens for a while. Here, pass me your phone, Levi."

Levi rummaged in his jeans pocket, unlocked the screen, and wordlessly passed his device to Pipa. She opened a map app and scrolled to Greenland. After a moment's consideration, she pinned a location to the map.

"There." She handed the phone back to Levi. "That's where the villages are. Keep that a secret. If you want to go, watch your back and don't tell anyone about your healing abilities."

"Thanks." Levi stared at his phone as if it held the answers of the universe. For him, I supposed it did.

Levi suddenly slumped against me, and I held him up in surprise.

"What's wrong?" I asked.

"So tired." He tried for a weak chuckle, but it came out as more of a wheeze. "I don't think I can drive us to your place."

I pulled out my own phone. "You don't have to. I've got this."

Byssa roared up behind Levi's truck fifteen minutes later. She leaped out of the driver's seat and ran toward our log.

"Lune! Levi," she gasped. "Is everyone okay? What

happened? You're all hurt. Can Levi heal you? Oh no, he's going to fall over. Catch him, Lune!"

"I'm fine," Levi slurred, wobbling as he tried to stand with my arm around his chest. "Just tired."

"Everyone in the car," Byssa said firmly. "Right now. I'm taking you to Dr. Mazzaella's. Lune, you can tell me everything on the way."

We packed the three others in the backseat of Byssa's little hatchback, and I slipped into the front passenger's seat with a groan of pain. Byssa glared at me and turned the key in the ignition.

"You'd better start talking," she said. "And is Squirter okay?"

"Squirter is fine," I said, my voice brimming with gratitude. "Levi's partly so tired because he healed him."

"Good." Byssa pulled away from the curb and drove down the road. "Now, tell me everything."

During the drive, I gave Byssa a run-down of Levi's kidnapping, the battle, and Pipa's revelations. Byssa was an excellent audience and kept her questions to a minimum, but she threw me a few pointed glares from time to time.

"And you didn't think to phone me or Hades for help at any point during these shenanigans?" she said once I'd wrapped up my explanation.

I shrank down in my seat. I hated disappointing Byssa. "I'm sorry. I was so frazzled by Levi's disappearance that I couldn't think of anything except jumping in the water."

Byssa sighed, but she patted my arm. "I get it. I'm

still mad, though. You all could have been captured or killed.”

“I know.” I shuddered as the full import of her words sunk in. I hadn’t let myself consider the consequences of today fully yet, but now the danger was past, they ate at my mind.

“Nicely done on influencing Marina, though,” Byssa said.

“I thought you didn’t approve of sirening. Influencing felt like the ultimate compulsion.”

“As an alternative to murder? And against an enemy who would kill you otherwise? Compel away.”

We smiled at each other, then I glanced at the quiet backseat. Levi and Echo had passed out cold, and Pipa gazed out of the window at approaching cars. She gave me a swift, brief smile that held none of the smugness I’d grown used to seeing from her. It made me wonder if Pipa might be a decent person to know, after all.

Probably not. She was annoyingly good-looking and a liar to boot. Even so, maybe she had a few redeeming qualities.

Dr. Mazzaella opened her lower door wearing a tomato-splattered apron, but she quickly whipped it off to tend to our ragged group. Levi barely woke for long enough to stumble from her office back to the car after his treatment, then he slept the whole way to my apartment.

By that time, my bandaged wounds had reduced their stinging throbs to dull aches, thanks to Dr. Mazzaella’s ointments. At my apartment building, Pipa and I hauled Levi out of the car, and each of us put an arm under his shoulders. We heaved him to my door with him stumbling between us, then we dropped him on my bed. He curled up and his breathing steadied into sleep. We gazed at him for a long moment.

"Don't let him get trapped at the villages," Pipa said at last. "He has a good life here, and someone to come back to. That's worth preserving."

She left without looking at me. I gazed at Levi for a while longer, pondering the intricacies of other people's motivations. Then, overwhelmed by exhaustion, I crawled into bed next to Levi and was asleep within seconds.

I awoke that evening to the sounds of quiet chatter and hushed footsteps. Levi was still asleep next to me, so I crept with aching legs to the door and peeked my head out.

Byssa was there, waving at Echo and Pipa to follow her. Jules hovered in the doorway, and I hid my grin. Maybe Byssa didn't need my matchmaking help after all. She seemed to be doing just fine on her own.

Byssa must have brought crutches for Echo, because the seal shifter was wobbling toward the door on her new metal legs. Pipa followed, brushing her hair with her fingers.

Byssa spotted me and whispered across the room, "I'm taking them out to dinner. You must all be starving after this morning. Want to come?"

"Thanks, but I want to be here when Levi wakes up," I replied.

Byssa nodded with a knowing smile, and the three exited the room. I breathed a sigh of relief when my apartment was quiet once more.

When I snuggled back into bed, Levi reached out for me with a sleepy arm.

"We have to stop doing this," he murmured.

"Doing what?"

"Falling into bed exhausted. I want to show you a good time, but I can hardly keep my eyes open. I promise I have more to offer."

"You have potential," I teased. When he opened his swirly blue and green eyes indignantly, I wriggled closer and laid my cheek against his bare chest. "You can show me that good time later. For now, heal yourself."

"I wish I could," he groaned. "But if I heal my cuts and bruises, I'll make myself even more tired. I have to suffer a slow healing process like a regular person."

"How tedious." I ran a finger down Levi's bare arm, and he shivered. Gratified, I kept up the motion while I spoke next. "Have you thought about what you're going to do now? About Greenland, that is."

Levi sighed and rolled onto his back, pulling me along with him until I laid on his chest. When he spoke, his voice rumbled into my ear directly from the vibrations in his lungs.

"I have to go," he said, almost pleading with me. "I discovered where I came from. It will eat me up to have that knowledge dangling in front of me and ignore it."

"Yes, you have to go," I agreed. Had he thought I

would say the opposite? "It's best if I don't come, though. This is something you need to do on your own."

It hurt, saying those words. I wanted to be there for Levi, to protect him from whatever he might face at the hands of his people. I wanted to guide him in the right direction.

But my presence in the villages would only hamper him, if the other sea dragons held back on my account. I had to trust that Levi would make the best decisions for himself. And if that meant staying in the villages, then so be it.

The thought still hurt like a hot vent, though.

"Just be careful about it," I said. "If you want to come back."

"If I—Lune." Levi pulled my chin up so he could look into my eyes. "There's no 'if' about it. I'm coming back. I'm not leaving my life here, the Lodge, my family." He frowned at me. "I'm not leaving you."

I blinked a few times at the traitorous moistness that threatened to overflow its bounds. "Just remember that I understand if you want to stay. They are your people, and you might find that you belong there. You might feel like you've come home, and that your life here isn't what you want anymore. And that's okay. I would understand."

Levi breathed out a curse, then his fingers gripped my chin more firmly. "I will come back. I don't care how great the sea dragon villages are, my life and home are here. That's a promise."

I wriggled out of his grasp and buried my face

against his chest. I wanted to believe him, but deep down, I knew the pull of belonging that went far beyond mind control. I wouldn't hold him to his promise.

But we didn't need to belabor the point. He was adamant, and I would let him believe what he wanted to. He would remember my words if he needed them.

"How will you explain yourself there?" I asked. "I gather sea dragons don't get out much."

"I'll have to ask Pipa." He rubbed my back in large, reassuring circles. "She'll have some ideas. Maybe I can pretend to be related to someone other than my biological mother, someone who's dead and can't deny it. Pipa said they take lengthy journeys when they come of age, so there are probably a few sea dragons whose son I can pretend to be, someone who doesn't carry the healer bloodline. And as long as I don't heal anyone while I'm there, it shouldn't come up."

I nodded, comforted by the thought that sea dragons had questionable ethics. What with their sacrifices, mind control, and hypervigilance toward strangers, I didn't see Levi fitting into their society that well. Maybe he would come back, after all.

I raised my head and leaned in close to Levi.

"You might be leaving," I said. "But you're not gone yet. What about that good time you promised me?"

When Levi grinned and pressed his lips to mine, I tried to let go of my worries of the future. I owed Branc two unbounded favors, the scope of which made me shudder. The rogue faction was a simmering threat, and Marina's words about the rogue faction at our final battle haunted me with foreboding. And Levi was leaving me. He might think he was coming back, but I couldn't count on it.

But we had this moment together. I would savor it with all my strength.

ALSO BY EMMA SHELFORD

Depths of Magic
Sea Fire
Sea Song
Sea Dragon

Nautilus Legends
Free Dive
Caught
Surfacing
Hooked
Riptide

Magical Morgan
Daughters of Dusk
Mothers of Mist
Elders of Ether

Immortal Merlin
Ignition
Winded
Floodgates
Buried
Possessed
Unleashed
Worshiped
Unraveled

Forest Fae
Mark of the Breenan
Garden of Last Hope
Realm of the Forgotten

ACKNOWLEDGEMENTS

Thank you to Tessy Dockery, Steven Shelford, and Nadene D for helping me polish this book, to Vincentas Saladis for the beautiful illustrations, and to Miblart for another lovely cover.

ABOUT THE AUTHOR

Emma Shelford feels that life is only complete with healthy doses of magic, history, and science. Since these aren't often found in the same place, she creates her own worlds where they happily coexist. If you catch her in person, she will eagerly discuss Lord of the Rings ad nauseam, why the ancient Sumerians are so cool, and the important role of phytoplankton in the ocean.

Emma is the author of multiple urban fantasy series, including Depths of Magic, Nautilus Legends, Magical Morgan, Immortal Merlin, and Forest Fae.

www.ingramcontent.com/pod-product-compliance
Lightning Source LLC
Chambersburg PA
CBHW061316190726
48288CB00002B/525